THE PILGRIM SOUL IN YOU

THE PILGRIM SOUL IN YOU

A STORY OF
LOVE, LOSS, AND REDEMPTION

MARTIN MUTKA

*This book is dedicated to
all those who have lost someone.*

When You Are Old

When you are old and grey and full of sleep,
And nodding by the fire, take down this book,
And slowly read, and dream of the soft look
Your eyes had once, and of their shadows deep;
How many loved your moments of glad grace,
And loved your beauty with love false or true,
But one man loved *the pilgrim soul in you*,
And loved the sorrows of your changing face;
And bending down beside the glowing bars,
Murmur, a little sadly, how Love fled
And paced upon the mountains overhead
And hid his face amid a crowd of stars.

—WILLIAM BUTLER YEATS

PROLOGUE

LONG BEFORE LAURA, whom I came to love and cherish more than anyone, I knew or thought I knew how precious life is, that the choices we make often decide our fate for years if not an entire lifetime. No one ever had to remind me what dreams are made of, or that we only live once. Nor did I need anyone or anything for inspiration—that came from something deep down, which I carried as a constant reminder from fateful yesterdays and promises for tomorrow. What I didn't know was whether my dreams were in vain—some hopeful wish I was trying to live out. In some ways, I'm still unsure because I've not decided if such bliss can endure the pain that life too often inflicts on us. What I do know is, as we go through life, we leave behind a part of ourselves with all those we come to know and love and appreciate, no matter for how long or how fleeting a time. That intimacy is what makes life precious—to allow others to see inside our heart, live fully, and make lasting memories we can embrace and hold on to as a reminder of not only what was, but what could have been.

PART ONE

"BLISS"

JULY 1981–JULY 1984

CHAPTER 1

I MET LAURA on July 23, 1981, at a graduate and law school open house for incoming students. I had graduated from Syracuse University three years earlier and spent most of the time after that restoring old houses in my hometown of Buffalo and following the stock market in my free time. I was an above-average student at 'Cuse and found I had an aptitude for math. I applied for the MBA program at Golden Gate University in San Francisco to study what I thought I might want to do—trade options at the Pacific Stock Exchange, where a cousin of mine, Jim Mathis, worked in their systems department. My other reason for applying was a desire to escape the long, frigid winters of upstate New York. I never expected that Thursday evening would change my life. But then, when do we ever think anything we do will have such profound consequences?

As I entered the large first-floor reception area, where tables were taped with flimsy white A–G, H–M, and N–Z placards, I walked towards the center table to get my registration packet and name tag. I signed the list and was handed the orientation materials for the Graduate School of Business. Behind me, although I did not know it at the time, was Laura McKenzie, who was entering law school. She overheard me say my name and sensed a friendliness she told me later. After the hour-long program, a break-out session, and a tour of the library, everyone returned to the reception area where soft drinks, cheese, fruit, and boxed wine were served.

During my session, we took turns introducing ourselves. The guy sitting next to me was Mike Foster, who had his BS in Computer Science from UC Berkeley. He was pursuing an MBA in Information Systems, and worked in the systems area at the Pacific Stock Exchange, PSE, or "The Exchange," as I learned it was called. I wanted to ask if he knew my cousin Jim, but the opportunity didn't present itself. But as I walked back to the hall toward the refreshments, I saw him standing with a girl who looked to be in college—maybe an undergrad volunteer, I thought. I held my stare a moment, then another, unable to divert my eyes from her face. She smiled, perhaps a little self-consciously, as she noticed my prolonged gaze. Mike caught my eye and motioned me over.

"Hey. Mike Foster," he said, reintroducing himself.

"Will Merritt," I replied.

He turned to the girl.

"And this ingénue is my cousin, Laura McKenzie. She's starting law school—one of those tree huggers who wants to save the planet," he announced, with feigned condescension.

I extended my hand.

"Will Merritt. Nice to meet you, Laura. I like trees too."

"What, another environmental fanatic?" Mike laughed.

"You seem very opinionated for a techie nerd," I said, hoping to get a reaction from Laura.

"I like that. My cousin Mike, the techie nerd! It sounds like a TV show."

"Hey, Mike, do you know Jim Mathis at the PSE?" I asked.

"Yeah, why? He's a real tech nerd."

"He happens to be my cousin. I haven't seen him since he threw up orange pop at my First Communion party."

"That sounds like Jim."

"Ah, an East Coast Catholic," Laura surmised.

"Pop instead of soda?" I inquired.

"Yes, plus I was behind you in registration and saw your address."

"She's clever that way. I'd love to stay and discuss global climate change, but I have to be at work at five thirty in the morning," Mike joked, as he said goodbye to us.

"Nice meeting you, Mike—guess I'll be seeing you around here in a few weeks."

"You too, Will. Goodnight, Laura," he added, as he headed out.

I looked at her for insight.

"He's crazy, but in a good way."

"So, you like trees?" I asked.

"I do," she replied, tilting her head in acknowledgment.

"And this our life, exempt from public haunt, find tongues in trees, books in the running brooks, sermons in stones . . ."

". . . And good in everything," she added, finishing the quote. "A Renaissance man?"

"I'm not sure about that."

"What are you sure about?" she asked.

"I'm sure I can't drink more than one glass of this boxed wine."

"Agreed."

We left the reception and walked toward the Market Street BART station.

"So what brings you out here for school?"

"Well, you know what Horace Greeley said."

"Go West, young man?"

"Yes, and someplace warm. I could have stayed at Syracuse, or gone to New York, but I wanted a change."

"A new beginning?"

"Exactly," I said, considering her words, "a new beginning."

"Sometimes that's harder than you think," she admitted.

"Sounds like you've had experience with change?"

"It's always been difficult for me," she conceded.

"Perhaps we can try this new beginning together."

Laura looked at me as if I'd read her mind and smiled.

"I'd like that. I'd like that very much, Will," she replied, as she pulled the ends of her blonde hair behind her ears.

It felt late, maybe because of the long day at the DMV and other errands, the socializing, the bad wine. Laura looked tired too as she watched her train approaching. I realized the conversation hadn't reached a conclusion and asked, "So how should we begin?"

She perked up, perhaps because she was waiting for me to offer an invitation, or at least a hint of suggestion.

"I was thinking of hanging out for a while on Sunday in Golden Gate Park. If you want to meet up? I could show you—"

"Some trees?"

"Yes, and I might even make you hug one."

"Sure, that sounds great."

"Meet me at the Japanese Tea Garden at two thirty."

The train pulled in, and over the screeching, I repeated, "Okay, two thirty, see you then."

"Bye, Will," she said, turning to board the closest car.

"Laura," I shouted over the noise, perhaps a little too loudly, "thanks."

"For what?"

"For making the thought of graduate school more tolerable."

"Do you know how cheesy that sounds?"

"I do."

"Good night."

"Goodbye, Laura."

The train sped away and I unconsciously waved to the image of her seated there alone in the brightly lit car. A broad smile washed over her face as she disappeared from view. I walked the few blocks to the Tadich Grill on California Street. It was cooler now and the sun was almost gone in the western sky. The bar area was nearly empty at 9:00 p.m. on that Thursday night. A few tables of tourists were finishing dinner while "Piano Man" played on the sound system.

"Anchor Steam," I said, to Fred the bartender with whom I'd developed a rapport on my prior visit.

I had arrived in San Francisco a few weeks earlier, just after Independence Day, and heard about the Tadich from one of my professors at Syracuse. I liked it and planned to be a regular, or at least as much of a regular as I could be on my savings and the part-time job I secured at E.F. Hutton—handling buy and sell orders for vacationing brokers—given the funds held in trust for my benefit were for less indulgent purposes. I had acquired my Series 7 securities license back in New York the summer after college, through a connection from school, and was offered the position over the phone before I arrived.

"You look tired, kid," Fred said, with a mischievous look on his face.

I looked up from the glass.

"But maybe a good tired?" he inquired, sensing my pleasant preoccupation.

"I just met someone. Her name is Laura."

Billy Joel finished and Fred picked right up, "Laura is the face on the misty night."

"In the misty light," I corrected him.

"Oh yeah, whatever. So where'd you meet this dame?"

"Fred, she's not a dame, she's a young woman—a girl."

"Okay, so we've established her gender and age. But where?"

"At school, an orientation for new students. She's going to study law."

"Law! A lawyer? Forget it, those types are ruthless."

"She's twenty-one. She finished high school in three years, and Berkeley in three-and-a-half."

"Berkeley! What is she, a commy rabble-rouser?"

"Fred, where'd you pick up this lingo? Dames? Rabble-rousers?"

"Hey, I've been around. Three years in the Army—Korea. I was twenty. That was thirty years ago—do the math kid."

"Fair enough, Fred, but she ain't, I mean, she isn't a rabble-rouser. She's . . ." I was searching for the word.

"Rich?"

"No, sweet," I said.

"Sweet! They're the worst. They take your heart and squeeze it and . . ." his thought trailed off.

"I have to go," I said, as I finished my beer.

"By the way, how old a fellow are you?

"Twenty-five," I replied.

"Twenty-five," he repeated approvingly.

"Be careful, kid, you don't wanna end up like me."

I detected a hint of sadness in his eyes.

"Okay. I'll watch for those dames out there."

I rose from the bar stool.

"You better believe it, they're scoundrels."

"Goodnight, Fred," I said, as I headed for the door.

"See ya around, kid, drive safely."

No one in the city drove anywhere, except maybe to Stinson Beach on the weekend. I treated myself to a cab ride to Cow Hollow, below Russian Hill, where I had rented a one-bedroom apartment with a view of San Francisco Bay and the Golden Gate Bridge.

The phone rang at seven in the morning on Friday.

"I wake you?"

"Who's this?"

"It's Mike Foster."

"What?"

"Your long-lost cousin wants to meet you. Lunch today, his treat—us three, if that's okay?"

"Sure, where?"

"Tadich Grill, one thirty, after the market closes."

Tadich Grill, I thought, *I just left from there.*

"Hey, Will, you there?"

"Yes, okay, one thirty at the Tadich," I replied.

The lunch was unremarkable other than reliving the orange pop incident. Halfway through, Jim was paged and had to go back to work. I feigned regret and saw it as an opportunity to find out more about Laura.

"Laura? Why are you interested in her?" Mike asked protectively.

"I don't know; she seems . . ." I used the word I did with Fred, "sweet."

"Sweet? Listen, Will, she's a sweet girl, but she's just that, a girl, innocent; she's been sheltered. Her mother and our grandparents, it's . . ."

"It's what?"

"It's been hard. Her father died when she was six. He was a bond trader at Witter. Come to think of it, you have something in common—he was from the East too, born in Rye, New York, went to Fordham, and then Stanford for his MBA. He stayed in California rather than work on Wall Street. A year later in '56, the PSE opened. Anyway, she's . . . it's just been difficult for her, her whole life. I was six too when Uncle John died. My brother Stephen was eight. It's sort of hard to remember him—he worked a lot, but he was a wonderful father and husband as far as I knew."

"So, wait you are?" I hesitated.

"Laura's mom is my mother's sister."

"And you have a brother?"

"Yes, Stephen, he's a civil engineer. He works at Bechtel, the engineering company. He spends most of his time in China, building dams."

"And Laura, does she have siblings?" I asked.

"She has a brother, Rob, two years younger. He's kind of messed up on drugs. He lives somewhere down in East Palo Alto."

Even as a recent resident of the Bay Area, I knew from newspaper accounts that EPA was a haven for drugs, gangs, and violence.

On Sunday, I met Laura at the Japanese Tea Garden. We sat under a huge oak tree on a nearby meadow of lush green lawn where the air was filled with fragrances of camellia, azalea, and bougainvillea—flowers I'd never heard of before. The sandwiches she made were delicious because I felt too anxious to eat that morning—two cups of coffee was all I managed. I changed my shirt once, then twice, until I settled on a light blue plaid cotton button down. The cold lemonade she brought reminded me of a far-off memory: my family picnicking at the lake on a summer afternoon. It was June 6, 1966. I recalled this because of the date 6/6/66. I was ten years old, and the Vietnam War was nothing more than a newspaper headline or a story on the evening news—Walter Cronkite or Huntley-Brinkley. It would be two more years before I grasped the horrific extent and toll of the war on American GIs. I remembered the Tet Offensive and then nothing else, except when our neighbors' son, Douglas Miller, was killed. One April morning, as I was heading to school, an Army Chaplain arrived in front of our house. A captain, in the driver's seat, got out of the car along with the Chaplain. As I walked by, one of them asked if that was the Miller residence and pointed to the house next to mine. I knew Doug had died. Even at my young age, I had seen enough war movies to know how next of kin notifications went.

"Yes," I said, and then proceeded on as if school would provide me with the knowledge that would explain this senseless death and give me insight into how to escape such fate.

The lemonade was refreshing. I lay back on the blanket, to soak in the warmth of the afternoon sun, and put Doug Miller out of my mind.

"Thank you, this was great."

"You're welcome. For a moment there, I thought I put you to sleep."

"Ah, 'to sleep, perchance to dream'," I replied opening my eyes. "No. Thank you, I haven't had a picnic like this in a long time."

"I'm glad that I could make you feel . . . at home."

"Thank you, Laura. I was, I don't know, nervous I guess about moving out here."

"And now?" she inquired.

"Now it seems like my destiny," I said freely.

"Maybe that's what attracted me to you—we're both sort of alone like that."

"But you haven't really told me . . ."

"You know what?" Laura asked.

"What?"

"I think you're great."

I sat up on the blanket and replied incredulously, "What?"

"I think you're great, Will," she repeated. "I see it in your eyes—you have soulful eyes, and a reserved sense of kindness."

I took her hand in mine and, in a slight tone of admonishment, said, "Laura, you don't really know me. I mean, I am a good guy, and I like you too, but you don't—"

She interrupted my babbling by leaning over and kissing me. It was a soft prolonged kiss. When we paused, I blurted out, "You taste like strawberry."

"I do, don't I? I still had a lip gloss in my bag from high school and didn't realize it until today."

"High school! Like short plaid skirts and white shirts and ties?" I exclaimed.

"Whoa, slow down, it's just flavored lip gloss."

"Yes, but it's your lip gloss from high school."

I drew her close to me. As we hugged and laughed together, I knew I was beginning to have feelings for her. Laura would tell me later it was a combination of the food and the sun and the surprise of the strawberry lip gloss that caused some momentary hallucination in me. I told her it was her kiss. It was her impulsive nature and uncanny ability to be so certain about how she felt that I found most endearing; she was so comfortable expressing her feelings in such an open way. We parted that day, as we had before, walking to a BART station for her ride back to the East Bay, though this time with a stop for ice cream along the way. At the train platform, she lowered her cone and I kissed her goodbye.

"You're an excellent kisser too," she smiled, taking a lick of mint chocolate chip.

"With a reserved sense of kindness?"

"Yes, very reserved," she laughed, as she turned to board the train.

After she left, I stood there for a moment, feeling both weary and exhilarated. I could think of only one place to stop before I turned in for the night. I hailed a cab outside the station, seeing the sun now just below the tall cypress trees studded throughout the park. I was greeted by a friendly face—it was Sunil, from my neighborhood deli, and he smiled a hello.

"I see you have had a wonderful day, my friend."

"Yes, it was good. How about dropping me at Balboa Café on Fillmore?"

"Oh yes, I mean no, go home and sleep my friend. I fear you will need your strength for that woman."

"Woman, what woman?"

Sunil smiled again.

"The one you are obsessed with, my friend."

"Well, I'm too drained to argue, Sunil, better steer this ship back to home port for the night."

"As you wish then," he replied.

As we rode off, I wondered how he could be so happy driving a cab on a Sunday evening when the rest of the world was likely at home with their families, unwinding from the weekend. Heading up Lombard, I asked Sunil why he drove his cab so much even on weekends.

"Because," he began in a serious tone, "I need to feed my family. They depend on me. My wife, my children, my wife's parents too."

"Of course, I'm sorry. It's just you work so hard yet seem happy whenever I see you."

"This is true my friend because helping my family makes me pleased."

"That's a good thing," I added, as we pulled up to my corner. I included a little extra in the tip because I felt stupid quizzing this man who had his priorities straight. As I unlocked the door of my apartment, I heard the phone and hurried to answer it.

"Hello," I gasped.

"Are you out of breath?" Laura asked.

"Ah, no, why? Are you home already?"

"Yes, I caught the express even though it wasn't labelled an express. I guess on the weekends no one checks those things. So, you're not out of breath?"

"No, I just ran up three flights of stairs and heard the phone."

"Oh good."

"Good?"

"Yes. Because if you aren't out of breath, maybe you'd like to join us at Yosemite for our annual weekend."

It seemed a lot to take in, and I really was out of breath. Back in the cab, Sunil had slipped me a flask of his father's home brew and insisted I take a swig or two—150 per cent pure fire, which I wasn't expecting. When I coughed up half a lung, he glanced at me in the rearview mirror with a look of satisfaction and exclaimed, "It is good, no?"

I nodded in semi-grief. Now, on the phone with Laura, I discerned the words "us" and "Yosemite."

"Yosemite?" I managed, as if I had never heard the word. "And, who's us?"

"Well, that would be my family. We've gone to Yosemite every Labor Day weekend ever since before I was born."

"You want me to spend the holiday weekend with your family?"

Laura's voice shifted to a sincere tone.

"Yes, Will, I'd like you to, very much."

There was a pause, probably not as long as it seemed, as I processed the significance of her words. When I replied, I delivered a rather unemotional response.

"Yes, I would like to, it sounds like fun."

Fun? Fun? Why did I say that?

"Okay, I have to go, but I'll talk with you soon," she concluded.

As we hung up, I sank down on the kitchen chair—wind burned, sunburned, somewhat dehydrated, slightly poisoned from Indian liquor, and still recovering from being kissed by this incredible woman. I grabbed a beer from the refrigerator and started to talk to myself out loud.

"I would like to? It sounds like fun? Her family? Most likely her entire family, extended family—cousins, uncles, aunts, grandparents."

I swallowed the last sip from the bottle.

"What's your damn problem?"

I thought about it and wondered if seeing Laura's happy family would remind me of what I had lost. I couldn't possibly be that selfish, could I? Or was it some subconscious instinct toward self-protection that was making me conflicted? I grabbed another beer from the fridge but didn't open it. I set it on the table and announced for no one other than myself to hear:

"I'm going to bed."

Yet, like the stage direction in the last scene of *Waiting for Godot*, I did not move. How can a picnic turn into a weekend? I had no answers to any of these questions.

Monday arrived sooner than I wanted. An early morning phone call from my cousin Jim summoned me to my new position at the Exchange.

"Hey, buddy boy, rise and shine. I've got good news."

"It better be at this hour."

"My newbie busted his knee on a bike ride over the weekend up in Sonoma. You want a J-O-B?"

"With you?"

"No, B of A, they need a new CEO—yes, with me here at the Exchange."

I was awake now and sitting up.

"But I know nothing about systems."

"You probably know nothing about getting laid either, but did that ever stop you from trying?"

"When?" I asked.

"ASAP, baby, money don't sleep. Bring a driver's license and a passport if you have one. Page me when you get here and I'll send someone from security to escort you to HR. Any questions?"

"Suit and tie?"

"Hell no, buddy boy, we're in the basement with the rats, just kidding, no rats, casual—it's California, dude."

With that, he hung up and my unexpected J-O-B was about to begin. I made a quick call to the E.F. Hutton broker with whom I was filling in to explain the situation. He told me not to worry and that the opportunity at the Exchange would be far better, and wished me well. I made it to the PSE by 6:30 a.m.—the exact moment, trading began. The rest of the day was a whirlwind, but at one o'clock Pacific Time, at the closing bell, they hailed me a hero for surviving trial by fire. I caught a mathematical glitch where three extra zeros were added to a transaction I was monitoring.

"Hey, buddy boy, my boss heard about your little catch and wants to meet you. Don't get a big head, we would have caught it in after-hours audit and busted the trade, but you saved a lot of paperwork for some house, and he wants to give you the official welcome."

"But I don't know anything about systems. Isn't he going to ask me something I don't have the foggiest idea how to answer?"

"Just ask him about golf, the rest will take care of itself. Relax, Will, you did good. I guess the apple doesn't fall far from the tree."

"Jim, we're cousins, not father and son."

"Whatever. Come on, he's eager to get to the course for a quick nine."

Jim walked me halfway to Wilkinson's office and pointed to the end of the hallway as I continued on alone. I knocked on the open door and stepped into the doorway.

"Will, Phil Wilkinson, it's a pleasure to meet you."

Wilkinson was fifty-ish and heavy set. I wondered how he hit a golf ball at all with his massive girth.

"Thank you, pleased to meet you, sir."

"I understand you just moved here from the East for grad school."

"Yes, that's correct, Mr. Wilkinson."

"Call me Phil. Thank you for stepping in on short notice, and also for catching that fly ball this morning."

Mixed metaphors were flying everywhere.

"I heard you have a tee time," I said.

"Yes, you play, Will?"

"Not in a while, but I was on the golf team in high school— about a six handicap."

As I said the words, I realized my faux pas.

"Six, huh. I've been stuck at thirteen for years. Unlucky thirteen."

"Well, it's the challenge, the fun, just to be lucky enough to be out on the course, right?" I said, trying to recover.

Phil smiled and stood up extending his hand.

"Nice to have you aboard, Will. Maybe we can play sometime?"

"I'd like that, sir . . . I mean, Phil. Enjoy your round."

I left feeling tired and sweaty. The basement was divided into two large rooms—a server farm with separate temperature control and the systems room filled with desks and phones and computer screens with minimal cooling.

"Hey, buddy boy, a few of us are heading over to the HC— The Holding Company—for a few brews. You in?"

I looked at my watch—it was 1:56 p.m. Who drinks at two o'clock in the afternoon was my first thought. I had nothing else to do, except maybe sleep, so I replied, "You read my mind."

It turned out brokers, traders, and back-office workers drank on Mondays and Thursdays and usually at the HC. On Mondays, it was only a couple beers before heading home to their families. Thursday, the heaviest trading day, was a little less tame and tequila shots were not uncommon. Fridays, I was told, were for those looking for some action—you could spot the interested secretaries by the small overnight bags they carried with them. But on that Monday, in my semi-celebratory mood, it was rather quiet as I became acquainted with the guys who worked at the PSE and the brokerage houses.

"Will, I'd like you to meet Henry Wilson, one of our most esteemed colleagues. Henry is a broker at Dean Witter," Jim said.

"Will Merritt," I said to Henry.

"Yes, I heard about what you did today; that's why I came over. I haven't been here in years, but I wanted to thank you for catching that error."

"You haven't joined these guys on a Monday in years, but today you stopped by to thank me?"

Admittedly, I felt a little tipsy after two beers and no lunch, except for a bag of chips.

"That's right, Will. I want to thank you."

"It wasn't a big deal—anyone would have caught it."

"Well, it is to me," Henry insisted.

"Say, Henry, do you by chance remember a bond trader named John McKenzie?"

His eyes lit up when he heard the name.

"John McKenzie! Of course, I knew him—everyone back then knew John."

"What can you tell me about him?"

His whole demeanor changed with my question. He relaxed and a smile appeared as he began his warm, nostalgic recollections of his friend.

"John was the most magnanimous and considerate individual you'd ever hope to meet. Smart as a whip, but never let it go to his head. He made sure that people were taken care of—you know—that they got their fair share—raises, bonuses—secretaries, janitors, everyone. He was a friend to everyone and made the bosses a lot of money along the way."

Henry stared into the distance for a moment before asking, "How did you know John?"

"I didn't. I know his daughter, Laura."

"Laura," he exclaimed. "Why, I remember him bringing her onto the floor when she wasn't more than five or six years old. It was . . ." he hesitated.

"Shortly before he died?"

"Yes," Henry replied. "He was a good egg. Left a wife and those two little kids—way too soon."

I drained my glass of beer.

"He was thirty-five," I answered.

"Hey, buddy boy." Jim had returned from the other end of the bar. "Why so serious?" he asked.

"Just talking about old times," Henry responded.

"Yeah, buddy boy knows a lot about old times on the job one day."

"Jim, stop."

"Okay, Will, today you're the man."

"I need to go," Henry said.

"Me too," I added.

When I got back to my apartment, I decided not to call Laura. I was too tired from the long day. I did, however, call from work the next morning. I waited until eight o'clock, unsure if it was too early that she might still be asleep, but also realized she had a tutoring position at a local junior college. As it turned out, I just caught her.

"Hey, Will, what's up?"

"I got a new job yesterday at the Pacific Stock Exchange. I'm at work right now."

"That's great, congratulations."

"Thank you. I can't talk, but was wondering if you'd let me take you to dinner to thank you for the picnic last weekend?"

"That sounds great. When were you thinking?"

"How about Saturday night?"

"Saturday, yes, okay. Do you want to meet in the city or come over here?"

"Why don't I pick you up? Is seven o'clock good?"

"Seven is great. I look forward to hearing all about the new job."

"Wonderful, I'll see you then."

"Thanks, Will, I've got to run."

"Okay, bye."

"Bye, Will."

As I hung up the phone, I heard a shrill, disembodied voice repeating, "Why don't I pick you up? Is seven o'clock good?"

Jim appeared behind me, having overheard most of the call.

"You see that ⅛ tick?" he said, pointing at a yellow bar on the computer monitor in front of me.

"Yes."

"See that ⅝ tick?" he continued, pointing at a red bar.

"Yeah."

"The red trade is mine. You watch the yellow calls—and the puts too."

It made little sense to me.

"Why?" I asked.

"Because, my tick is bigger than your tick," he said, roaring with laughter, amusing a few others nearby.

"That's your idea of humor?"

"Hey, what can I say? By the way, the old man heard you were asking around about Chez Panisse. That have anything to do with seven o'clock?"

"Maybe."

"Don't get coy with me, young man," Jim laughed.

"We're the same age."

"My point exactly. Anyway, he wants to see you."

"Wilkinson?"

"Yes."

"When?"

"You can go now if you make it short."

"Okay," I said.

"Yeah, the news of your little 'stunt' yesterday spread upstairs and Phil got props from the Big Guy."

"The Big Guy?"

"Bob Richardson, VP of the division."

I got up from my chair and hurried to Wilkinson's office, where I knocked on the open door.

"Will, come in. I heard from Jacki, my assistant, you were asking around about Chez Panisse?"

"Yes, I was hoping to get a reservation on short notice."

"Ah, the normal reservation wait is four weeks for weeknights, and about ten weeks for weekends."

"I know, that's why I was asking around."

"I see. When were you hoping to go?"

"This Saturday," I sheepishly admitted.

"This Saturday?"

"Yes, I know, something came up last minute, and I was trying to . . ."

"Impress a lady?"

"I guess you could say that."

"Well, if eight o'clock works for you, you're in luck."

"How? Do you know Alice Waters?"

"No. My wife and I have a reservation on Saturday at eight."

I looked at him puzzled.

"You mean you're giving me your reservation?"

"Yes, that's what it means."

"Mr. Wilkinson, I mean Phil, that's very generous, but I can't accept the offer. I'm sure your wife is looking forward to it."

"No worries, Will. We have two. My assistant made one for eight and my wife made one for six o'clock. She wants to go earlier. I had just told Jacki to cancel the later reservation when she mentioned you were asking about the restaurant."

"Wow, that's a coincidence," I said.

"It's an omen—of great things to come," he insisted.

"Well, thank you very much, I appreciate it."

"You're welcome. I'm glad I could make you feel at home around here," he said, looking down at his watch.

"I've got to get back," I said, gesturing toward the doorway.

"Yes, by all means, go."

"Okay, thanks again, Phil."

I called Laura that Saturday afternoon to tell her where we had a reservation in case it mattered how she dressed. I remembered seeing a movie where a woman was horrified for being underdressed at some country club dinner party. I didn't think Laura cared much about fashion, but thought it was best to tell her where we were going.

"Chez Panisse—how did you get a reservation there on such short notice?"

"That's a long story, which I'll tell you about tonight."

"Sounds like we have a lot to talk about."

"I hope I don't bore you."

"I doubt you can bore me honestly. Thank you for letting me know. I have something I've been saving for a special occasion."

"Okay, well, I'm going for a run now."

"That's funny, I'm about to go running myself. Wow, another thing to talk about."

"I'd better make a list."

"Okay, you do that. Enjoy your run."

"You too. See you later."

"Can't wait."

"Bye, Laura."

"Goodbye, Will."

Laura lived with her mother in Albany, just north of Berkeley, in a large brick Victorian home. I arrived with a bouquet of white calla lilies—her favorite flowers, she told me, while walking through Golden Gate Park together. I rang the bell, expecting her mother to answer, but Laura opened the door to greet me. She was wearing a light purple, which she called lilac, print dress and comfortable-looking taupe-colored Cole Haan flats.

"For you," I said, handing her the flowers.

"They're beautiful, thank you," she replied, kissing me as we embraced. "Let me put these in water," she said, turning to walk to the kitchen.

"This is a beautiful home."

"And large," she laughed.

She reached for a vase from the cupboard and asked if she could get me anything.

"Maybe a glass of water. I jumped in the shower right after my run and didn't hydrate much."

"I'll join you," she said, pouring two glasses from the tap.

As she arranged the flowers in the vase, I said, "I remember you telling me how much you like calla lilies."

"You must have because I do."

"I remember you telling me something else you liked," I grinned, sipping the water.

"What?"

"The way I kissed you."

"No? Did I say that?"

"You did."

"Well, I don't remember saying that," she teased.

"Perhaps this will refresh your memory," I said, kissing her gently.

"Nope."

I kissed her again, and she put her arms around my neck.

"My memory is returning."

"Good. By the way, you look pretty in your special occasion dress."

"You like it?"

"Very much, and I like the casual footwear thing you've got going on."

"Yeah, I'm a casual kind of girl."

"But you're wearing makeup."

"Yes."

"You didn't at the park."

"Ah, yes, a little."

"Well, you don't need it."

"Flattery will get you everywhere."

"Is your mom home?"

"No, she's at church—some special Saturday evening novena."

"I'm sorry I missed her."

"You'll get to meet her at the cottage. If you join us."

"I said I would."

"Yes, but I detected a hint of reservation in your voice."

"No, I was just surprised, it was kind of sudden that's all. Speaking of reservations, we should get going."

"Okay, let me grab my sweater," she said, returning to the hallway before we stepped out the front door.

At the restaurant, Laura and I were seated promptly. There was a small bowl of dark purple irises on the table and their color nicely complimented her light purple dress. When I commented on the contrast, Laura corrected my description with, "lilac." Maybe she did care about fashion more than I thought—perhaps we all do at that phase of a relationship. I scanned the room to see if Phil and his wife were still there, but they were not.

"Have you been here before?" I asked.

"A couple times for lunch, but not in a long time."

I ordered a bottle of wine and noticed her smiling.

"What?" I asked, after the waiter left.

"I remember my first time here. It was with my mother, brother, and grandparents."

"When was that?"

"In 1974, to celebrate my eighth-grade graduation. I was fourteen."

"I bet you had quite the supply of strawberry lip gloss then?"

"Apparently, since I still do."

"Has anyone ever told you how beautiful you are?"

"What? Stop—you're making me blush. So, tell me about this new job."

Over dinner I told her the entire story, including meeting Henry Wilson and hearing his fond memories of her father.

"I don't remember him."

"You were five or six."

"Funny, so many people know so much about my father and I know so little."

"Well, from what Henry said, he was wonderful man."

"Thank you for telling me all those things he had to say."

"I think since we both ran today, we're entitled to dessert," I said, picking up the menu on the table.

"I like that rationale."

We talked for another hour over crème brulée and a lemon raspberry fruit tart about my family, Syracuse, and moving to San Francisco. Much to our surprise, when I asked for the check, the waiter told us that a Mr. Wilkinson had seen to it.

When we arrived back at her house, she invited me in. On the kitchen counter was a note her mother left—she was staying overnight at her parents, who lived not far away, in the Berkeley Hills.

"She does this sometimes when she's feeling lonely. She doesn't know I know the reason. My grandfather told me. I guess she doesn't want me to worry about her."

"But you do."

"Yes."

"Of course, but what can you do?"

"Not much, that's what makes it so hard."

"I didn't mean to suggest . . ."

"No, it's okay. It's been like this a long time. I just try to be a supportive daughter."

"Still, it has to be difficult for her, to see you move on and have your own life."

"Yes, I suppose it is."

"I'm sorry. I didn't mean to make you feel bad."

"You haven't. It's been a long road and she knows I've achieved a certain independence and will be on my own soon."

"What about your brother?"

"He's not around anymore. He's got his own troubles."

"Maybe I should go."

"Oh God, am I scaring you off?"

"No, not at all."

"I know it's a lot to take in all at once," she apologized.

"No. I want to know everything about you and your loved ones, and everything that's important to you. Thank you," I said, embracing her.

"For what?"

"For feeling comfortable enough to share all these things about your family."

"You did too, over dinner."

"But I'm not still bearing responsibility for them. They're the ones looking over me."

"That's a nice way to think about it," she said.

"I've rarely felt the need to discuss them. It's never been important for me to share with anyone."

"I'm glad you feel comfortable sharing your feelings with me."

"I do," I replied, leaning down to kiss her. She returned my kiss and a mutual feeling of passion grew. It was something that could not be denied.

"Stay with me tonight."

"What?"

"Stay with me tonight, Will."

"Are you sure?"

"I am. I'm not sure why, but I am. I feel so comfortable being with you."

That night, in the McKenzie home, we made love for the first time.

"Oh God, Will, I've never felt like this in my life," she exclaimed, when we finished and fell into each other's embrace.

"Neither have I."

"Really?"

"Yes."

"So, it's a first for both of us."

"It's incredible making love with you," I smiled, kissing her gently.

"I'm glad. I haven't had a lot of experience."

"You're wonderful," I assured her.

"Are you sure?"

"Yes, I'm sure."

"Will you hold me all night?"

"I'll hold you forever," I answered, surprising myself.

"Don't say that if you don't mean it."

"I do mean it," I said, looking into her eyes.

"How did this happen?" she asked.

"I don't ask those questions anymore. I'm just thankful that fate somehow brought us together."

"Fate? We must have been attracted to one another."

"Yes, we were. So why isn't that fate?" I asked.

"Maybe it is. I don't know—right now, I don't care. All I care about is that you are here with me."

"We've found each other," I said.

"Well, as cheesy as that sounds, yes," she replied.

"One question?"

"What?"

"When will your mother be home tomorrow?"

"Ah, good question. I'm sure not until noon after mass."

"That gives us the entire morning together."

"Do you have a one-track mind, Merritt?"

"Not at all, I can multitask quite well."

"I think I'll test that out first thing in the morning."

That was the first time we spent the night together. It was the night that changed my life and the way I perceived myself in the world—no longer alone, but part of a couple, connected to someone in a special way that only we understood. As I lay there beside her, I suddenly remembered something I had written in high school English class and whispered the words to her:

Love is the miracle of sudden intimacy.

There, across a crowded room,

is a look, a smile, an attraction,

that cannot be questioned.

"That's beautiful, who wrote it?"

"I did. And I'm just realizing it's true. It's absolutely true."

She leaned over and kissed me.

"I'm fading, Will," she said, as she closed her eyes. "Will you be here when I wake up?"

"I'm not going anywhere."

Laura's bedroom windows faced east and the sun filtered in through the shades around six o'clock. I could see her dimly lit, peaceful face now. She leaned her arm over toward me touching my hand.

"Ah good, you're still here."

"I told you."

We embraced and made love again with an incredible intensity that neither of us had experienced before the previous night. And then we fell back to sleep until we awoke again and made love once more before I realized it was time for me to leave.

In the weeks leading up to Labor Day weekend, I learned much more about Laura's family. Betsy Capshaw, her grandmother, was the quintessential matriarch. Her husband, Andrew, a tall man with broad shoulders and piercing blue eyes, was her "knight in shining armor." Andrew grew up in Sacramento. His mother was a seamstress and his father oversaw the state forestry reserves. In the late '40s, John Capshaw came into money and bought a tract of timberland just north of Yosemite. He and his son Andrew became timbermen and, with the profits for high-demand lumber to build post-war homes, they expanded their property holdings farther north and east. Andrew saw the potential in California real estate and was careful in managing the forest lands they owned. He had seen many others deplete tree stock for a quick buck. By the late '60s, with John's passing, Andrew Capshaw had built a mini-dynasty of residential developments throughout Northern California. Near the end of the Vietnam War, before a national recession hit, he sold off forest property to the federal government to preserve wilderness areas around Yosemite National Park. Andrew wisely retained a few dozen acres, where he built a beautiful summer home for his family along the Tuolumne River.

Andrew and Betsy had two daughters—Anne and Ellen, Laura's mother. Laura, being the only granddaughter, was the apple of her grandfather's eye and she loved spending time with him and Betsy outdoors at their summer oasis.

My arrival at the "cottage," as they called it, was met with a downpour of rain not uncommon during late summer in the mountains. Despite my best effort, I was soaked as I ran up the front porch steps with my backpack and blanket in tow. The first family member to greet me was Sergeant, a full-grown chocolate-colored Labrador Retriever, who barked twice and then took pity on me. Ellen appeared behind the screen door. Laura told me her mother was forty-seven, but she looked younger and I saw the resemblance. She was thin, fair-haired, and slightly taller than her daughter.

"Mrs. McKenzie, it's nice to meet you. Laura has told me so much about you. I'm glad we can spend some time together."

"Ellen, please. Gosh, you're drenched, please come in," she said.

As she opened the screen door, Sergeant retreated from the porch into the cottage as I followed him in.

"Laura and the boys went into town for some supplies."

I looked at her quizzically.

"They ran out of beer and wine last night. Guess the first night celebration went a little longer than expected."

"Oh, well, I brought a bottle of wine," I said, handing it to her. "This should last until they get back," I joked.

"Let me show you where you can put your things—at least the dry ones. The others you may want to drape over the mantle."

A modest wood-burning fire was crackling in the living room just beyond the front room.

"You're with Mike on the first floor in the back bedroom just past the living room. We thought since you know him, it wouldn't be much trouble," she explained.

"Oh, yes, that's fine, wherever it's dry is great."

Andrew and Betsy were warm and loving. Ellen was charming and not as reserved as I expected her to be. Stephen, Mike's brother, was smart and affable, as were their parents, Anne and David. They were the epitome of a close, tight-knit, successful, upper-middle class family. I felt relaxed around them and we engaged in conversation and even debate on a variety of things: politics, sports, business, and banal topics like how to make ice cream or tie a fishing knot. My ease and comfort around the family was a welcome surprise and I realized my self-conscious worry about my reaction was unfounded. Being with her wonderful family was endearing and, if anything, renewed my sense of promise for tomorrow. That was the weekend I knew I was falling in love with Laura. She was her grandparents' granddaughter, her mother's child, her cousins' pride and joy. She lit up the room and cherished her family, and they loved her in return. As difficult as it must have been to lose her father at six years of age, she embraced what she still had, yet didn't lose sight of what she had lost.

The following afternoon, Stephen and I went for a hike in the woods. I asked about Laura's brother. He explained that no one knew where he lived; he floated from friend to friend. Rob was only four when his father died, and afterwards Ellen doted on Laura, while he remained aloof and withdrawn. His first experience at preschool ended when he knocked over a pitcher of milk and then ran off and pulled a fire alarm. Ellen was summoned to retrieve him, and his teacher suggested he needed more careful parental oversight. Laura was enrolled at The College Preparatory School in Oakland, which her grandparents insisted she attend given her intellect and musical ability. The private school was known as an outstanding educational institution both for scholarship and music. Piano was her passion. Ellen and Rob attended her recitals and, as the years passed, it became increasingly obvious her talent and academic achievement outshined anything he could produce. Ellen privately blamed herself for his lackluster aptitude and inability to fit in with his peers. She was lost herself—mid-thirties and grieving the loss of her husband while raising two children. It was all too much for Rob, and Ellen found it increasingly difficult to deal with his truancies and suspensions for drinking. He finished public high school and moved out the day after graduation. Ellen shielded Laura from most of it, and her focus on school and music was a positive distraction from what was going on with him. So, it was not unusual that Rob didn't take part in the annual family summer outing. Stephen confessed that no one knew the extent of his involvement in drugs down in East Palo Alto that summer, and it was something no one wanted to talk about. I didn't bring up the subject again.

On the third day, I was feeling so comfortable that I offered to make dinner. After a few modest protests from Betsy, she agreed. I sent Mike and Stephen to town for provisions in the midafternoon. No one remained in the house except Betsy, who headed to the porch for a nap as Laura stood standing in the kitchen doorway, still looking surprised at my offer.

"Can you cook?" she demanded.

It was a legitimate question since until then, we had only eaten in restaurants.

"Laura, today I feel like I can do anything."

"Well, that's fine and dandy, but my grandpa will want dinner, real dinner."

"Yes, I can cook. I can braise, I can boil, I can blanch, I can bake, I can broil, I can—"

"Okay!"

"Laura," I said, in a more serious tone.

"What?"

"I think I'm falling in love with you."

"I think I'm falling in love with you too," was her response.

"No, I mean it."

"I know you do."

"You do?"

"Yes, Merritt, I've known since the afternoon in the park."

She walked toward me and we embraced. I could feel her heart beating against my chest. I kissed her and she kissed me back.

"Make love with me," she said.

"Here?"

"Yes, upstairs, in my room."

We quietly climbed the stairs and spent almost two hours together.

"You're a wonderful lover," I told her.

"You bring something out in me. The universe stops when we're together like this. I'm so happy, Will, you make me so happy."

She started to cry.

"Why are you crying?"

"I've never been in love before."

I held her tightly until her crying turned to soft laughter.

"Ah, that's better," I assured, and then retreated down the stairs to the kitchen.

Dinner turned into a feast with everyone enjoying my beef bourguignon served with vegetables, new red potatoes, and arugula salad. David opened a bottle of Beaujolais Nouveau he had been saving. For dessert, I made a melon compote garnished with fresh huckleberries, nutmeg, and a splash of champagne.

"Kudos to the chef," Andrew said, after his second bite of "beef stew" as he called it.

"You'll make a fine catch as long as the girl isn't a vegetarian," he mused.

He was referring to Laura, who didn't eat meat, but who insisted I make something that would be "edible" for her family.

"Well, I've been known to make quite a tasty quiche," I said.

"Oh, listen here. Two months in San Francisco and the boy knows what the gays eat."

"Grandpa, stop it," Laura scolded.

"Ah, too much wine for this old man," he said, apologizing. "It makes a man . . ."

"Drunk?" she asked.

"Let's not quarrel before dessert is served," Betsy said.

More fruit jokes was my momentary thought.

"Andrew, you can't fool us," Betsy continued. "You employ straight and gay people."

Ellen changed the subject by asking where I learned to cook.

"Mostly from watching Julia Child. And my grandma was a superb cook and baker."

"Well, Laura is quite an accomplished baker too," Betsy boasted.

"Oh, I had no idea," I said, turning to look at Laura, who was seated next to me.

"I'm good at a lot of things," she offered, putting her foot against mine under the table.

"Well, we'll see next week when you're steeped in Contracts, Torts, Property, and Criminal Law," I replied meanly.

"Oh, don't remind me. This is my last weekend of freedom for three years!"

Grandpa Andrew looked at her with his kind blue eyes and spoke, "You'll do fine, Laura, don't worry."

His words felt so reassuring as if he knew what would become of her and everyone else in the family.

"And you too, Mike, and you too, Will. I wish you all the best," he said, raising his glass.

With that Ellen arrived at the table, carrying my dessert, which was enjoyed without comment, except for a few complimentary remarks about the champagne kicker. After dinner, we all sat around the fireplace in the living room, except for Andrew and Betsy, who retired for the evening.

"Gramps had a few wines in him. Think he'll be getting some tonight?" Mike smirked.

"Michael," his mother scolded, "you mustn't talk about people that way, especially your grandparents."

It was obvious Anne and Ellen felt uncomfortable with the subject of sex. Maybe that's why Ellen remained a widow after her husband's passing, I thought.

"I think old people should have sex," Laura countered.

"Okay, you two. Well, I guess that's our cue," Ellen said, as she and Anne headed upstairs. David followed shortly thereafter.

"Well, it's getting late," Mike joked, looking at his watch. "Eight forty. Where did the time go? Three down and two to go."

"What's that supposed to mean?" Laura demanded.

"Well, little cousin, you didn't invite this feller up here just to fix you dinner, did you?" he asked coyly.

"As a matter of fact, I did."

"Hey, Will's a stand-up guy though, maybe he can't stand up right now," Stephen laughed.

"Speak for yourself," I said, getting up to put another log in the fireplace. "I'm here to ensure this fire doesn't burn the house down," I continued, wielding the brass poker.

Stephen produced a bottle of bourbon, which we waved off having consumed a copious amount of wine. I wanted to hold Laura and somehow she sensed it because she stood and then joined me on the sofa across from the roaring fireplace. Sergeant appeared for a moment, then headed back to his bed in the corner of the room. Mike and Stephen sat at opposite ends of the sofa in large brown leather chairs with huge armrests as if standing, or more precisely sitting, guard over the grand proceedings.

"Hey, guys, you know I love you oodles and oodles, but I'd kind of like you to get lost so I can neck with my boyfriend."

"I'm getting the distinct impression we are being asked to leave, brother," Stephen said.

"Leave this wonderful, warm, and cozy chair in front of the fire?"

"Leave, please," Laura pleaded.

"Yes, ma'am," they answered in unison.

And with that, we were alone again. We fell asleep in each other's arms as we would for many future nights, after long hours of classes and study and meals together. In fact, it became a pattern to the point that we found it difficult to fall asleep without the other beside, and that is how Laura became my roommate after Thanksgiving. The rest of the weekend was a blur of idyllic family activities right out of a page from the *Saturday Evening Post*. A few days later, classes started, but I found myself going back in my mind, from time to time, to that true beginning of my love for her.

CHAPTER 2

THERE WERE READING assignments for the first day of classes unlike undergraduate school, where you didn't even buy books until you were certain you would not drop the course. Laura had a lot of reading too. And while we were in the same building at 536 Mission Street, law students drifted to the law library or elsewhere off campus to study in solitude.

September 23 was a Wednesday, which meant Laura had Torts at nine o'clock. I arrived at 8:20 a.m. with a dozen red roses wrapped in cellophane and placed them on her assigned chair. A half hour later, with most students in their seats, she walked in to find the flowers. Smiles greeted her as she read the card:

"This bud of love, by summer's ripening breath, may prove a beauteous flower when next we meet."
You have given me the best two months of my life. Happy Anniversary.

"Well, I'm glad everyone is in such a spirited mood for a Wednesday morning. Who can give us the facts in *U.S. v. Carroll Towing Company?*" Professor Johnston inquired, as he briskly entered the classroom.

Laura placed the roses on the floor next to her and raised her hand in response to his question. He called on her to recite the case facts, which she did without looking at her notes.

"Very good, Ms. McKenzie. I assume those flowers you were trying to secrete are not meant for me?"

"Correct," she replied.

"Very well then, who can tell us the holding in this case?" he asked, as the class continued.

Laura tracked me down at eleven thirty after my corporate finance class while I was on my way to the library.

"Hey, you," she shouted from across the hallway, "what's the deal with the roses?"

"Roses? Johnston gave you roses?" I replied.

"No, it wasn't Johnston, it was you, you big liar. Come here, I have to give you something."

As I approached, she jumped into my arms and kissed me.

"What was that for?" I asked.

"For leaving them in my Torts class rather than Contracts."

"Ah, I see, I thought it was a thank you kiss."

"No, you'll get your thank you on Friday. I'm coming over and making you dinner."

"Dinner? Is that a euphemism?"

"Do you want it to be?" she smiled.

"Yes."

"Okay, then it is. And I might feed you too."

"That sounds like a bargain," I joked.

"A bargain can be a legal contract."

"Okay, counselor. I've got an accounting quiz in an hour."

"Then go study," she insisted, turning around with roses and books in her hands. "See you Friday."

"Is that a verbal contract?"

"Wouldn't you like to know."

I aced my quiz on retained earnings, dividend distributions, and equity dissolution. Thursday I was slammed with work at the Exchange, classes, homework, and then a stop at The Holding Company. It had been a good day. Everyone was in friendly spirits because summer was over and the hassle of kids and vacations had disappeared with families falling back into a routine—school, work, weekends. September was typically the warmest month of the year and lent itself to warm sunshine through late afternoon, which everyone enjoyed from the outdoor patio at the HC. The mood was upbeat with much anticipation about favorable tax changes from Washington. I got in and out in under an hour because I was trying to stick to my running schedule. The topic du jour was the risks of writing naked options on margin, which I listened to intently while sipping on a single draft beer. I did my four and one-half mile run at the Marina Green well before dark and settled into studying stock transfer entries for the Series 24 General Principals exam. By Friday night, my brain was fried, but I made a trip to Safeway on my way home to make Laura's dinner offer easier. She looked tired when she arrived, but I noticed a bulging overnight bag.

"Just so you know, I'm getting my period," she announced.

"What do you think I am, a sex maniac?"

"Yes, and a devoted one."

"Hey, why don't you take a nice relaxing bath and I'll make dinner?"

"Are you sure?"

"Hearing no objection, so ordered," I replied.

That night after dinner, we sat on the balcony and watched the last ray of sun fade over the Golden Gate Bridge.

"This is silly," I said.

"What?"

"All this transportation, lugging stuff back and forth. Why don't you move in with me?"

"My mother wouldn't like it, neither would my grandparents."

"Are you sure?"

"Yes, and besides . . . don't you need your space?"

"Laura, when I'm alone, all I think about is you. Seeing you— talking, just holding your hand, is the highlight of my day. I can't imagine my life without you."

"Wow. I think that's maybe the first time I've ever heard you express your true feelings. You've given me something to think about, but right now I need to get some sleep."

She went to the bedroom and fell asleep under the blankets and comforter, while I sat alone on the balcony, looking at the lights reflecting off the water in the Bay. What was it she was anxious about? Was it her father's death, feelings of abandonment, or did she believe her mother's disapproval was something she couldn't ignore? Whatever the reason, I didn't know the answer and drifted into thoughts about my own parents.

My days at Syracuse seemed like a distant memory. My father had been a workaholic who ran a small, but profitable, tool and dye machine shop that specialized in high-end, customized marine machinery. Given Buffalo's proximity to the Great Lakes, and the many boats and ships that traveled those waterways, the business retained prestige and profitability even after his death in my senior year of high school. My mother, a nurse, doted on him, my brother Tom, and me until the day Tom drowned out on the lake. He was seventeen, a year younger than me, full of "piss and vinegar" as my father used to say. We lost both of them that year. I graduated near the top of my class with a scholarship to Syracuse in spite of everything that happened. Only my mother was there to see me walk across the stage to accept my high school diploma. A year later, she was gone too from breast cancer. While I mourned her loss, I needed to reconcile with those feelings in college, so it wouldn't consume me. By my sophomore year, it hit me: I was alone with no one—no family, at least no one close, to rely on.

I finished my second year of college and applied for a Fulbright Scholarship. It required an essay on what I would change in the world given the means and opportunity. I wrote my first draft about eliminating nuclear weapons and, with help from a teaching assistant at the Maxwell School, I managed to craft a cohesive and convincing essay. That effort, along with the fact that my parents were deceased, earned me an "Honorable Mention," which meant absolutely nothing. However, the award boosted my grades for the remaining two years as sympathetic professors aligned in my favor. In the end, I graduated magna. *So what?* I thought. When my older cousin Robert and his wife drove in for graduation and took me to dinner, I remember him asking "What did you learn?" and my response: "I learned how little I know." I recalled how I felt an inexplicit sense of abandonment back then—by my father, my mother, even my brother. I obviously knew it wasn't their fault, but nevertheless couldn't rid myself of that uneasy feeling for some time. After graduation, I took my frustration out on two-by-fours, rehabbing old houses back in Buffalo.

My thoughts returned to Laura. The woman I hoped to spend the rest of my life with, and be the mother of our children, was sleeping peacefully in the next room. What could give me more happiness? *Absolutely nothing*, I thought, *absolutely nothing*. The next morning, I got up and went for a run. I was full of energy and returned to find her still asleep. I showered and slipped back into bed as she woke up.

"You ran because you needed to release your sexual tension," she mused.

"Yes, and now I need you to rub my back, since I was sitting out on the balcony until after midnight in that metal chair."

Laura's strength was pathetic, but she tried to massage my muscles anyway. After a few minutes, I took pity on her and rubbed her, then I leaned down and kissed the back of her neck.

"How about some breakfast?" I asked.

"Why are you so good to me?"

"Because of my reserved sense of kindness."

"What?"

"It's what you told me on our first date, that I have soulful eyes and a reserved sense of kindness."

"Very prescient of me, huh?"

"Eggs?"

"Scrambled, please."

"Oh, you mean like your brain after Contracts?"

"No, Contracts I get, it's Property that's my problem."

"Property? A Capshaw-McKenzie not understanding Property Law?"

"Oh no, I understand the law, I just don't agree with it."

"That sounds about right. So after eggs scrambled, what's your plan?"

"Library all day," she replied. "And you?"

"Library all day. But I have a date tonight," I smirked.

"Really, with who?"

"You mean with whom?"

"With whom," she repeated, making a face.

"Ingrid Bergman . . . and Humphrey Bogart, Claude Rains, Peter Lorre, Sydney Greenstreet."

"And an annoying female law student?"

"Annoyingly beautiful."

"And hungry."

I brought her breakfast in bed before we spent the day studying.

Casablanca was every bit as good as I remembered. The first time I watched the movie was at 'Cuse my freshman year with Lisa Karen Singer. Lisa was a Poli-Sci major from Long Island, destined to marry rich, and live out her days lunching and bitching. At nineteen, Lisa was a looker, smart, and opinionated, which proved to be both an attraction and a challenge. But at nineteen, I was up to the challenge. We fucked on the first date and the second and the third. After that, the dating formality was dispensed with, and she'd just show up at my dorm room whenever the mood struck her, and it struck her often. Lisa was a great kisser and despite her big breasts, which she liked to display by wearing tight-fitting white tops, she was an insecure Jewish princess whom no one understood except, for some reason, me, which suited me fine. I had access to alcohol, pot, and concert tickets—all three of which she enjoyed. The tickets came courtesy of my freshman year roommate who was from Kenmore, a suburb of Buffalo. He grew up with Todd Beckenstein and his older brother, Jay, who was the saxophonist and co-founder of the band Spyro Gyra. Their first album came out when we were juniors, but they played the Jabberwocky, or "The Jab" as it was called, in the basement of Kimmel Dining Hall our first year, so we got to know the regulars and scored first dibs on tickets. By junior year, Lisa had switched majors twice: first to History and then Sociology.

"Sociology?" I inquired once with obvious bad timing.

"Don't be insensitive," she demanded. "Yes, Sociology, you know Max Weber, Emile Durkheim, Karl Marx."

"Not Chico, Harpo, and Groucho?" I smirked.

After that, the relationship ended, although I continued to procure concert tickets for her from time to time, and she introduced me to a few girls with whom I shared movie nights.

Rick remained in Casablanca, while Ilsa and Victor Laszlo escaped like they had the first time I saw the movie, only now Laura was holding my hand the whole time, which added a nuance of emotion to the love story. Afterwards, we went for a walk in the warm September night, listening for the occasional foghorn in the distance. Summer was ending, but our love was only just beginning to grow.

September became October and midterms preoccupied our lives. I didn't bring up the subject of living together again because I knew she was stressed from classes and I also didn't want her to be the subject of her family's disapproval. They had a preconceived notion of Laura, a collective confidence in her to do the right thing, and they were as supportive as any family could be. Still, I thought it was a lot to bear and wondered if I was a distraction.

"What are you saying?" she demanded, one Sunday evening when I hinted that she didn't need to always make me her priority. I thought her focus should've been on midterms. It was a poor choice of words and I tried to correct them.

"I don't want you to feel like you need to spend your entire weekend with me."

"Entire weekend? We spent twelve hours yesterday and today in the library. We slept nine that leaves three hours. Are you saying you don't want to spend time with me?" she cried.

I had let my exhaustion get the better of me.

"I just want you to do well," I said.

"I will do well, if I know I can depend on you to be there when I need you regardless of when that is."

The words came out of her mouth so quickly I'm not sure she realized their significance. It was apparent that I was the first man she trusted and now I felt like I had disappointed her. We stopped the discussion due to pure exhaustion, and in the morning we were up early, engrossed in reading our notes over coffee.

I had come to realize my concern had more to do with some insecurity I was feeling—like everything might come crashing down, and I didn't want Laura to suffer from collateral damage. There was no basis in my insecurity, other than I was in uncharted waters alone in San Francisco with no close family or friends to lend moral support. I recognized this feeling, albeit infrequent, happened when I was overly tired and feeling vulnerable. Fortunately, the night's sleep had excised this concern, and I sat there, trying to think of what to say to explain myself. After a few minutes of silence, I got up put my hands on her shoulders and whispered, "I love you."

"I know you do, and I love you too, but you don't need to handle me," she replied.

"Handle you?"

The words slipped out before I could catch myself.

"Yes, I can decide for myself if I need time without you to get things done. It isn't up to you to decide that—unless you feel the need for time alone?"

"Laura, it's not that at all. I cherish every moment I spend with you, but I don't expect you to spend every moment with me."

She turned and looked me in the eye.

"Fair enough, Merritt. I know I get a little defensive."

"Okay, so we aren't going to see each other anymore?" I kidded.

"Nope, this is it, this is goodbye," she replied, as she stood up and kissed me.

In that kiss, we were together, lost in each other's skin and breath and hair. We made love hastily, realizing the time. We had an hour to get downtown and sit for our last midterm. Later that day, she had planned to join me at The Holding Company, but some fellow law students enticed her to meet them at the Tadich Grill. I checked my answering machine at five o'clock and listened to the message about her plans and invitation to join them. I decided to ask Jim to accompany me over to the Tadich.

"Oh shit, Will, they banned me from there back in '80 when Reagan was elected."

"What happened?" I asked.

"I poured an Irish whiskey over some liberal bastard's head who was making a rude comment about Ron and Nancy."

"Well, you were justified, weren't you?"

"Ah, the asshole was a manager at Shearson. He called my boss and we caught all kinds of shit. But you go, Will."

When I arrived, the place was packed with out-of-town advertising executives who were attending a convention down the street at the Hyatt. I spotted Fred behind the bar and he pointed to a table near the front window where Laura and her friends were seated. Five others had just left and the remaining two friends were keeping her company until I arrived. I walked over, leaned down, and kissed her.

"Hi," I said, in a loving voice. "Sorry, I'm late."

"Hi," she replied. "Someone's in a pleasant mood."

I put my hand out and introduced myself.

"Lisa Singer," came the first response. I grinned, not about to relay the name coincidence. "Larry Martin," came the second.

"Would you excuse me a minute? I want to say hello to someone."

I walked over to the bar to check in with Fred.

"So that's the dame, huh, kid? I recognized her from the photo you showed me."

"Fred, this isn't 1945."

"Don't knock '45, it was a good year, VE Day, VJ Day."

"Fred, can I get water, no ice?"

"Geez, she got you on the wagon?"

"No, I'm just thirsty . . . been off from work this whole week sitting for exams."

"You hungry?" he asked.

"Hungry? Ah, maybe."

"I can get you comped tonight, just tell me when you're ready."

On that cryptic note, I returned to the table as Lisa and Larry, who were engaged I learned, were on their way out.

"Hey, Will, Laura finished the Property midterm first," Larry said.

"Oh," I responded, not knowing if that was good or bad given her previous comment about disagreeing with the law in that course.

"Well, we're beat," Lisa said.

"You two have a good night," I offered, as they said goodbye to Laura.

As I watched them leave, I caught Fred motioning out of the corner of my eye. I raised both hands and mouthed, "What?" In return, he motioned with his hands as if he was eating, so Laura and I walked the length of the bar to the dining area.

"Two big shots cancelled a Chef's Table for six. I got two open seats. It's paid. You want to eat in the kitchen?"

At first, I was confused until he repeated, "Chef's Table."

"Oh, Fred, I'm sorry. This is Laura, Laura McKenzie."

"Fred Connors, pleased to meet you, Laura."

"Pleased to meet you too, Fred, and yes, we'd love to dine at the Chef's Table."

Moments later, we were seated in the kitchen next to the area where plates were prepped for serving, but far enough from the stoves and ovens where the real noise and congestion occurred. At the table were seated a husband and wife from Los Angeles and two inebriated middle-aged women from Chicago in town for the ad exec convention. Laura pretended to be a journalist writing about Charles Manson and I, she related, was a New York City detective in the Art Theft Division here to investigate a stolen Matisse painting. The LA couple ate their meals quietly, while the other two barely managed to get the food from their plates to their mouths. We finished dinner, thanked Fred, and headed back to my place tired, but satisfied and relieved that midterm exams were over.

The Golden Gate University Graduate School and Law School Student Associations cosponsored a Thanksgiving Day meal in the Tenderloin, a seedy section of downtown, where many of the poor and homeless resided. Laura and I volunteered to help as did several others. I had served meals at a soup kitchen back at Syracuse on a fairly regular basis and found it to be a humbling experience. Laura told her mother we would miss dinner, but she insisted we come by later anyway.

On Thanksgiving, we drove to the community center on Geary, arriving just before noon. Food had been prepared since earlier that morning, and as we pulled up, a line had already formed at the door. We went inside and were put to work right away. It was a long afternoon, and by six o'clock, we were beat. At one point, I looked over at Laura, who was serving corn and mashed potatoes, while I was in the kitchen, washing pots and pans. Her hair was mussed and a strand of gold curl, from under her Sierra Club baseball cap, was hanging down one side of her face. Both cheeks were flushed as she cheerfully continued to serve the seemingly endless stream of people. It was the children that particularly evoked emotion in us with their assortment of family members: a parent, an aunt, sometimes a grandparent or two, but always so many children—some with smiles, but others with hopeless expressions of need on their faces. When

I finished washing, I walked over, handed her a glass of water, and kissed her cheek.

"I love you," I whispered in her ear.

"Thanks, I needed that," she replied.

By the time we arrived at her mother's house, dinner was over, but dessert had yet to be served. We both poured ourselves cups of coffee and glasses of wine, unsure of what we needed first. Stephen and his girlfriend Caroline Robbins, a fellow Easterner, announced their engagement after we had said our hellos, and everyone was overjoyed for them. Laura and I found ourselves exchanging a knowing glance at one another. Everyone was excited, though the news wasn't a complete surprise to us. Seeing them so happy only helped to reinforce the bond that we felt toward each other. It truly was a day for thanks and giving.

Caroline was a geologist and MIT grad, who worked with Stephen at Bechtel. Her parents were middle class—her father was an electrician and her mother a school teacher. I felt a connection with her background and the fact that we were both from the East was endearing. After dessert, Laura and I took our wine out onto the huge wrap-around porch and Stephen and Caroline joined us.

"Caroline, are you from Boston?" I asked.

"No, from a small town near Albany, New York," she replied.

"Really, which town?"

"Rensselaer. Have you heard of it?"

"Yes. So, why not RPI?" I asked.

"I was accepted there, but hey, MIT and Boston, how could I say no? And you?" she asked.

"Buffalo. Syracuse undergrad," I replied.

"My sister went to Syracuse. What year did you graduate?"

"'78," I answered. I detected a playful look on Laura's face, waiting, I suspected, to comment on the conversation.

"My sister was there then, she graduated in '80."

"What was your major?" Caroline asked.

"He double-majored in sex-ed and co-ed fornication," Laura interjected.

"That gives Women's Studies a whole new meaning," Stephen laughed.

"Don't encourage her," I said, referring to Laura. "Actually, I majored in math."

"Sarah, my sister, was a bio major. She's in dental school now at SUNY Buffalo."

"Well, you two have something in common," Stephen said.

"So what brought you out here?"

"Laura. We've been pen pals since she was eight and I thought it was finally time we met."

"Yes, he promised me eternal happiness," Laura mocked, in a lithe Daisy Buchanan-like voice.

"Well, it looks like it's working," Stephen replied approvingly.

He cared about the family as much as anyone, except perhaps for Andrew. As the oldest grandchild, Stephen was especially protective of his only female cousin. They shared a passion for music. Like Laura, he played classical piano, perhaps even better, but was prodded by his father to find a suitable profession, which left little time for music lessons. Uncle David, who was an attorney, was pragmatic about things like that and civil engineering was a more acceptable choice for his son.

"You remind me of my Uncle John," Stephen said.

"Well, I've heard wonderful things about him, but I'm not sure they apply to me."

"I think you have some of his traits. You're smart and intelligent."

"Aren't those the same?" Laura interjected again.

"And you're tolerant of interruptions," he continued.

"That's kind of you, but I think tonight should be about you and Caroline, so let's raise our glasses. Best wishes and much happiness," I said.

We spent the entire weekend after Thanksgiving on term papers and studying. On Sunday evening, we hosted a pot-luck-leftovers dinner for some of Laura's law school friends while we watched *On Golden Pond* on the VHS tape player I bought. Henry Fonda played Norman, and Katharine Hepburn his wife Ethel. Laura's grandmother had been suggesting it since Labor Day weekend and we finally understood the "knight in shining armor" reference.

"I wonder if we'll be like that when we're old?" Laura asked, as we were cleaning up after everyone left.

"You mean senile and hard of hearing?" I asked.

"No, I mean, will we still love each other?" she asked pensively.

"Of course, we will."

"But, will we still be 'in love' with each other?"

"Laura, I will still be 'in love' with you until the day I die. I may not know who you are, but I'll still be in love with you."

She smirked at my remark.

"Okay then, that's all I need," she replied.

"That's all you need for what?"

I knew her well enough to know something was going on inside her head.

"Whether I should move in with you."

"McKenzie, you are one strange girl."

"But I insist on paying half the rent."

"If you insist, there isn't any point in trying to change your mind."

"That's right, there isn't."

"Great, I'll just use my savings for poker night and cigars."

"You don't gamble or smoke."

"Well, no, I couldn't afford to before now."

"You'd better save it for a hearing aid. I'm not going around shouting all the time like Katharine Hepburn."

That night, for the first time, I wondered what life would hand us. What was in store for us in ten, twenty, forty years? I nodded off thinking of Norman, Henry Fonda's character, and how old and frail he had become. *Would that be me? Would I be so lost?* No, I concluded, not as long as I had my Ethel—my sweet, beautiful Laura McKenzie.

December was busy but then, with exams over and three weeks off before classes began, Laura and I became resident tourists and visited all the sightseeing spots—galleries, museums, Fisherman's Wharf—even taking cable cars whenever we could. It was a fun time for us to relax after a hectic semester. On Christmas Eve, we attended Midnight Mass at Saints Peter and Paul Church in North Beach. Even though we were both pretty much atheists, we were lapsed Catholics, who wanted to experience the music and joy of our long-lost childhoods. The words to the songs were familiar and Laura sang along with the choir.

"Sing, Will, sing," she pleaded, as I joined her.

Laura didn't stop attending church after her father died—she was too young to decide for herself, but that was when she stopped believing, she told me.

"How could a merciful God take a parent from a six-year-old?"

I had no reason, nor did I try to answer her rhetorical question.

"When did you stop believing?" she had asked me, on a late-night walk some time back in October.

"I'm not sure I ever really believed. Despite twelve years of parochial school, I never once felt the need to believe in something greater than myself. I always felt that whatever obstacles or misfortunes I suffered, I was the only one who could fix them. No one, or no God, would ever do any heavy-lifting for me."

"I know what you mean," she replied, and then nothing more, as if her silence was tacit understanding. That's what I loved about her—she could talk and argue and debate and even filibuster, but when someone was talking about something sincere, even sacred, she would listen and reserve judgement, sometimes responding with as little as "hmm" as if to say, "Yes, I get it." After Mass, we parted for the first time since she moved in. She had promised her mother she would stay the night at her house to help prepare for company. Ever since Laura was born, her family had hosted the extended family on Christmas.

"You understand, don't you?" she asked, for the third time that evening.

"Yes, of course. I just hope Santa knows where to deliver your presents."

"Well, be sure to bring anything with my name on it to my mom's tomorrow."

"Okay," I promised.

Laura dropped me at the apartment and drove off in my black Plymouth, which I barely used in the city. I called my cousin, Jim. His answering machine picked up and I realized he was down in Palm Springs, visiting his sister and her family, so I hung up without leaving a message and went to bed. The next day, I did my usual four and one-half miles and then, for no particular reason, I ran another four and one-half. I had nothing to do until it was time to leave, so when I got back, I crashed on the sofa, drenched in sweat. I drank several glasses of water and lay there staring at the ceiling half-bored, half-lonely. I knew it was silly. I would see Laura in a matter of hours, but at that moment, I felt alone—no family of my own to spend the holidays with. Grades had been posted, four As and a B+, so I knew it wasn't that—things I had control over—it was this other thing, this feeling that life had a way of altering the plans you made that was causing my anxiety.

"Screw this," I said to myself, and headed to the bathroom to shower and shave.

I arrived at Ellen's just after two thirty. Laura answered the door.

"You came!"

"Of course, I came, I was invited, wasn't I?"

"I don't know, were you? I certainly didn't invite you. Mother?" Laura yelled, "Did you invite this young man carrying two bags of gifts?"

From the distant kitchen, I heard her reply, "Laura, can't you give Will a break for once? It is Christmas."

"I guess you'd better come in," she said, with a huge grin.

I set the bags down and she threw her arms around me.

"I missed you," she said.

"I missed you," I smiled.

"Good! Want some eggnog?"

"Sure, let me say hello to your mother and family first," I added, noticing that almost everyone had arrived.

"Yes, splendid idea. I'll meet you in there with the eggnog."

The living room was decorated with Christmas ornaments and wreaths and toy Santas and a ten-foot Douglas fir with ornaments, lights, and tinsel. Christmas music played on the radio in the background and I was greeted with a handshake or a hug and a warm smile. Everyone could tell how happy Laura was and knew I was responsible for at least part of that joy. Later that night, Ellen confessed she and her parents saw a similarity between me and John. Laura hadn't made that connection, at least not consciously, since she was so young when he died.

"It's flattering you think so," I managed. "I only hope I can be as good as he was."

I stopped short of saying "as good a husband," not wanting to forecast anything I wasn't sure would happen.

"Go sit with her, Will," Ellen insisted.

"Ellen, I love your daughter very much."

"I know you do, and I know she feels the same about you."

The evening continued with food and drinks and presents. After everyone left, and Ellen went upstairs, Laura and I sat alone on the sofa with the room lit only by the twinkling lights on the tree.

"You did good today, Merritt. Everyone was glad you were here with the family—especially me."

She leaned over and kissed me gently on the lips. I pulled her closer and she could feel something in my jacket pocket pressing against her.

"What have you got in there, a revolver?"

"No, it's your gift."

"I thought you gave me my presents—the sweater and the hat, the book, the watch."

"This is a special gift," I said slowly.

"Special?"

"Very special."

I reached into my pocket and produced a small unwrapped box. It was old and the fabric was worn through with age.

"This was my mother's," I said, as I opened it to reveal a two-carat diamond ring.

Laura gasped.

"Will you marry me?"

Her eyes were filling with tears. It was only the second time I had ever seen her cry.

"Don't cry," I smiled.

"Yes, yes, I will marry you," she smiled, hugging me tightly.

CHAPTER 3

"SON OF A gun!"

I heard Laura yelling from the hallway outside our apartment. I opened the door to see her with a huge grin on her face, holding the mail with an opened letter on top.

"I made *Law Review!*"

They only selected six second-year students. It was November 1982, almost a year since our engagement.

"That's wonderful, congratulations."

She looked at me and said, "Thank you," with regained composure.

Once inside, she read the letter again in the bedroom as she changed her clothes.

"Holy shit!"

"I hope this new position isn't going to reduce your speech to profane outbursts?" I shouted from the kitchen.

"Son of a gun."

"You said that already. You'll have to expand your vocabulary."

"Hell, yes," she said, reappearing in the kitchen in running clothes. "Let's go for a run."

I was about to point out Wednesday wasn't one of my days to run, but agreed.

"How far?"

"How far? I don't know—until we're tired."

I looked at her semi-crazed countenance.

"Ah, five, no six."

"Six miles?"

"Yeah, what's the matter? Afraid you can't keep up?"

"Oh, I can keep up," I said, as I went to change.

At the Marina Green, the six miles were fairly easy. Laura ran at a twelve-minute pace, but I let her believe I was struggling over the last lap as she pulled ahead and finished almost a quarter mile before I did.

"Keep up, huh?" she taunted, when I finished the lap.

"It's Wednesday. I'm not used to running on Wednesdays."

"Excuses?" she teased.

"Hell, yes."

"Hey, that's my swear word," she demanded.

The best part of running with Laura, as a card-carrying member of the Sierra Club, was her insistence on conserving water, which meant we showered together on occasions like these.

"Ah, the sacrifices I make for the environment," I said smiling.

"Sacrifices? You see any flab on that?" she asked, pointing to her well-toned thighs. "Or here?" patting her flat stomach.

She knew it would turn me on and it did. The run too had energized us both and we made love in the shower.

"You feel so good," she said, kissing me passionately.

She came with an intense orgasm and we lay in bed afterwards, cuddling for a while until her stomach growled.

"Hungry?" I asked.

"Ravenous."

"Oh, just ravenous? Not, Goddamn fucking ravenous?"

"You're mocking me, right? This is mocking."

"Yes," I said, as I stood up to go make grilled cheese sandwiches.

That second year passed with a much greater workload because of *Law Review*. I finished my MBA summa cum laude and quit my job at the Exchange. Starting work at 6:00 a.m. had lost its appeal; it lost its appeal the first month, but I needed something impressive on my resume. But now, instead of joining the workforce, I decided to go one more year on scholarship to get a second master's degree in Taxation. Laura and I discussed it at our mutual birthday dinner on March 17—she was turning twenty-three and I was twenty-seven.

"You'll work the rest of your life. Why not take one more year and do it—we'll finish school together," she urged.

It didn't take much convincing with the scholarship offer. The boys down in systems at the PSE told me to do the extra year. Even Phil Wilkinson called to give me his two cents.

"Will, it's only another nine months. You'll be done before you know it. It's like a baseball season—spring training, right through the summer into postseason, and then the World Series."

The analogy didn't quite fit, actually it didn't fit at all, but his sentiment was sincere.

"Thanks, Phil," I replied, when he was through with his diatribe.

"And you know you can always use me as a reference."

"I appreciate that, and for the great opportunity to work with you."

"No, thank you, Will. You've done outstanding work for us."

As I relayed all this to Laura at dinner, I realized I had monopolized the conversation.

"What about you? When will you hear from the Sierra Club?"

She had applied for a summer internship in their legal department.

"April 1, April Fools' Day."

"Don't be silly, I'm sure with your grades and references and *Law Review . . .*"

"We'll see," was all she could manage.

"Is something wrong?" I said, noticing she had barely touched her food.

"No. I don't know. I've been having a hard time focusing this past week. I'm tired I guess."

"Well, you've been working all the time and—"

"I'm late. It's . . . just from stress, but I wanted you to know." She looked at me plaintively. "In case, you know."

"Laura, it would be okay," I said, trying to reassure her.

"No, it wouldn't. I'm twenty-three. Twenty-three today— that's too young to have a baby and be a mother."

"Why did you let me go on talking when this was on your mind?"

"Because it's probably nothing—just anxiety and stress. I'm not pregnant!" she said, in a raised voice.

"You missed your period, but you know for certain you're not pregnant?"

"Yes."

"Then why are you drinking Perrier?

"Will, please stop."

She was on the verge of tears.

"I'm sorry. I didn't mean to make you cry."

"I'm not crying. I'm just upset."

"I can see you're upset. Would you like to leave? Do you want to go home?"

"Yes, please," she said, in the feeblest voice I ever heard.

"I'm sorry I ruined your birthday."

"You didn't ruin my birthday."

"Yes, I have."

"Laura, stop."

"Okay, can we please go?"

When we returned to the apartment, she announced she was going to bed. I kissed her and held her for several minutes.

"I love you, Laura. No matter what happens, I'm here for you."

"Thank you."

I tried to read, but my mind was filled with so many competing thoughts. I took a sleeping pill—a habit I had fallen into since I was going to bed later because I didn't have to get up early for my job anymore. I slipped into bed as Laura was sleeping. When I woke up the next morning, she was gone. A note on the kitchen table read:

> Off to school. See you tonight.
>
> Love L.
>
> P.S. I got my period!

On the first Saturday morning of April, a letter arrived with a Sierra Club return address. I realized it was more than one sheet as I grabbed it from the mailbox. Laura was still asleep when I got up to the apartment and peered into the bedroom. Her body felt warm as I lay down next to her and she exhaled, realizing I was there. A minute later, she opened her eyes.

"Hey, beautiful," I said.

"Hey."

She had pulled an all-nighter writing a *Law Review* article on *Agins v. City of Tiburon*, a 1980 Supreme Court decision involving a zoning law and the Takings Clause of the Fifth Amendment.

"I think I'm the bearer of good news," I said, producing the unopened letter.

"What is it?" she asked, with her eyes still bleary from sleep.

"It's from Publisher's Clearinghouse. You may already be a winner."

"What are you talking about?" she said, half awake.

I handed her the envelope and her eyes focused in on the return address. She ripped the paper and read the letter.

"I got the internship!"

"That's awesome—congratulations."

"Yes, it is. To tell you the truth, I didn't think I stood a chance. There are lawyers who've passed the bar, who were competing for this."

"Even more reason to be proud."

"Thank you, Will."

"For what?"

"For believing in me, and for all the supportive things you've said these past few months."

"I'm very happy for you."

"For us," she said.

"Okay, for us."

A month later, Mike and I graduated and Laura attended the ceremony. She was dressed in a navy suit and wore heels.

"Oh my God, you're a yuppie," Mike shouted, when she walked into the very same room where I had first met them two years earlier.

Even I had to admit it was a departure from the tattered gray Berkeley sweatshirt she practically lived in—size extra-large with the sleeves rolled up, covering half of her five-foot-three body. The graduation ceremony was long. A few small children squirmed in their seats as each graduate's name was announced alphabetically, except for Mike, me, and one other student—the summas. Mike told me he was disappointed he wasn't allowed to speak, which I mused was an obvious oversight that would likely be rectified by a huge reduction in his student loan. He was headed to Dean Witter for a job in their Information Technology department. I was staying on for a second master's, which Mike thought had more to do with me wanting to be with Laura in her third year. He said it was a romantic gesture on my part. I'm sure she had something to do with it, I confessed, but only to myself.

After the ceremony, Mike's parents, Anne and David, invited us to lunch at the Sheraton Palace Hotel. The family had patronized the hotel for years. Stephen and Caroline joined us, and because their wedding was going to be held there the following month, the executive chef arranged a private room and prepared a special meal. Although Laura and I had been engaged for just under a year and a half, there had been no real discussion about a wedding date. I think we just assumed that would happen after law school since Stephen and Caroline were getting married this year. Lunch included a champagne toast, which both Laura and Caroline begged off. I half-expected Mike to make some comment about Caroline being pregnant, but since his parents were present, he didn't.

"Calories, I need to fit into my wedding dress," she explained.

"Gratuitous Transfers, Evidence, and Conflict of Laws finals," Laura replied.

"Well, more for us," Mike said. "Conflict of Laws, that's a course?"

"Yes, unfortunately for me, it is."

After a third cup of coffee, Laura rose from her chair. She thanked everyone, walking around the table to say goodbye. She received one more compliment from Anne on how professional she looked in her new suit. When she reached me, I rose and she took my hand.

"I wish I didn't have to go," she said.

"I know. Are you going to study at the library or the apartment?"

"The apartment, I have to get out of this suit. But you go see your broker buddies."

"Okay, I'll keep an eye on your cousin," I said.

"Congratulations again, and for making summa, so my cousin couldn't boast."

Mike overheard her comment.

"And, can you imagine if he had McKenzie genes too?" she teased. Everyone laughed, including Mike. "Sorry, Uncle David," she quickly added.

"No offense taken, counselor," he replied.

"Ah, yes," she said, looking at her watch. "Not unless I pass my finals."

Laura departed with everyone watching her walk away in amazement. It was the first time they could remember seeing her in heels.

After we left the hotel, Mike and I headed over to The Holding Company. It was almost four o'clock when we arrived and the regular crew of brokers and traders was there.

"Hey, boys, been waiting for us?" Mike smiled.

A broker from Paine Webber named Sam Wilde, who had lost a bundle to Mike in a recent poker game, was quick to respond.

"No, Foster, computers were down for two fucking hours. We had to stay late and execute everything on paper."

"Well, let me buy you drink," Mike offered.

Sam's demeanor changed, perhaps because he was surprised at the gesture. Mike could be unpredictable like that. He could turn enemies into friends with his boyish looks and Irish charm.

"Thanks," Sam said, when Mike handed him a Chivas and water.

"How'd you do, Sam?"

Mike was in the zone now—all empathetic and heartfelt.

"We did all right this week; this first half of the quarter too. It's just tricky when the network's down and you're doing everything in your head."

"But you go on instinct and experience, am I right, Sam?" I asked.

"Yeah, I suppose. Hey, congrats to you."

"Thanks, Sam. You know I'm headed to Witter," Mike said.

"I heard, we all heard."

"We're gonna eat your lunch," Mike replied, after his second shot of tequila.

"Sam doesn't eat lunch, he's too busy making money, right, Sam—fill or kill?" I asked.

"I try. Hey, thanks for the drink but I have to catch the four fifty to Tiberon."

Sam finished his drink, congratulated us again, and headed out to the Ferry Building.

"I'm gonna hit the can," Mike said. "I'm not sure champagne and poached lobster followed by Anchor Steam and tequila is such a good idea."

While Mike was gone, I noticed a tall redhead sipping her drink and standing somewhat alone, away from the rest of the crowd. I went over and introduced myself, seeing that she had watched my conversation with Sam so intently.

"You know Sam?" she asked, as I approached her.

"I do. And you?"

"Yes, I'm at Merrill on the retail side of the house," she answered. "Lynn McCracken," she continued, extending her hand.

"Will Merritt," I replied.

"Say, what happened to the other guy in the black pin stripe?"

"Oh, he'll be back."

"Can I buy you a drink?" she asked.

"Maybe in a bit, I still have this one."

"Well, in a minute, I might not be here."

"Then I guess I'd have to buy my own."

"You're pretty cocky."

"Me? Wait until you meet Mike—the guy in the black pin stripe."

"I'm sorry, I just had a rough day."

"No need to apologize. You're in a tough business—sales is stressful."

"It's also dominated by men and some are real assholes," she added. "So what do you do?"

"I work, well worked rather, at the Exchange in systems and operations and I graduated with my MBA today."

"Congratulations. Worked?"

"Yes, I retired a few weeks ago," I mused.

"So that meant Series 24 or 27, handling options trades, authority to DK?"

"Yes, and a lot of audit stuff."

"Are you feeling okay?" I asked, when Mike reappeared.

"I'm feeling better now," he said, looking at Lynn's large chest pushing out against her tight green dress.

"This is Lynn McCracken."

"Mike Foster."

"Hello," she replied, turning back to me to ask, "Are you really retired?"

Mike laughed.

"Yeah, he's retired from hitting on hot women—actually any women."

"I quit. I'm going for a second master's and then into M&A, I think."

"M&A?" Mike said. "You never said anything about investment banking!"

"Well, I've been fielding some offers, we'll see."

"Say, Lynn, can Will buy you a drink?"

"I offered to buy him one, but he declined."

"I didn't decline, I deferred," I said.

"Well, I'd like a drink,' Mike replied.

I caught the bartender's eye and ordered a round for the house, which at that point was about a half dozen back-office people in systems, all of whom we had worked with, including my cousin Jim, who arrived late because of the network problem.

"Gentlemen and Lynn, Will and I graduated today with our MBAs, ranked first and second in the class. It has been a distinct honor and privilege to have joined you these past few years. I am moving over to Witter, while my esteemed colleague will enjoy another year of graduate school. Thank you and have a pleasant evening."

Everyone raised their glass and drank and came over to buy us more. By six thirty, we were inebriated. Lynn and I put Mike into a cab.

"He's going to Eighteenth Street on Potrero Hill. Mike, what's the number?" I asked.

Mike gave the cabbie his address and they drove off.

"Can I buy you a drink now?" Lynn asked.

"Sure," I said.

"Where?"

"I know a place."

"Harrington's?"

"No."

"MacArthur Park?"

"No, the Tadich Grill."

"Oh okay, I haven't been there in a while," she replied.

As usual, Fred was behind the bar. He was mixing Manhattans for a group of lawyers who had just won a large settlement.

"Will, and beautiful redhead, take a load off," he said, motioning to two empty stools at the end of the bar nearest to the dining room. "What brings you out on a beautiful May evening?"

"Booze," I replied.

"Well, you've come to the right place. The usual?" he asked.

"No. How about a Manhattan like you just mixed for the trial bar over there?"

"Hey," Fred whispered, leaning across the bar, "they just got an $18 million award."

"Me too," Lynn said.

"I'm sorry, Fred, this is Lynn."

"Fred Connors, at your service," he replied, turning to mix our cocktails.

"He gets sentimental at times," I said.

"That didn't seem sentimental."

"Well, you kind of have to know him to realize when he's being that way."

"I think you're cute," Lynn said.

"More like drunk."

She looked over my shoulder and noticed a table of people eating dinner.

"Oh shit!"

"What is it?"

"It's my ex with a group of clients. I don't think he saw me."

"Do you want to leave?"

"No, I want to taste one of those $18-million Manhattans."

"Well, if we split that money, it would be a $9-million Manhattan."

"I knew you were a math whiz."

Fred returned with his shaker, poured its contents into two long-stemmed glasses, and garnished them with cherries.

"Cheers, you two," he said.

"Thank you," Lynn replied. "So you must come here often—Fred asked if you wanted the usual."

"Once in a while. I come to watch the people, the bustle of their lives, business dinners, tourists, married guys with their mistresses. Fred will tell you; he's seen it all."

When he heard his name, he turned back to us.

"What's up?"

"Lynn asked why I stop in every once and again."

"Well, it isn't for the cheap prices I can tell you that," he replied.

"No, I mean for the color," I said.

"Coloreds?" Fred replied.

"No, the color, the vibe, the people coming and going. 'Men came and went, they passed and vanished, all were moving through the moments of their lives to death.'"

Lynn put her hand on my thigh while I quoted Thomas Wolfe.

"Geez, Will, that's morbid. Drink your Manhattan; it'll cheer you up," he said.

"I'm not depressed, Fred. I'm simply answering the question why I come here."

"You're depressing me, kid. What about you, Lynn? Is Will depressing you?"

"Not at all. I think he's just making an honest observation about life that most people choose to ignore."

"Oh boy, you two are a pair," he said, putting his hands up as he walked over to the lawyers.

"Are we?" she asked.

"Are we what?"

"A pair? Or at least a pair for the night?" she whispered, biting her full lower lip.

"I—"

"Don't say anything to spoil the moment."

She leaned over and kissed me with her pouty lips.

"Lynn, I'm engaged."

"So?"

"So, I can't do this."

She sat upright on the stool and turned to face the bar.

"Well, you're certainly the moral one, aren't you?"

"Lynn, Lynn, look at me."

She turned her head and stared into my eyes.

"You're a beautiful woman, but I can't betray what I have, what I never even knew existed until I found it."

Her stare didn't waver until she said, "It's okay, like I said, I just had a bad day, a really bad day. I'm going to leave before it gets any worse."

She gestured with her eyes toward the table where her ex was seated.

"Good night, Lynn," I replied, as she rose from the stool and walked away.

Seeing her leave, Fred walked back over to me.

"Say, Will, I know it's none of my—"

My glare cut him off.

"I need the tab."

"She dropped two twenties at the end of the bar on her way out."

"Oh. I'm gonna head home."

"Okay, kid, you do that, and get a good night's sleep, you'll feel better in the morning when the sun comes up."

It was after 10:00 p.m. when I got back to the apartment. Laura was curled up asleep on the couch with all the lights on and a casebook next to her. I placed the book and her notes on the table, turned off the lights, and put a blanket over her. Best not to have a conversation, I thought as I went to the kitchen for a glass of water and headed off to bed. Within minutes, I too was asleep and, in the morning, awoke to the sounds of Laura stirring in the living room. After a quick shower, I made coffee. It was barely seven, but the sun was out just as Fred had predicted. I sat down on the sofa next to Laura, and she opened her eyes.

"The sun is so bright, it's only six something."

"It's seven o'clock," I said.

"Seven! Oh, I have my Conflicts final at nine."

I tried to kiss her, but she protested, "Morning breath."

She jumped up past me to get into the shower. Laura McKenzie was a determined second-year law student focused on those last three final exams, but she did kiss me goodbye before leaving. I wished her well and went back to bed, wondering if Mike felt as hungover as I did.

On Sunday, Anne and David hosted a family brunch for Mother's Day at their home on Russian Hill—a ten-minute walk from our apartment. Laura still had two finals before we started our summer jobs, but took a break to spend time with the family. As we sat down to eat, her grandfather mentioned that he and

Betsy were going to the cottage for a few days to install some bathroom fixtures.

"I understand you know a bit about plumbing," he inquired, as Stephen and Mike were carrying platters of food over to the table.

Mike gave me a quick glance, eager to hear my response.

"Yes, I've done some."

"Can you solder copper fittings?"

"Yes, and I can solvent weld PVC pipe."

"Well, how about giving me a hand installing new sinks in the bathrooms?"

"Sure, when are you going?"

"Tuesday. We're driving up Tuesday and coming back Friday afternoon. The sinks and bathroom fixtures have already been delivered. They're sitting in crates on the front porch."

Up at the cottage, we spent Tuesday afternoon unpacking the crates and moving everything into place. Over the next two days, we pulled out the old sinks and replaced them with new ones. Of course, Betsy insisted we stop for lunch, and help with some other chores of her own, so the work took both days to complete. By Thursday evening, we were worn out from the physical labor and fresh mountain air. Betsy made a late dinner of pan-fried trout she caught herself. After we cleaned up the kitchen, she decided to turn in for the night. Andrew and I sat out on the enclosed porch together.

"What are you reading?" he finally inquired.

"Graham and Dodd's Security Analysis."

"No, I mean the other book," he said, pointing to a small paperback.

"Oh, it's a collection of poetry Laura gave me for graduation."

"Ah. Who you got in there?" he demanded to know.

"Wordsworth, Keats, Byron, Shelley, I think, some Tennyson, Yeats."

"Shelley? What do you have by him?"

"Take a look," I said, flipping to the table of contents and handing the book over to him.

"Let's see here, hmm, yes here it is," the old man announced, *Adonais: An Elegy on the Death of John Keats*. He found the page and began reading aloud, "Oh, weep for Adonais—he is dead! Wake, melancholy Mother, wake and weep!"

Andrew stopped and continued to read silently until he spoke again.

> "Afar the melancholy thunder moaned,
> Pale Ocean in unquiet slumber lay,
> And the wild Winds flew round, sobbing in their dismay . . .
> Touched by this spirit tender,
> Exhales itself in flowers of gentle breath;
> Like incarnations of the stars, when splendor
> Is changed to fragrance, they illumine death
> And mock the merry worm that wakes beneath."

He closed the book, staring at it for a moment and then looked up.

"I read that at John's funeral," he confessed. "Such a sad thing."

"It must have been very hard on Ellen," I said.

"It devastated her."

"I'm sorry."

"We all were, still are."

"Of course," I said, as he handed the book back to me. "Oh, I almost forgot. I brought you a gift."

"A gift?" he replied, now newly intrigued.

"Yes," I said, producing a cigar from my jacket pocket. He smiled as I handed it to him.

"Good thing you waited until Betsy went to bed, she doesn't exactly approve of this sort of thing."

"Well, we accomplished a lot these past few days, so I think you deserve a little treat, don't you?" I asked, as I turned off the overhead light.

"Absolutely, my boy," he replied, as he lit it. "This is a fine cigar, Will, thank you."

"My pleasure."

We sat there, silently looking up at the clear, dark night as a shooting star raced across the sky.

"You know, being old isn't so bad considering the alternative."

"Yes, I guess so."

"It must have been hard for you too, Will, losing your parents and your brother at a young age? Laura told us. I hope you don't mind?"

"No, I don't mind, for me it feels like something that happened long ago. After college, I spent almost three years doing manual labor rehabbing houses just to preoccupy my mind—it was like therapy, I guess. I knew I wasn't ready for grad school, for that mental commitment."

"Timing," Andrew said.

"Timing?"

"Yes, it's the element of life we so seldom have control over. Good timing allowed me to meet my Betsy. Bad timing, well, we try not to dwell on too much."

"Tell me more about Laura's father."

"He was a fine man. Handsome, smart, kind, patient. John was humble, in that he recognized how fortunate he was. When Laura was born, he took two weeks off from work— something unheard of back then. He took some ribbing for it too, but he didn't care. He loved my daughter and was devoted to her and his family."

His voice trailed off.

"Am I keeping you up?" I asked.

"Yes, but you need to know these things. Who else is going to give you the unvarnished truth?"

"Laura doesn't remember much about him, except for what her mother told her."

"And now she'll have a partner. She's happy, Will, everyone can see that, and you're a large part of that happiness. Your parents would be proud of you."

"Thank you, Andrew. Another brandy?"

"A short one," he replied.

I poured us each another.

"Here you go, brandy, cigar, fresh air, what could be better, right?"

"Here's to you, Will," he said, raising his glass. "Thank you for all your help this week."

"It was my pleasure. I'm glad I could help and spend some time with you and Betsy."

"You know one day, you and Laura will come up here with your own family. I'll be long gone . . ."

"No, not for many years."

"Maybe so, maybe so."

"Hey, who will help me take care of the place? Not Stephen or Mike. You have to stick around, Andrew, I'll need you."

"Okay, it's a deal," he agreed, with a smile of contentment. I could see he was tired.

"But right now, I need you to turn in and get some sleep."

"Good idea," he said, without objecting. He stood up from his porch chair and walked inside.

I remained there alone on the porch. I noticed the vast silence and wondered how the years at the summer cottage would unfold. I thought about calling Laura, but knew it was too late. Tomorrow was her last exam, so she was sleeping or studying—either way I didn't want to disturb her.

The trip back home on Friday was fun. I offered to drive, and Betsy sat in the passenger seat, regaling me with stories about their many travels back and forth. She recalled one particular drive home when Anne and Ellen were very young. An escaped convict from San Quentin was roaming the state and road blocks were set up to inspect vehicles. They were pulling an open bed trailer with various baby supplies—cribs, strollers, toys, a playpen. When the family came to one of the stops, a surly state trooper demanded to know what was in a certain container that was theoretically large enough to hide a man in the fetal position.

"Dirty diapers," Andrew complied.

"Oh really? That's a large container for diapers," the trooper asserted. "I'll just take a look," he said and opened the lid.

With that the smell of two-week-old soiled diapers practically knocked him over. Betsy loved to tell funny stories like that and carried on for most of the drive home.

To our surprise, Laura was sitting outside their house when we pulled in the driveway just after three thirty. Andrew had napped most of the way and was delighted to see her upon waking.

"How did exams go?" he inquired.

"They went," she replied sardonically. Then realizing that was an unsatisfactory response, she elaborated on each exam for ten more minutes. After we unpacked the car, Betsy insisted we stay for dinner.

"We'll just order a pizza and I'll make a nice salad. Andrew, I think we have a bottle of red wine in the pantry," she said.

I could see Laura was beat from the long week of exams, but, nevertheless, cheerfully assisted her grandmother.

"Let's just sit in the living room for a while until it's time for dinner," Betsy suggested.

We played a couple games of bridge, something I had picked up at Syracuse, until Andrew decided it was time to order the pizza. By quarter to eight, we were on the Oakland Bay Bridge, heading home.

"You need a shower."

"Yes, I do," I acknowledged.

Laura was practically asleep by the time I got into bed after a long, hot shower.

"So, it went okay—with finals?" I asked.

"Yes, it went fine."

"Your grandfather is a slave driver."

"Well, it's a good thing you won't have to work that hard for a living."

"You bet it is, otherwise I'd be too tired to make love with my favorite attorney."

"Law school student," she corrected.

"You're not going to be a law student forever."

"Amen to that," she said. "Hey, seriously, it was very sweet of you to help my grandparents."

"I'm just glad bathroom fixtures last a good thirty years."

"But you had some fun too, right?"

I told her about the night before sitting up with her grandfather, what he said about us going to the cottage with our own family someday, and how I thought it was important to have spent time with them.

"Well, tomorrow you can spend time with me, okay?"

"Okay," I replied.

"I love you," she said softly.

"I love you."

"I can't keep my eyes open, Will, I'm fading."

"Go to sleep," I said, as she curled up in my arms.

On Saturday afternoon, we took the bus downtown to Union Square, where we bought business clothes for our new summer jobs. We celebrated with dinner at Alioto's at Fisherman's Wharf. Despite it being a tourist destination, the food was good and we could walk there in fifteen minutes. Afterwards we stopped at the bakery in Cannery Row owned by my classmate Alex's parents.

We spent most of Sunday in bed, sleeping and reading. In the late afternoon, I suggested we go for a run or a walk. Laura opted for the latter, so we walked up Russian Hill to check on her aunt, Anne, who was alone because David was in Los

Angeles on business. We took our usual route along Macondary Lane—a quaint two-block stretch from Leavenworth to Taylor Street, stopping at our favorite spot under the shade of a trellis of draping purple wisteria with a picturesque view of the Bay. We arrived at her aunt's rejuvenated by the uphill walk and Anne offered us iced tea, which we gladly accepted. I recounted my trip to the cottage with her parents and she was grateful I could help her father. He was seventy-six, but didn't believe he needed help with most things. It was a testament to his independent spirit she said.

On Monday morning, we rode the bus downtown to start our respective summer jobs. For maybe the first time, I saw Laura not just as a law student but rather a dedicated, soon-to-be lawyer who was passionate about her profession and chosen career. My five o'clock quitting time no longer afforded me the ability to stop at The Holding Company because by then everyone would be gone. Laura and I met up and took the bus home together. We talked about our day while changing into running clothes. On that day, and all subsequent days that summer, we recognized something new in each other. There was an air of purpose and seriousness in our conversations now when we discussed work. The realization was palpable that in less than a year, we would be full-time working people responsible for things beyond just ourselves.

My visits to the Tadich became less frequent that summer. Occasionally, when Laura attended a Wednesday evening meeting with the Sierra Club Board of Directors, I would stop to see Fred and sit alone with this newfound seriousness. My summer job in the Mergers and Acquisitions Department of Wells Fargo Bank was high stakes in a private and often nebulous atmosphere. M&A was a secret world of attorneys, accountants, and investment bankers. Because the industry involved a lot of banking money, I encountered a very guarded community of players, much different from the brokers and traders I knew. Discretion was the watch word.

"What's the matter, kid?" Fred would ask. "You look glum. Is it the dame?"

"No, Fred, it's just business stuff," I'd reply.

On this day, however, I was feeling especially down and still in shock from the news of Dennis Barnhart's fatal auto accident. His company's public offering had opened that morning at $13 a share, reaching $17 before closing at $15.50. The news came across the wires just before five o'clock and I instinctively punched the ticker symbol into my Quotron machine even though the market had closed four hours earlier. The white numerals 15.5 flashed against the green screen. I looked at Fred, who apparently had been talking to me the whole time.

"You don't drink half what you used to; hell, last time it was one beer," I heard him say.

"Watching my weight."

"You can't fool me, kid. It's the dame, isn't it?"

"No, Fred, Laura and I are fine—as a matter of fact, we're engaged."

Until then I had avoided telling him.

"Yeah, when's the wedding?"

I remembered why I kept it from him. His words hung in the air. *When is the wedding?* I wondered. Laura and I had never discussed a date. She had another year of school, so I think we just assumed after that.

"Soon," I replied.

"A young man not yet, an elder man not at all."

"You know Francis Bacon?" I asked.

"Some, I got two years of college courses."

"Good for you, Fred."

He pointed to the door. Laura was walking in.

"Hi," she said, sitting down on the bar stool next to me. I leaned over and kissed her.

"Hi, Fred," she added.

"Hope you can do a better job cheering up Mr. Glum here."

"Mr. Glum?" she replied.

"That's Fred's new name for me."

"Why?"

"I don't know. Hey, Fred, why am I Mr. Glum?"

"'Cause you're glum, you're moping around, staring into space, ain't drinking, just nursing a beer."

"Yep, that definitely qualifies as glum," Laura agreed.

"Let's go," I said.

"I just got here," she cried.

"See, that's what you need, kid, some spunk like Laura here."

"Thanks, I'll take some spunk on the rocks," I said.

"Fred, may I have a glass of Chardonnay?" Laura asked.

"One Chard coming right up."

"What's wrong?" Laura asked.

"Dennis Barnhart, the CEO of Eagle Computer, was killed this afternoon in a car crash in Los Gatos."

"That's awful, wasn't Eagle's IPO today?"

"Yes. Hambrecht will have to rescind it. I saw him last month. He was so excited about going public."

"I'm sorry, was he married?"

"Yes. He had a son and two young daughters. Let's talk about something else," I said, thinking of two more little girls who would grow up without a father. "When am I going to make an honest woman out of you?"

"Where did that come from?"

"We should set a date."

"A wedding date?"

"Yes, a wedding date."

"Well, okay," Laura replied. "When do you think we should get married?" she asked.

"This fall."

"This fall? This fall I'm in school."

"Okay, next spring on our birthdays; it's even a Saturday."

"What brought this on?"

"Fred asked and I didn't have an answer."

"Well, I'm not sure Fred's concern should drive this question."

"Laura, it's a legitimate question."

She looked at me and could tell I was sincere. She put her hand to my cheek.

"How about after the bar exam?"

"When is it?"

"July."

"When in July?"

"The eighteenth and nineteenth," she replied.

"Okay, then July."

"Or August."

"No, July," I insisted.

"Most places are probably booked for next summer."

"What about Phil and Carol Wilkinson's home in Belvedere? Remember how beautiful it was when we were there on the Fourth of July?"

"I do," Laura smiled.

"No, save those words for next July."

I called Fred over, waving my empty glass.

"Now that's more like it," he said, taking my glass. "You ought to hang out with this woman more often."

"I intend to, and by the way, we're getting married next summer in July."

"Congratulations," he said, setting a glass of Anchor Steam down in front of me. "This one's on old Fred."

He was about to get Laura another glass of wine, but she waved him off.

"No, thanks, Fred, one's my limit during the work week. I'll have a club soda with lime."

"Okay, fair enough, counselor," he replied.

When we finished our drinks and headed over to Sutter Street to catch the bus, it was chilly with a heavy summer fog settling in. I put my arm around her shoulders as she wrapped hers around my waist. Later, we lay in bed, listening to the foghorns out on the Bay. It was a comforting and rhythmic sound which lulled us, and perhaps everyone else in the city, to sleep that night.

I called Phil Wilkinson the next morning and left a message. The following day, he called back to tell me they'd be delighted to host our wedding.

"Let me run the date by Carol. She's in the city today. We're having lunch."

"July 28," I said, and quickly added, "1984," just to make sure he didn't think I meant next month.

That afternoon, Phil called back. I had been reading the news on the wires that the Washington State Supreme Court ruled that contracts obligating local utilities to pay off $2 billion in construction bonds for two nuclear plants were invalid. The muni bond market was reacting, as most traders suspected an imminent default on the bonds. Little did I know at the time that this "WHOOPS bond" default would be the largest in history. Phil sounded frazzled, but assured me that Carol was thrilled as well about hosting our wedding. Apparently, Laura had made quite an impression on her at their party and, as it turned out, Carol's father also knew her father, John, back in the '60s. With that important task taken care of, I could focus on my work.

Wells had an IPO coming up and they based most of the final projections on my analysis. The two leads were pulled away for another project and I was tasked with finishing their work.

"So you think you may have screwed up?" Laura asked, one evening when I was trying to explain my concern.

"No, the math is right, it's the numbers."

"Then, what's the matter?" she asked.

"These IPOs—more than half the time they fizzle. They aren't based on any historical data. They base their forecasts on cockeyed optimism—sales projections produced by caffeine fueled best case scenario artists."

My concern, as it turned out, was unfounded. The IPO launched on Monday, June 13, opening at 13 and by the closing bell on Friday, it was up 13% closing at 14 ⅝. The Dow managed a 3.9% gain for the week, while the NASDAQ was up just under 3.5%, buoyed by the news that Reagan was about to reappoint

Paul Volcker Fed chairman. My phone rang just after 1:00 p.m. It was my cousin Jim.

"Hey, buddy boy, are you a wizard or what? Open at 13, on June 13, and close up 13% for the week!"

"Yep, we're into symmetry around here," I responded.

"And some fucking lumber company?" he continued. "Who the hell is buying lumber?"

I was about to ask if he had seen the recent housing starts numbers, but instead asked, "What's up?"

"Hey, no, I was just calling to say congrats. You gonna see any of that juice? Oh wait, you're just a salaried intern. By the way, I thought you were into biotech?"

I knew he had something to tell me.

"Hey, Jim, sorry I haven't been around the HC."

"It's okay, buddy boy, that McCracken chick has been sharing the wealth if you know what I mean."

"So biotechs, what have you heard?"

"Alex Brown filed an offering today—two million common for Chiron. You see that on the wires?"

"I did, Jim. I have friends at AB—been following it for two years. Genentech, XOMA, Amgen."

"Oh, I hear Amgen is announcing this Friday. Those boys at Smith Barney and Witter have been on the phone with their institutional clients for the past three months. Word is two million plus shares at 18. Does that wet your whistle?"

I knew he was asking if I could meet at the HC for drinks.

"Can't do it. I'm here until five o'clock. Hey, Jim, I got two calls here I have to take."

"Okay, buddy boy, I understand. Money don't sleep, right? I just wanted to say congrats and all."

"Thanks, Jim, I appreciate the call."

I took the calls from Credit Suisse and Goldman, and afterwards stopped by my boss Jonathan Marks' office to check on the four o'clock conference call with the lumber company's CEO and senior management.

"Hey, we're all good here, Will," Marks announced, as I walked through his doorway. "You've got a family thing tonight, right?"

"Yes, a wedding rehearsal and dinner," I replied.

"Okay, well, I know it's been a hectic few weeks, but we appreciate your effort on this and I'll see if I can't get you a weekend down at Pebble Beach. You play, Will?"

"Yes, but not in a while."

"Good, well, you have a great weekend and I'll see you Monday."

Marks was an asshole, but good at his job. What he lacked in people skills he made up by lavishing bonuses and perks on his minions, including the summer interns. I learned a lot because of his open-door policy, which meant he allowed you to attend all meetings and conference calls with the understanding that he would personally dismember you and dispose of your body parts in San Francisco Bay if you leaked anything. No one ever did. I was back at my desk by quarter to five, having changed my shirt and splashed on some cologne. As I passed the receptionist desk, Sandra, a tall, attractive Black woman commented, "Oooh, somebody's got something going on tonight!"

"It isn't what you think, Sandra," I smiled, as I walked back to my cubicle.

I checked my Quotron one last time as the phone rang. It was Mike, calling from downstairs while Laura sat in a cab in front of

420 Montgomery. I met him in the lobby and ten minutes later, we were exiting the taxi in front of Grace Cathedral on Nob Hill for Stephen and Caroline's rehearsal. As we walked up the steps of the Gothic structure, I took her hand and put my arm around his shoulder.

"Now pay attention, Mike, because you're going to have to do this again next year."

"You mean you want me to be your best man?" he asked, with surprised emotion.

"Well, as long as you don't screw it up tomorrow, I think you've got a good shot."

Mike stopped and hugged Laura and me both. The three of us had spent a lot of time together at school—studying, debating, drinking, even dancing at a few clubs—so it was only natural he was my choice.

"Let's keep this amongst us for now," Laura insisted. "After all, this is Stephen's weekend."

The rehearsal, the wedding, and the reception were all flawlessly executed and extravagant in the way expensive weddings are. They had decided on a small wedding party. Caroline's sister Sarah, the dental student, was her maid of honor and her best friend growing up, a neighbor friend from Rensselaer named Kevin Mason, who lived in Colorado, was a groomsman. Stephen chose his brother Mike as his best man and Laura as their bridesmaid.

Rob McKenzie's name always drew a variety of responses anytime he was mentioned and it was always painful for Laura to hear. So when he arrived at the wedding on Saturday morning, dressed in a gray suit and clean-shaven, everyone welcomed him with a warm smile and hug albeit with somewhat reserved affection. He sat with his mother and me, and as the hymns were sung and the liturgy was recited, he sat stoically silent. The two Christmas holidays I spent with Laura and her family didn't include Rob as he vacationed in Cabo San Lucas funded, Stephen and Mike surmised, by selling drugs in the South Bay. He would call Laura on her birthday, or more often than not a day or two later, and for weeks she would drift in and out of a sullenness from those conversations. As for Ellen, she was too weak to deny any of the allegations and too sheltered to believe them. She was numb to the idea that her son was a dealer and an addict. The rest of the family seemed to take his comings and goings in stride. They made sure he got medical care, but never gave him gifts he could turn around and sell. But sitting there next to him, I couldn't help thinking he was just a lost soul trying to survive any way he could. He had been a handsome child and was still good-looking with the same long brown hair he had as a kid. But he was too thin for his clothes and had a gaunt face. He looked pale and old for twenty-one. His occasional facial grimace, a tic really, reflected how he had lived these past few years. During the sign of peace, he hugged his mother while she stood stiffly with her arms at her sides. He then turned to me and shook my hand.

"Peace be with you, Rob," I offered.

"Peace, man," he replied, with no inflection in his voice and then returned to a blank, off-in-space gaze.

At the reception, he stood alone at the bar, downing shots of vodka. Later Laura approached him to dance, but by then he was too drunk to even move. Mike and I got him into a cab shortly thereafter. The cabbie was my friend Sunil, whom I was happy to see despite the circumstance. I introduced Mike, who instructed him to drive Rob back to East Palo Alto. Mike handed him one hundred dollars and his business card in case he owed more. I gently placed my hand on Rob's head as he bent down to get into the back seat.

"And under no condition give him any money, understood?" Mike instructed.

Sunil looked at me for confirmation and I nodded affirmatively. He was silent, but understood the situation and drove off with Rob now half-reclined in the back seat. Mike and I returned to the reception and headed straight for the bar.

"Two shots of Jamison," Mike instructed the bartender. Turning to me, he raised his shot glass and sighed, "Thank you."

We drank the whiskey together and I said, "I have to go."

"What do you mean?" he asked.

"I need to find Laura; we haven't danced yet."

"Boy, are you whipped!"

"See you later," I said, leaving him standing there with the bartender.

When I found her, she was coming out of the ladies' room with her mother and grandmother.

"Where have you been?" she asked.

"At the bar with Mike." And then a moment later, when we were alone, I added, "We were putting your brother in a cab."

"Oh."

"Mike had an address and I knew the cabbie so he'll be okay, I mean, Sunil will make sure he gets home."

"Thank you," she said.

"You don't need to thank me."

"No, but I do," she insisted.

The band started to play "Blame It on the Bossa Nova."

"Okay, well, then dance with me. You can't have a bad time dancing."

"Who said that?" she asked.

"I think I just did."

We began to dance "swaying to and fro" and, as she sang the words, I knew she was having fun. We took a break when the cake was cut and sat down for dessert and coffee. The evening continued with more dancing until the band finished for the night. Impulsively, Mike grabbed the microphone and introduced Laura and Stephen, who sat side by side at the grand piano and played a Bach concerto for two to the applause of the dozen or so guests still lingering. Stephen and Caroline said goodnight to everyone and then left as Mike, Laura, and I headed for the elevator.

"It's a good thing we're staying here and not driving home," Mike said, on the ride to our floor.

"You think?" I replied mockingly.

"Will you be needing a turn-down service?" Laura asked him.

"No, he gets turned down enough," I replied.

"You two are two funny kids."

"Good night, Mike," we said, as he opened the door to his room.

"Do you think he made it to the bed?" Laura asked.

"Hope so," I replied.

Laura and I took a warm, soapy shower together and then lay down on the huge, king-sized bed. She moved close to me and I wrapped my arm around her waist.

"Did you have a good time?" I asked.

"Yes, did you?"

"How could I not when I'm with you?"

"That's sweet," Laura said. "Now I'm going to sleep, so you can do me in the morning."

"Yes, ma'am."

"Hey, I'm not a ma'am yet," she objected.

"Sorry, by the way, whatever happened to that strawberry lip gloss you used to carry around?"

"You mean from high school?"

"Yes."

"I don't know. Want me to go down to the gift shop and see if they have any?"

"Nah, you can wait until morning," I smiled, fearing getting hit with a pillow.

The next day, at brunch for out-of-town guests, we were seated with her uncle David's father, David Sr., his mother, and their friends, Mr. & Mrs. William Clark, Jr. At the time, Clark was National Security Advisor in the Reagan administration, but was about to be appointed U.S. Secretary of the Interior—a not so secret he shared with those at the table. Senior and Junior, as they referred to one another, had met at Stanford and became lifelong friends, both serving in various capacities over the years in the California Republican Party, renewing their friendship with annual fly-fishing trips to Wyoming, where Clark had a summer home. Once again Laura easily ingratiated herself into the conversation and by the entrée, Clark suggested she apply for an externship for the spring semester with the Interior's Office of the Solicitor. The regional office was located in Sacramento, but they had a field office in San Francisco. Laura thanked him while I kept his wife, Joan, company.

We talked about their three grown children and I brought her cookies and fruit from the buffet table.

By three o'clock, Laura and I were exhausted. As it was Father's Day, Laura gave her grandfather a framed photo of the entire family, including me, taken at the summer cottage that first Labor Day weekend I spent with them. I had reserved a room for Saturday night and then, when my IPO successfully closed up on Friday, I added Sunday night as a personal reward, knowing Laura and I would be there alone—the last two guests. Later that evening, we came back down from our room and walked through the large, empty reception hall. We strolled silently holding hands and smiled knowing that we were next and how wonderful that would be.

The following Sunday, we visited her college friend Richard and his partner Jose's home for brunch. While Richard was taking biscuits out of the oven, and Jose was stirring Hollandaise sauce, they bickered over whether the gay bathhouses should be closed. Richard, a lawyer, was taking a civil liberties position, while Jose, a nurse at San Francisco General, was making a pragmatic argument in favor of closure in light of the AIDS epidemic. Laura tried to diffuse the situation by asking Jose if he knew anything about the Shanti Project. One of her professors had helped secure funding for the first AIDS clinic in the city. I wandered from the kitchen to the living room, where eight of their friends were sipping mimosas. I realized I was the only straight man in the room, but nevertheless felt at ease. I'd gotten to know gay men and women at Syracuse and many more while living in San Francisco, where it was a way of life that was lived openly and proudly. After an incredible feast of

Eggs Benedict with smoked salmon and fresh papaya and mango, everyone walked down to Castro and Market to catch the muni downtown. The 1983 Gay Freedom Day Parade, as it was called then, drew the largest turnout in history. It was my second year attending, and the high spiritedness of the parade marchers and crowd was no less celebratory that year.

"You know you don't need those," Laura said, when we were getting ready for bed that night.

"Need what?"

"Those condoms you put in the drawer. I saw you take them when they were handing them out at the parade. I'm on the pill."

"I know you're on the pill."

"Then, why did you take them?" she persisted.

"I was just being polite."

"So you're not thinking of switching teams?" she teased.

"Come over here," I demanded, pulling her close to me. She yelled gleefully in surprise.

"You're the only teammate I'll ever want."

"Are you sure?"

"I love you so much it hurts," I replied.

"It does?"

"Yes, it does."

She kissed me softly and we held each other, drifting off into contented and quiet slumber.

CHAPTER 4

SUMMER FLEW BY with the hectic pace of work, but Laura and I managed to get to the cottage almost every other weekend—a welcome break relaxing with her family in the mountains. Friday, September 2, was my last day at Wells Fargo and Laura's final day at the Sierra Club. I was able to get out early for Henry Wilson's retirement party at the HC. I had met Henry on my first day working at the Exchange and thought it fitting to see him on his last. I stopped at the lobby stand in my building, bought a box of Montecristo's, and walked over to the Embarcadero on that sunny and exceptionally warm afternoon.

"Will," someone yelled from across the crowded room. It was Mike Foster waving me over to a crowd of tech guys he was standing around.

"Hey, here's a man I haven't seen in a while," he said, introducing me to several of his new colleagues and pointing to Phil Wilkinson, who was standing a few feet behind me.

"So, this is basically an incestuous group of systems guys from Witter and the PSE," I said, looking at the crowd surrounding him.

"Yeah, most of the traders are outside catching some sun, and the broker crowd is huddled around Henry over there."

"And I see a few hacks from Wells," I said.

"After three months you've figured that out?"

"No, it only took a month, but I needed the job."

"Those tools fuck with their socks on," Mike said.

Phil Wilkinson came over to say hello.

"Hey, Will, how was it at Wells?" he asked.

"Tough. No teamwork over there—everybody trying to outdo everyone else. A lot of favoritism—you know, the whole Stanford and SC cabal."

"Hell, don't sugarcoat it like that, Will. Tell us what you really think," he laughed.

"Investment banking isn't for me," I said.

"Well, at least you found out now before you went to work for those pricks, right?" he replied.

"Right."

"And how's Laura doing? You guys are still coming for dinner?"

"Yes, Laura's great. And thank you again for offering your home for the wedding."

"You don't need to thank me every time we see each other."

"Okay, Phil."

"Good to see you, Will. I'm going to make the rounds and head out."

"Say hello to Carol," I said, as he walked away.

I joined Mike at the bar.

"Here you go," he said, handing me a shot of tequila.

"Just what I need," I replied facetiously. I had forgotten what it was like to drink in the afternoon. I asked if he knew where Henry was, as I had lost sight of him.

"Over there with the brass," he replied, pointing toward a group of strangers.

"I'm going to call Laura and ask her to join us."

"Don't you want to spend time with your buds here? Free booze! They got a cake coming."

I ignored his question and went to the pay phone in the hallway to call her. I made my way through the crowd over to Henry.

"Will, good to see you," he said, as I shook his hand and handed him the box of cigars.

"Thank you, that was very thoughtful. I understand you're engaged to John McKenzie's daughter."

"I am. You certainly have your information network well deployed."

"Got to. It's how we survive. Congratulations, Will, to Laura too."

"Actually, you'll be able to do that in person, she's stopping by."

"Excellent. What's she up to these days, other than getting engaged to a handsome young man?"

"She's about to start her third year of law school. She just finished a summer internship at the Sierra Club."

"Does she like it, law school?"

"Very much, she's focused on environmental law."

"Good for her," he said.

"And what about you?" he asked.

Just as I was about to answer, the Senior VP for Institutional Investing at Witter approached us with a glass of orange juice for Henry.

"My sugar is a little low," Henry explained, taking the glass.

"Thank you, Carl. Will, I'd like you to meet Carl Maddox," Henry said.

Aware of who he was, I said, "Senior VP for Institutional Investing. Will Merritt, nice to meet you."

"Nice to meet you, Will," Maddox replied.

"So, Will, finish your answer," Henry insisted. I took notice of his mild disregard for Maddox's seniority, which I attributed to his impending retirement.

For Maddox's sake, I added some background.

"Well, I moved here in July of '81, went to work in systems and operations at the Exchange, got my MBA this year, along with your new IT guy Mike Foster, and spent this summer interning at Wells in their M&A department."

"How did that go?" Maddox asked.

"It was . . . interesting. I'm not sure I'm cut out for investment banking."

"How come?"

I thought back to a conversation I had at brunch before the gay pride parade at Richard and Jose's apartment.

"M&A, at least now, is kind of like anesthesiology. It's rather routine until something goes wrong, and when it does, it goes terribly wrong."

"That's a good analogy," Henry said laughing.

"I mean Micropolis, Eagle, Key Tronic, Wilcat Systems, Computer Shop, Computer Craft, PC Telemart, and Kaypro. Eight tech IPOs in the last ninety days and most will likely fail."

"Fail?" Maddox interrupted. "You're not giving away insider information, are you?"

"No, not at all, Mr. Maddox."

"Carl, please."

"I just don't believe they can survive. They're undercapitalized from the start, their marketing plans are shit."

"So where do you see the tech industry going?" Maddox asked.

"I think this is a short-term phenomenon until IBM and HP can retool from mainframes to micros and desktops. And Apple is possibly another long-term player—maybe one or two new entries."

"What are you doing now?" Maddox asked.

"Today was my last day at Wells. I'm going for another two semesters to get a second master's."

"And then?"

"A job."

"Will, it sounds like you might fit in at Witter."

"Doing what?" I asked.

"Securities analyst for the technology industry. I agree with your assessment of those offerings," he said, handing me his business card. "Call me at the end of the semester and I'll buy you lunch. Henry, I gotta run, but we will see you at this year's Christmas party—that's my last official order," he said, shaking both our hands.

I caught a glimpse of Laura standing near the entranceway and waved to her. She smiled broadly as she walked over to us. She was wearing a beige linen suit, which she complained about having to iron every time she wore it. Around her neck was a string of pearls her father had given her mother on their tenth wedding anniversary a few months before his death. Ellen, in turn, had passed them on to Laura when she graduated from college—a memento from her father. I leaned down and kissed her.

"Laura, this is Henry Wilson."

"Henry, Laura McKenzie."

"Mr. Wilson, it's a pleasure to see you again after all these years."

"The pleasure is mine, Laura."

"Congratulations on your retirement," she added.

"Thank you. And congratulations to you and Will on your engagement. I hope you two will be very happy."

"Thank you," she replied.

"Say, if you don't have any plans, I'd love to take you to dinner tonight."

"Henry, that's very nice, but don't you need to hang around here? After all, you're the guest of honor."

"Yes, a while. I've got to cut a cake!"

"We'd love to have dinner with you, Mr. Wilson," Laura replied.

"Call me Henry," he insisted. "Why don't we meet back here in an hour?" he suggested.

"Okay," I said.

Laura and I left him to go talk with Mike.

"Laura!" Mike shouted, noticing her walking toward him. "Hello, did you see Henry?"

"Yes, he's a very sweet man."

"Yeah, old Henry is salt of the earth, we're gonna miss him. How about a drink?"

"Chardonnay," she replied.

"So how's your summer been?" Mike asked.

"Good. You know, busy. I spent most of August reviewing 36 CFR 219."

Mike looked at her quizzically as he handed her the glass of wine.

"The new federal regulations that came out last year for updating the planning process to the National Forest Management Act."

"When was the law enacted?" he asked.

"1976."

"And it took seven years for final regs to be issued?"

"Yes," she said.

"And I thought securities regs took a long time."

"They all do," Laura said.

Later, a cake was wheeled out on a cart with a single lit candle on top. Everyone sang "For He's a Jolly Good Fellow." Henry cut the cake and said a few words about his years at Witter and how much it meant that everyone had come out to celebrate his retirement. He made his farewells and we met him at the entrance.

"No cake?" Laura asked.

"I'd better not, my diabetes," he replied. "So where would you like to eat?" he asked.

"Well, if you ask Will, he'll say the Tadich Grill," Laura replied.

"Excellent choice," he said.

As we were seated, "A Summer Wind" by Frank Sinatra was playing on the sound system.

"Ah, a great song," Henry remarked.

The song was a favorite of mine too from the jukebox at the "Jab" back at Syracuse. Not so much for the melody, but rather the wistful lyrics.

"Just have to watch out for those piper men, right, Will?" Henry said unexpectedly.

"Plenty of them at Wells," I responded.

"Aren't they everywhere?" Laura asked. "Aren't you talking about character, and whether or not it's corruptible?"

She had taken the meaning in a different direction. Henry smiled.

"You remind me of your father," he said.

"How?"

"He saw everything in black and white, right or wrong, good or bad."

"Yes, I've heard similar sentiments. Unfortunately, the world is a more complicated place now with shades of gray taking up more space than either black or white," she replied.

"You're absolutely right, Laura, and that's why I'm retiring. I belong to another generation, a simpler time, when trust was measured by your word rather than a notarized signature on a contract."

"Do you think it would have been difficult for my father to negotiate the landmines, the ethical lapses, the naked greed?" she asked.

"I think it's difficult for anyone, but I also know he would have been up for the task."

She leaned across the table and gently squeezed his hand. A tear ran down her cheek, which she tried to fight back with a smile.

"Laura, know this, your father was no more or no less a man with human faults like the rest of us. What distinguished him was his uncanny ability to see the best in people, so they in turn saw the good in themselves. He inspired others to avoid the pitfalls and temptations which only lead to downfall and disgrace."

Henry continued speaking for several minutes until our dinners arrived.

"Cioppino with garlic bread!" he remarked, as the oversized bowl was set down in front of him. "Best in the city," he continued, looking up with a smile of satisfaction on his face.

By the time we finished our meal, he had peppered her with many questions about her family, her college days, and law school. I sat silently, eating, listening, and smiling—occasionally picking up some bit of information about her I hadn't known before. We all declined dessert and when the check arrived, I offered to split it with him.

"Nonsense," he insisted. "It's my pleasure—and don't forget that transaction you resolved for me."

I couldn't argue and instead asked what his plans were for retirement.

"Retirement?" he replied incredulously. "I'm teaching at San Francisco Community College starting next week—two evening classes."

"That's wonderful," Laura said.

"Yes," I said. "Henry, if you ever need any research help, let me know."

"Thanks, Will. Right now, I need to catch a cab. It's been a long day for me."

"Let me get one for you. Sit here with Laura and I'll come back when the cab gets here."

"Fair enough," he said.

"Where are you headed?" I asked.

"Presidio Heights," he answered.

"Well, then, let's share a cab and you can drop us, if that's okay?"

"It's more than okay," he replied.

I walked outside just as a cab pulled up. It was Sunil.

"Sunil, I'll be right back."

"Okay, my friend," he said.

I returned to the restaurant and motioned to them. Henry insisted on sitting in the front seat to give us more room. I introduced them to Sunil and, as he pulled away from the curb, I caught him smiling in the rearview mirror.

"You told me she was very beautiful, Will, but surely you underestimated your description."

"Undoubtedly," I replied.

"Laura, may I call you Laura?" Sunil continued.

"Of course," she answered.

"I drove Will home after your first date in Golden Gate Park."

"You did?" she replied.

"Oh, yes. I could tell even then he was a smitten man, smitten, I tell you."

"Well, your dad's hooch might have had something to do with that."

"Oh no, my friend. I only offered you that to calm you down. Your heart was beating out of your chest—ca boom, ca boom."

Sunil was tapping his chest with his fist as he made the sounds.

"Well, this has been an enlightening evening, including the cab ride," Laura remarked, when we pulled up to our corner.

I handed Sunil enough cash to pay the entire fare.

"Please take good care of our friend Henry here," I said, as we exited the cab and said goodnight. There was a certain irony because it was Sunil who had driven Laura's brother back to East Palo Alto from the wedding reception. I saw no need to bring it up. After all, Henry had recalled some wonderful stories about her father, which I knew she was delighted to hear.

"He's quite a character," she said, as we walked to our door.

"Who? Henry or Sunil?"

"Hmm, come to think of it, both of them. We should invite Henry to the wedding, don't you think?"

"Absolutely! Anyone who can afford to live in Presidio Heights is welcome," I said facetiously.

"And here I bought into all that stuff you said about not wanting to get caught up in the greed."

"I don't. But I'm willing to accept a gift from honestly made money."

"You're incorrigible."

As we turned into the alcove of our building, I grabbed Laura and kissed her.

"Oh, so you think I've never been kissed like that in an alcove?"

"No, I don't."

"Well, the mailman gives me one every time I come down for the mail," she kidded.

"Well then, I guess you're an EAK?"

"EAK?"

"Experienced alcove kisser."

"I certainly am."

"Hey, wait a minute. I'm the one who gets the mail."

"Oops, I lied," she said laughing.

I was glad Henry could bring that light-hearted feeling out in her. The talk about her father made her happy rather than sad.

"Thank you," she said softly.

"For what?"

"For tonight, for everything."

"Anything I do for you doesn't require a thank you."

"Well then, thank you for not requiring me to thank you."

"You're giddy. I've never seen you giddy before."

"Is it a good thing, this giddiness?" she asked.

As we opened the door to the apartment, we heard someone leaving a message on the answering machine. It was Betsy, asking if we could stop on the way to the cottage tomorrow to pick up some sweet corn and an assortment of fruit for the annual Labor Day weekend get-together. Laura grabbed the receiver just in time. I took her linen suit jacket off as she talked and hung it on a hanger. Then I came up behind her and unzipped her skirt. As it fell, I picked it from the floor and hung it up too. I went to the bedroom and hung up my suit, returning to the living room wearing only boxer briefs. I turned the lights off and started kissing the back of her neck. She kicked off her shoes and turned around to face me.

"Okay, Grandma, I have to go, see you tomorrow," she said, hanging up the phone. "This might be our last opportunity for a while. Grandpa has strict rules about cohabitating, or rather non-cohabitating, before marriage on any Capshaw property."

"That didn't stop us before?"

"Yes, well, I think there's a higher degree of scrutiny now since we're living together," she said.

"Then we better make this last, is that what you're saying?"

"Yes."

That Labor Day weekend was much like the previous two with one significant difference—the announcement of our wedding date, which we agreed to hold off sharing until the last night. On Sunday, Laura and I prepared dinner. We made Trout

Almandine, string beans, fresh bib lettuce salad with pecans and cranberries, and, much to Andrew's delight, charcoal-grilled baked potatoes. Laura baked two peach pies. Before dessert was served, Andrew initiated a series of toasts to thank everyone for being there and to extend his and Betsy's best wishes for everything that had transpired since last Labor Day—birthdays, promotions, vacations, graduations. When he finished, I stood up with my wine glass in one hand and Laura's hand in the other.

"Betsy, Andrew, Ellen, Anne, David, Caroline, Stephen, Mike, you have welcomed me into your homes, you have offered me your affection, and I'm thankful for your kindness and generosity."

Sensing Mike was about to interrupt, Laura gave him a look that stopped him in his tracks.

"Just over two years ago, Laura, your Laura, came into my life and I into hers, and for whatever reason or reasons that I don't know, and perhaps will never completely understand, she fell in love with me and that has made me the luckiest person in the world. My love for her has no bounds, my commitment to her is absolute, and on July 28 next year, we will vow our love to one another. I wish to propose a toast to my bride-to-be—my friend and soulmate."

"Here, here," Andrew said.

Everyone drank from their raised glasses and for the next ten minutes, we were all hugging and kissing and laughing in celebration. Mike interrupted, "Can we have dessert now?" to a round of jeers and more laughter. After the pie and more wine, Stephen, Caroline, and Mike cleared the table and cleaned up the kitchen. Laura and I were forbidden to help, but were instead bombarded with questions from Ellen and Anne and Betsy. I rose from my chair when David stood to stretch his legs.

"Congratulations, Will."

"Thank you, David. That means a lot coming from you."

"Let me know if there is anything I can do?" he added.

"Well, we want a civil ceremony, so I imagine you know a judge who could officiate?"

"I'll get to work on it right away," he replied.

"Great, thanks."

Later that evening, when everyone had gone to bed, Laura and I stretched out on the large sofa in front of the fire. Sergeant, sensing the warmth, jumped up to join us and settled near our feet.

"Well, you really did it, Merritt—not much chance of turning back now," she said.

"I don't want to turn back, or go back, or even look back. Everything in my life is ahead of me, ahead of us."

"You really believe that, don't you?"

"Yes, absolutely, don't you?" I replied.

"Yes, but your past is a part of who you are and, therefore, it's a part of your future."

"Your past influences your life while you live it, and then when the present becomes the past, it influences your future," I said.

"Have you been smoking something?"

"No, I'm just intoxicated with you," I replied.

Laura put a pillow over my face and laughed, "Are you sure you don't have any Irish blood in you? You certainly have the blarney."

"Not a drop."

"Well, I have enough for the both of us."

"That much I know for sure."

Laura's look turned serious.

"What do you think our kids will be like?" she asked, somewhat unexpectedly.

"If they're anything like you, they'll be angels."

"Jeez, Merritt, you're on a roll tonight."

"I'm just speaking from my heart," I said, smiling with happiness.

"And if they're like you?" she asked.

"God help us."

"I thought you didn't believe in God?"

"In that case, I'll start."

Apparently our laughter was keeping Sergeant awake, so he retreated to his bed in the corner.

"We'd better go to bed too," Laura suggested.

"We could sleep here in front of the fire."

"And have my grandpa find us in the morning? No, not a good idea."

"All right then. You go to bed and I'll stay here."

"Okay, in a few minutes. I want to remember this moment, us here, like this."

We sat there quietly, reliving the joy of the evening. I kissed her cheek, and then her lips, before she reluctantly rose to ascend the stairs alone.

CHAPTER 5

LAURA AND I returned to school shortly after Labor Day. It was her last semester of classes as she was practically certain of securing an externship with the Interior Department in the spring. She was taking Environmental Law and Policy, California Environment and Natural Resources, Water Law, and Land Use Zoning, plus serving as an editor-in-chief of the *Environmental Law Journal*. In addition, she continued working on *Law Review* as the notes and comments editor. As for me, after the second week of lugging two volumes of the Tax Code and four volumes of Treasury regs back and forth to school, I bought a second set and kept them in my locker. Our lives for the next three months were routine but busy. On Saturday nights, we'd go to a movie or out to dinner—usually the Pacific Café on Geary and Thirty-Fourth for grilled fish or Giorgio's at Clement and Third for calzones. Laura would shower, dress, and apply makeup, change her top at least once, and then carefully choose a necklace and earrings before announcing she was ready. I knew she was doing it for me, and I always complimented her on how great she looked. Those dates were the best part of my week. We forgot about school entirely and just had fun being out somewhere, enjoying each other's company.

By late November, we were feeling more relaxed about school with midterms over. On Thanksgiving, we served meals at the Shanti House in the Castro until 8:00 p.m. Afterwards, we were too tired to make the trek to her mother's. However, when Laura called her that evening, she sensed something was wrong.

"Mom, what's the matter?"

"Rob called late last night and wanted to know if he could come home."

"And?"

"He wanted to know if he could stay for a couple of weeks."

"What else?" Laura asked.

"He asked if he could borrow money."

"How much money?"

"$3,000."

"For what?"

"He didn't say, but I think he owes someone."

Laura grimaced as she let her head hang down.

"I'm sorry, Momma," she whispered.

When she got off the phone, she was in tears.

"Laura, I'm sorry," was all I could think to say.

"I know you are. I'm not equipped to deal with this, with him, now."

"I don't think anyone is expecting you to," I said, trying to console her.

"He's my brother. I should be able to deal with this, to fix this problem."

She was sitting down now, as if the gravity of the situation had forced her body into the chair.

"He's an addict. You can't fix that, only he can."

I watched as her hands drew to her face, and as tears flowed, she wiped them away.

"I know, Will, I know, but I'm not used to feeling helpless. All my life, I have . . ."

"Made other people feel better about themselves because you know how difficult it is to deal with the pain of losing—losing something or someone—but you can't change everyone, especially someone who doesn't want to change. Laura, you realize he's an addict, don't you?"

"Of course, I do."

The conversation had run its course. Neither of us wanted to continue with the futility of it. It had been an emotional day even before the call to her mother. Laura had learned a friend of hers had been diagnosed with Kaposi's sarcoma—a rare cancer affecting the skin and lymph nodes. She decided to take a bath. I was lying on the bed when she came into the bedroom wearing only a towel. I knew she was still tense, so I offered to rub her back after she changed into her "pro forma sweat shirt" as I referred to it.

"You must be the only woman in the world who can make a seven-year-old, worn out, sweat shirt look sexy."

"You think I'm sexy?"

"Yes!"

"I love you," she said, in a voice of certainty I wasn't sure I had ever heard before. "I can't imagine my life without you."

"Well, you don't need to worry about that because I'm not going anywhere."

"Promise?"

"I promise," I replied, sensing her vulnerability.

"I need to sleep," she said.

"Then come here and let me rub your neck," I offered.

She was asleep in moments.

We made it over to Ellen's on Friday night for Thanksgiving leftovers, where the phone call from Rob was rehashed.

"So, what did you finally tell him?" Laura asked.

"I told him he was welcome to stay, but only if he was sober and didn't bring any drugs into the house or have any of his friends over."

"And the money?"

"He hung up when I said I wouldn't give it to him."

The words hurt Laura and once again tears came to her eyes.

"What if he got treatment?" I asked. "Would you loan him the money then?"

They both sat silently, surprised by my somewhat obvious suggestion.

"If he owes money to someone, his life could be in danger. Maybe it would be an incentive to get treatment?" I wondered.

"Well, maybe, if he will try—I mean genuinely make the effort to quit," Laura offered.

"We should call him," Ellen insisted.

"Do you want me to call him?" I asked.

Laura looked at me the way only she could with her penetrating blue eyes and steady stare of sincerity.

"Would you?"

"Yes, of course. It might even be better coming from me."

We agreed I would call him the next day and tried to put the subject out of our thoughts for the rest of the evening.

Laura and I decided to spend the night rather than drive back to the city. Ellen put a toothbrush and towels out for me before she went to bed. We followed shortly thereafter to Laura's bedroom on the third floor. I felt awkward with Ellen in the house, and Laura delighted in my uneasiness, teasing me by applying strawberry lip gloss she found in her dresser drawer.

"So, how many boys have been up here?"

"You've been the only one."

"Really? Well, that must mean I'm special."

"You're special all right," she said, in a sarcastic tone.

"Are you teasing me?"

"A little," she replied, drawing me close to her.

"A little or a lot?" I asked.

"A lot, always a lot."

"That makes sense. You never do anything halfway!"

Laura kissed me and we sat back on the bed—her bed.

"Is this weird for you?" I asked.

"No, not with you, it isn't."

We made love slowly and gently before falling asleep in each other's arms.

"I've been thinking about your brother," Rob said, as he fingered the cocktail napkin in front of him.

We were sitting at the bar in the Tadich Grill, waiting for Laura.

"Really?"

"Yes, it's so unfair."

"Unfair, how?" I replied, already knowing the answer.

"I mean, I just started rehab, but already I've realized all people have problems—issues they either deal with or choose not to deal with."

"That's true," I said, prompting him to continue.

"But death offers no hope, no second chance. That's why it's unfair—your brother dying. At least I have the choice to ruin my life or try to make it better—either way I'm still alive, still living some existence."

"Self-respecting, I hope."

"Yes, Will, my life has value," he replied, suddenly with tears in his eyes.

I put my hand on his shoulder.

"Yes, it does, Rob—not just to you but to others, including me."

"I'm going to beat this. I'm going to make something of my life."

"Slow steps—it's not a sprint, it's a marathon."

Rob picked up the napkin and dabbed his eyes.

"Tell me more about your brother, about Tommy," he asked, trying to regain his composure.

I mentioned his love for baseball and it seemed to brighten his demeanor. He asked a few more questions until he saw his sister pass by the front window.

Laura walked into the Tadich Grill, wearing a crimson red dress and short black blazer. When she spotted Rob next to me at the bar, she frowned, but as she reached us and saw we were drinking ginger ale, her smile returned. Fred, the consummate gentleman, never said a word when I asked for ginger ale. He had heard my stories about Rob's problems and discerned why I ordered what I did.

"How was the party?" Rob asked, before I could get a word out.

I had told him she was attending the Sierra Club's holiday party before meeting us.

"It was fun," she replied, hugging him before turning to kiss me.

"Hello," she said, in an affectionate voice.

I caught the faint smell of wine on her breath.

"Hi," I replied.

"Well, you look quite dapper, Rob."

"Will bought me pants and this jacket," he said proudly, "an early Christmas present."

"That's quite a dress," Fred said, from behind the bar.

"Thank you, Fred."

"What can I get you?" he asked Laura.

"You know, I think I'll have what they're having."

I wasn't sure if it was a test or not but kept quiet.

"One ginger ale coming right up," he replied.

As her smile broadened, I looked at her as if to say, "What did you expect?"

"Thank you, Fred," she said, when he returned with her drink.

"Hey, Laura, I got my first sobriety pin," Rob announced, opening his jacket lapel to show her.

"That's wonderful."

"Thank you."

"Have you guys ordered yet?" she asked.

"Not yet, we were waiting to see if you wanted to eat or not. I'm not very hungry. What about you, Will?" Rob asked.

Before I could answer, Laura interjected, "Well, I'm famished."

"Will?" she said, looking for affirmation.

I realized if we didn't eat, the evening might end, perhaps leaving Rob alone in a place that served alcohol.

"I could eat."

Laura and Rob picked up the menus Fred had left on the bar.

"Will, you wanna look?" Rob asked.

"No, that's okay, I've read it a few hundred times," I smiled.

"And this is on me," Laura added.

"Well, then, you'd better find something on that menu, Rob," I kidded.

"I think I'll just have a bowl of clam chowder," he responded.

"Sounds good, I think I'll join you," I said.

Fred made his way back and took our order.

"And for you?" he asked Laura.

"Fred, I'll have the Dungeness crab salad."

Although Laura was a vegetarian, she occasionally ordered fish or seafood. I guess she considered this one of those special times.

After dinner, we caught a cab and dropped Rob at the halfway house where he was living—a requirement of the treatment program I was able to get him into in a relatively short time. It was one of the perks of working on Montgomery Street—a network of contacts from colleagues dealing with abuse due to the stress of high-pressure jobs. When he reached the top of the steps, he turned around and waved to us.

"How did you do this?" Laura asked incredulously. "He's tried before and failed."

"I know, he told me he's tried three times. I think, I hope, he's ready to do it this time."

"How can you be sure?" she asked.

"I can't, but we've talked, and I know he's come close to dying at least once. He's seen the destruction that booze and coke and pills have had on the people around him. I think he realizes he's at a crossroads."

"But what did you say to convince him?" she insisted.

"I told him about losing my brother. He asked a lot of questions about Tom. It brought back memories I'd forgotten. I shared how sad and abandoned I felt after he died. I think he may have understood how his death would affect you and your mother—how even more devastating it would be after having gone through what you did when you lost your father. It resonated with him—perhaps for the first time in his life."

"I hope you're right, Will, I really do."

"He still feels a sense of abandonment about your father's death. He believes he lost his family then, including you."

"I didn't abandon him! I tried to reach out plenty! He just never wanted to be a part of the family, he never wanted to listen to anything I had to say."

"I know you did. He didn't hear you, he wasn't listening to what you wanted for him. He couldn't process it, he was only reacting to how he was feeling and what he thought he needed, and no one could give him that."

"Until now?"

"I'm not sure, but he's trying."

"Because you helped him."

"I got him into a program, an expensive—"

"What? Wait . . . it's not county funded?"

I couldn't lie to her, especially about this.

"No, it's not. Laura, listen to me, it's working. It's my parents' life insurance proceeds. I invested it in the market. I've tripled it. I don't need it, we'll be fine. I want to do this. Please don't be mad at me."

"Does he know?"

"Of course not."

"That's good. I'm not mad at you. In fact, I don't know how I feel," she admitted.

"How about this, don't think about it right now? It's a four-month residency program, December through March, and another eight months of outpatient counseling and group-therapy sessions."

"But how much?" she asked.

I pulled a photo from my wallet and handed it to her.

"Tom's dead. Your brother is alive. His life can have meaning, some purpose. Don't you want that?"

"Of course, I do," she replied, somewhat indignantly.

"Then let me do this. Don't get me wrong, I'm doing this for Rob, but I'm also doing it for you. I don't want you or your mother to go through what I did—or what you went through when you were six—because it doesn't get any easier."

Laura sighed, a long sigh. I knew it meant she was either thinking or perplexed. In this instance, likely both.

"I'm uncomfortable about this," she said.

"It's working. That's all that matters."

"It's just so sudden, this turnaround."

"Laura, I don't know a lot about addiction, but I recognize when someone reaches rock bottom, it can empower them because there's nowhere to go but up, and that offers a promise of hope. Those moments come around once, maybe twice, in a lifetime."

We arrived at our building and walked the stairs to the apartment. She was in front of me and for the first time that night, I was really noticing her. Her muscular legs—she was a vison in that red dress. Laura was becoming a presence in this town—*Law Review* editor, Sierra Club member, stint at the Department of the Interior, soon-to-be environmental law attorney, not to mention a member of a prominent family and someone engaged to me. Maybe that's why I took such an interest in Rob and his redemption. Somehow, I thought maybe he was the key to Laura—the key to understanding everything yet, I knew that explanation was too simple. When I'd ask Mike, he would just nod his head and say, "It was like she raised herself." I understood what he meant, and why she was upset with me and my involvement with her brother. I think she just couldn't bear her own helplessness, or the thought of enduring another loss.

As the last few weeks of classes wound down, Rob and I had daily telephone conversations. Occasionally, we would meet for coffee in between my classes. To be honest, I wasn't sure what was motivating him to give the program a chance. I didn't allow myself to think it was me, that I had some magical power that finally convinced him. I sensed though he was looking for my approval. Perhaps he felt I was a clean slate, a tabula rasa, having no history or unpleasant interaction, and, therefore, no preconceived notion about what I thought he was or wasn't capable of achieving. I tried to maintain a nonjudgmental attitude and felt he understood and appreciated it.

Finals for Laura and me ended the same day, Thursday, December 22. Laura planned an impromptu happy hour with several classmates, as it was unlikely she would see many of them again until graduation in the spring. They met at the lobby bar at the Hyatt Regency, which featured live big band music a couple nights weekly during the holidays. I made a stop to drop off a paper and say hello to Barbara Kenny, my Tax Research professor and academic advisor, and invited her to join us. She had more work to do, but promised to stop by on her way to the BART station. I walked the short distance to the hotel, feeling relieved of the stress of exams and happy about celebrating the holidays with Laura.

There were about forty people when I arrived. I felt over-dressed in a suit because of the business lunch I had earlier with Carl Maddox from Dean Witter before my afternoon exam in Estate and Trust Taxation. I stood at a distance, momentarily observing the group, watching Laura talking and smiling. I loved her so much. I had confessed to Rob that morning over coffee that it hurt, that my heart ached at the thought of not being with her. Now watching her, my heart soared with happiness, knowing she loved me, that she was mine to love in return. She was wearing a black velvet pantsuit with silver sequins on the jacket, which, when the light caught it just right, sparkled. She turned around and saw me standing there and motioned to join her. I pointed at myself and mouthed "Me?" When she nodded "Yes", I put both my hands over my heart and smiled. I walked over and kissed her full on the mouth.

"Were you spying on me?" she asked.

"No, I was watching you having fun. I like to see you happy."

"Ah, I see. Would you like an adult beverage?"

"No, just being in your presence is intoxicating enough."

Several of her friends overheard me.

Adam Wagner, a 3L, who was in the Tax program with me, spoke up, "Will, your brain must be fried from that Estates final."

"Not at all, Adam. I'm in love with this woman and I don't care what anyone thinks about how I feel."

Laura's high school friend, Samantha Symons, an associate at Morrison and Foerster, who graduated a year earlier, interrupted. "Hey, Will, maybe you can bottle that and sell it?"

"Sam, love isn't something you can buy. Love is the miracle of sudden intimacy."

She seemed startled by my response.

"Laura, he's a keeper," she said.

"I know," Laura agreed.

"And a soon-to-be-employed one," I added.

Laura looked surprised and waited for me to continue.

"Witter offered me the security analyst position."

She hugged and kissed me.

"Congratulations."

Barbara Kenny walked up behind us and we turned around to greet her.

"I finished early," she said, hugging Laura hello.

"Did you tell her?" Laura asked.

"No, I wanted you to be the first to know," I said.

"That was sweet."

"Tell me," Barbara insisted.

"Dean Witter offered me a security analyst position."

"That's wonderful, Will," she said. "Say, when are you two getting married again?"

"No, not again, it will be the first time for us both," I kidded.

"July 28, a week after the bar exam," Laura replied.

"Congratulations."

We thanked her as she finished a glass of wine someone had handed her at some point during our conversation.

"I need to leave though. I've got to catch the train to Berkeley and then do some last-minute shopping."

"Well, thank you for stopping by. Happy Hanukkah, merry Christmas," Laura said. "Do you have this Homo Sapien next semester?" she asked, pointing at me.

"Partnership Tax," Barbara nodded.

"Thankfully, I only have three courses next semester. I have to take the Series 86/87 for the Witter job."

"I'm sure you'll do fine if this semester is any indication," Barbara offered.

As she was leaving, the band came back from break and started playing "Moonlight Serenade." I pulled Laura away from her friends and we danced to Glenn Miller and then Tommy Dorsey's "I'm Getting Sentimental Over You."

"By the way, I told Maddox I needed two weeks off in August for our honeymoon."

"I love you so much," she whispered back.

We had decided last minute to announce the wedding date over Labor Day weekend at the cottage. On the drive home that weekend, I had suggested a two-week trip to Alaska because of Laura's love for adventure and the outdoors. Neither of us was the type to lay on a beach all day, so when I proposed the idea, she thought it was the perfect choice.

As we made our way back to the group, we recognized people who had just arrived. Laura went over to say hello, while I headed over to Max Steinhart, my buddy from ERISA and Pension Tax class. It was an LL.M. course that we both petitioned to take, so we sort of bonded and ended up studying together.

"Hey, Steinhart, happy Hanukkah," I said, approaching him at the bar.

"Hey, Will, thought I'd see you here."

"You know me, 'Wherever there's a cop beatin' up a guy, I'll be there.'"

"Ah, still with the quotes. Who is it this time?"

"Max, I'm surprised you don't know. Someone from your own backyard—Steinbeck."

"Oh yeah, *The Grapes of Wrath*."

"You better stick to law," I said.

"Yeah, but labor lawyers don't get the hot women."

"What about those union babes?"

"What babes, like Cesar Chavez's sister?"

"You got a point. I suggest you attend shul on Fridays and find a nice Jewish girl."

"What do you know about nice Jewish girls?"

"Well, back at Syracuse, everything," I joked.

"I miss those college days. At Stanford, I knew all the Jewish female undergrads."

"When you say 'knew,' are you speaking in the biblical sense?"

Max laughed and raised his glass.

"Happy Hanukkah, merry Christmas," he said.

"L'chaim," I replied.

"Do you know where Laura is?"

I pointed over to a group of people where Laura stood chatting.

"I should go say hello, I can't stay long."

"You go. I'm heading to the men's room."

Max and Laura were ranked first and second in their class just like Mike and I were. As I made my way back through the crowd, I recognized someone I had seen quite a bit in the library.

"Hi. Will Merritt. Are you a 3L?" I asked.

"Well, 4L, I'm on the part-time track. Susan Taylor."

"Nice to meet you, I've seen you in the library," I replied. "You look almost ready to—"

"Yes, I'm forty weeks."

"Congratulations; is this your first?"

"Yes," she replied.

"Hi, Susan," Laura said, as she approached us. "Hanging out with pregnant women I see."

"Just one."

"I hear they're very sexy to some men," Laura suggested, looking at me.

"Not to Scott," Susan replied.

"I see you met Will."

"Oh my, that Will? This is your Will?"

"I'm afraid so," Laura smiled.

"Congratulations, Will. Laura's a sweetheart. I've known her, and her cousins, since Berkeley. And I work with Mike at Dean Witter."

"Really?" I asked.

"Yes, in compliance. Anyway, when are you two tying the knot?" she asked.

"I think the technical term is noose," I joked.

"Next July. You and Scott have to come," Laura insisted.

"That might be awkward since I dated Stephen, and Scott still hates him for it."

"Hey, all the more reason," I added unhelpfully.

"We'll see; he travels a lot on business, so maybe it'll just be me and Melissa."

"It's a girl?" Laura asked, placing her hand on Susan's enormous belly.

"That's wonderful, a Christmas baby," I said.

"My due date is December 25, so we'll see."

A while later, Laura made her way to the stage as the band was taking its last break for the evening.

"I want to thank everyone for coming tonight to share this noteworthy event with me. After five semesters of law school with you all, I am finished with classes and homework and exams, except for the bar. Unfortunately, this also means the end of all the good times we shared—the weekends living in the library and those long nights in the *Law Review* offices. Although I am continuing as editor of the *Environmental Law Review*, I'm unlikely to see many of you again until graduation. I just want to take this moment to thank everyone for all the help and support you have given me over these past three years. I wish you much success going into the final semester and wish you and your families a happy Hanukkah, a merry Christmas, and a blessed Happy New Year."

The cab ride home was quiet. As we approached Union Street, Laura asked if I wanted to stop for a nightcap. She never asked that question before, so I suspected she didn't want the evening to quite end—that when it did, it would bring a finality to her life as a student. I directed the cabbie to Prego on Union. The bartender, a woman in her early thirties, greeted us as she continued to wipe wine glasses with a white bar towel.

"What can I get you?" she asked.

"How about two Grand Marniers?" I replied.

"I'm Amy, by the way," she said, as she poured hot water from the coffee pot into two snifters. "Are you here for dinner?"

"No, just a night cap; I've been up since five this morning," Laura replied.

"Really, for what?" she asked, now dumping the hot water out and pouring a generous amount of liqueur into the snifters.

"Law school finals," Laura said, taking a sip.

"So, why didn't you want to go home and collapse? You obviously need sleep," I asked.

"I just want it to last a little longer. I can't believe it's over just like that—it seems so sudden, so abrupt."

"Kind of like life, I imagine."

I was tired and realized the analogy wasn't the best.

"Perhaps, but there's no control over death—it just comes when it comes. This is volitional, like I've chosen to end this and it's making me feel sad inside."

I put my arm around her shoulders.

"Change has never been easy for you. You mustn't look at it as losing something."

"No?"

"No, you will graduate and pass the bar and be admitted, and have wonderful colleagues you'll work with and clients you'll advocate for . . . Laura, you'll do great things, I know you will."

A smile formed around her lips.

"Hey, why don't we have a St. Patrick's Day party for your friends after midterms? We can celebrate your twenty-fourth birthday too," I said.

"And your twenty-eighth."

We finished our cordials and walked down Union Street toward our apartment. All the storefronts were adorned with Christmas decorations and the sidewalk was busy now with people shopping or heading to dinner. Everything was vibrant and alive with lights and music. Back at the apartment, we changed,

Laura donning her old gray sweatshirt. We plopped down on the bed and lay there, too tired to sleep but happy to stay awake and share the time together. Occasionally, one of us would say something random—something we'd forgotten to tell the other in the past few weeks because of all the craziness that the end of the semester brought until we fell asleep.

The next two days were filled with shopping, gift wrapping, and baking. Laura became obsessed and started making all sorts of cookies. She sent me to the Marina Safeway twice in two days for butter and sugar. On Christmas Eve, we invited Rob over for dinner. When he arrived a half hour late, Laura asked if everything was okay.

"Yes, fine. I just missed the bus and had to wait for the next one. I forgot they don't run as often on the weekends," Rob assured her.

Laura retreated to the kitchen and I ushered him into the living room, which we had lit with candles.

"Wow, what a great view," he remarked.

"Yes, it's spectacular, isn't it?"

"I've forgotten how beautiful it is, since I don't see the Bay or mountains much anymore."

"I've been wondering what to get you for Christmas."

"Oh, Will, you don't need to get me anything more."

"No, listen. How about we drive up to Point Reyes and do some whale watching. We'll bring hot chocolate and sit on the cliff with binoculars."

"That sounds great. I remember you told me about the first time you went up there with Laura—how sick you were and how cold it was."

"God it was cold, and I figured I was already so sick that I couldn't get any worse! You remember me telling you that?"

"Yes. When I started in rehab, you told me that story and some others. They were, I don't know, inspiring, I guess—your ups and downs. I tried to imagine how I would have felt."

I noticed Laura standing in the hallway, listening. She walked in with a tray of fruit juice and handed Rob a glass.

"There's nothing in here other than fruit juice?" he asked anxiously.

"No, just ice cubes," she replied.

When I took a sip of mine, I realized she had spiked it, and probably hers too, with vodka.

"Mmm," I said. "You should serve this more often."

She looked at me mildly annoyed, as if we were pulling something on Rob.

"Yes, Laura, it's very tasty," Rob agreed.

"Are you hungry, Rob?" Laura asked.

"Oh, you know me; my appetite isn't what it used to be."

"I've made your favorite—lasagna."

"It smells delicious."

"It's with spinach, which I know you like, but not meat since I don't eat it."

"That's fine. I know you don't eat meat. And if you want some wine with dinner, it won't bother me—I mean it won't tempt me—in case you were wondering," he said, in a convincing voice.

Now I felt like a fraud drinking in front of Rob. I'm sure Laura felt badly about it too.

"Actually, we don't have any," I said truthfully.

Laura asked me to help her in the kitchen, so I left him alone in the living room paging through a book of Ansel Adams' photographs.

"What's the matter?" I asked.

"I feel like a shit. Here he is trying to remain sober and we're sneaking alcohol," Laura admitted.

"Let's dump it out," I suggested.

We poured what remained of our drinks into the sink and filled them with water.

"I'm sorry, I made a mistake."

"We all make mistakes. Don't beat yourself up."

"You're a good man, Charlie Brown."

"You bring it out in me."

We decided to eat at our small table on the deck. It was a cool night, but we were wearing heavy sweaters. The air was still and the sky was crystal clear. As darkness descended, all the houses and apartment buildings were illuminated and the lights reflected on the water in the Bay.

"Laura, this is delicious, like Grandma used to make," Rob said.

"She still does," Laura replied.

"Is she disappointed in me?" Rob asked. "I know Momma is, but what about Grandma?"

"Grandma Betsy has always loved you. You were her favorite being the youngest grandchild. And Mom, well, you know, she's never gotten over Dad's death. She's always loved you, but if she was harsh with you, and I know she was, it was because she wanted you to be strong and not get caught up in drugs and alcohol. She's had a hard time reconciling how to be a good mother to you, but I know in her heart she truly loves you."

"You're a lot like your mother," I added.

"You think so, Will?"

It wasn't a compliment, rather an observation.

"Yes, Rob, I do. You're both very sensitive and . . ." I hesitated, not sure if I should continue.

"And what?" he pleaded.

"Truth?" I said.

"Yes, truth."

"And vulnerable," I responded.

"You mean weak."

"No, Rob, I don't mean weak. I mean you are vulnerable to other people's opinions and influence."

"I know. I've sometimes not been able to make the right decision. It was hard for me," he admitted.

"Listen to me—you are not a weak person. A weak person could not have done what you've set out to do. This program is one of the best in the country—on par with the Betty Ford Clinic. You've shown commitment and dedication and humbled yourself, accepting you need help, that takes guts and determination. You're not a weak person, you're a courageous one."

Rob was tearing up when I finished. I looked at Laura and so was she.

"Hey, what is this? It's Christmas Eve, we should be happy and thankful. Rob, go put on some Christmas music," I instructed him.

Laura leaned toward me, pressing her hands against my face. She pulled me close and kissed me.

"What did I do to deserve you?" she asked.

"Everything," I said.

"I can't believe the way he responds to you."

"My brother is dead, yours isn't."

She started tearing again.

"We should be celebrating not crying."

"I am celebrating," Laura pouted.

Rob returned to the patio and we cleared the dishes and moved inside.

"Hey, Will, Laura, if it's okay, I'm going to turn in. We had PT at seven this morning and I'm kind of beat."

"Yes, it's okay, Rob," she replied, blowing out the candles in the living room. I brought him a pillow and blanket for the sofa. Laura and I cleaned the dishes in the kitchen and poured ourselves a single vodka on the rocks, which we shared as we put away the food.

"Can you finish?" she asked.

"Sure," I said.

She disappeared into the bathroom. When I finished, I went to the bedroom and heard the squeak of the shower faucet. After several minutes, I got up and went into the bathroom, where I could hear her sobbing in the shower above the sound of the running water.

"Laura?"

"Yes."

"What's wrong?"

"Nothing," she replied, suddenly turning off the water.

I handed her a towel and she stepped out from behind the shower curtain. She threw her arms around me.

"How could I have been so selfish all these years?"

"Laura, it's not your fault. Stop blaming yourself for the past, you were a kid, you couldn't have—"

"I should have been a better sister. I should have done something."

I picked her up and carried her to the bedroom, placing her on the bed.

"I forgot to brush my teeth," she said sheepishly.

I picked her up again and carried her back to the bathroom. She reached for her toothbrush.

"Don't look," she demanded.

I walked back to the bedroom. When she returned and stood in front of the dresser, she applied lotion to her face and hands like I had seen her do every night since she had moved in with me.

"I love you," she said, in a serious tone, observing me through the mirror, then turning to look at me directly to reinforce her feelings.

"I love you too."

Tomorrow was Christmas Day. Rob would be joining us, and the rest of the family, for the first time in a long while. Their collective happiness was the only gift I could possibly desire. I couldn't help but think my brother Tommy would be proud of the small part I had played. Rob had begun to embody the brother I lost.

"Merry Christmas, Will," Laura said, now lying next to me in bed.

"Merry Christmas," I replied, with a feeling of joy I hadn't experienced in a long time.

CHAPTER 6

THE APARTMENT BUZZER rang just after seven thirty in the evening on New Year's Eve. Mike and his date were waiting downstairs.

"Are you ready? They're here," I asked Laura.

"You can take my bag and the cooler. I'll be down in a minute."

Stephen and Caroline had insisted we all sleep over at their condo. Mike was standing beside the limo, dressed in a three-piece suit, smoking a cigar.

"Hey there, Will, you look like a packhorse with all that stuff."

The chauffeur walked around the limo and opened the trunk, so I could place our overnight bags inside. He then proceeded to open the passenger door. I peered inside, observing a pair of shapely legs tucked in against the plush interior.

"Hi," I said.

"Hello."

"You must be Jane."

"Yes."

"Will Merritt, nice to meet you."

"It's nice to meet you too. Mike is excited about tonight. He's happy you and Laura could join us. He loves you both," she said, in an excited but nervous voice.

"Who are you?"

"Yes, I know, I'm just some outsider on a New Year's Eve date. Actually, this is our third date."

"Oh, I've got to know what the first two involved," I kidded. Jane smiled.

"He's actually a very sweet guy once you get to know him."

"I guess I never got past the insults phase."

"That can't be true. He told me you asked him to be your best man."

"A momentary lapse in judgment."

Laura poked her head in from outside and slid into the back seat next to me.

"Laura, this is Jane . . ."

"Nolan. I'm so happy to meet you, Laura. Mike has told me so much about you both but I'm still feeling like a real outsider right now."

"Oh, Jane, don't be silly. I'm glad we'll get a chance to spend some time together."

Mike finished his cigar and joined us in the limo.

"Hey, this thing has a bar and a telephone," he announced.

"When's the last time you were out?" Laura asked.

"1980."

"That sounds about right," Laura replied. "So how did you two meet?"

Mike's face turned serious.

"I was at SF General, checking on a buddy, and I ran into Jane in the cafeteria. I recognized her from the neighborhood; turns out, we live two blocks from each other on Potrero Hill. Anyway, she was friendly and offered to check on my friend Andy. Will, you remember Andy S. from the Exchange?"

"Yes," I replied.

"He had PCP, *Pneumocystis carinii* pneumonia, from AIDS."

"Oh, that's awful. He's just a kid, what, nineteen or twenty?"

"Yeah. Remember his mom would send in her homemade red sauce for us? Anyway, Jane volunteers on the fifth floor and it turns out she likes Western omelets like I do."

"How is Andy?" I asked.

"He died last month."

We sat there in silence a moment until Laura spoke up.

"Jane, what's the best part of being a doctor?"

"Delivering babies. I'm a second-year OB/GYN resident."

It was obvious Mike appreciated her changing the subject.

"You think we brought enough stuff?" he interjected.

"I hear they have a wood-burning fireplace," Jane said.

"That will come in handy after our midnight swim," Mike replied.

"You've got to be kidding?"

"Maybe you don't know Mike as well as you think? Laura and I will jump in, but that's it. I've seen *Jaws* and don't plan to be some great white's New Year's feast."

"You in?" Mike asked Jane.

"When in Rome. But I'll need a stiff drink first," she replied.

"Just one?" he kidded.

"I know we are well supplied in that department. Will and I dropped off several bottles yesterday when we delivered the seafood," Laura revealed.

"Can Caroline cook?" Mike asked.

"Well, she lived in Boston, where they have seafood, and she went to MIT, so I'm just spitballing here, but I'm guessing the answer is yes," Laura replied.

"Will, how do you deal with this McKenzie sarcasm?" Mike asked.

"When it gets too much, I withhold sex," I said, trying to maintain a straight face.

The limo turned onto The Great Highway, and in the darkness, we could barely make out the water.

"'When I see the sea once more will the sea have seen or not seen me?' What? No one's familiar with the Chilean poet Pablo Neruda?" I asked.

Blank stares greeted me. A minute later, we were pulling up in front of the condo.

"Will, put your money away, I've got this. Besides you'll need it tomorrow for the cab," Mike said.

"So will you."

"Yes, but I'm employed. You need to save your money for the honeymoon."

"That's true. Okay, but the next limo is on me."

"Deal," Mike replied.

The two-story condo had a sprawling living room window that faced west out over the highway, Ocean Beach, and the Pacific beyond.

"Only problem is we need to clean it every other day because of the salt spray," Stephen remarked.

"With a view like this, I wouldn't mind a little Windex routine," Jane replied.

"There's a certain serenity to living at the beach. You can walk it together or alone; it provides a solace from everything. It's funny to think; I grew up in a house overlooking the Hudson, I lived in Cambridge with a view of the Charles, spent summers in Wildwood, New Jersey, on the Atlantic, and now live here with a view of the Pacific," Caroline said.

"And you're a Pisces—a water baby like Laura and me," I added.

"Isn't it lonely out here when one of you is away on business?" Jane asked.

"Good thing you don't travel, Will," Mike injected. "Will here would miss Laura too much. What am I gonna do?" he mimicked in an Italian accent.

Stephen snickered at Mike's comment.

"Say, let's get those shrimp and clams going on the grill," Caroline suggested.

"Good idea, honey," Stephen said, carrying the tray of seafood out onto the deck.

"Laura, Jane, can you help me for a minute in the kitchen?" Caroline asked.

"Of course," they replied, leaving Mike and me standing in the living room.

"So, what's up?" Mike asked.

"Nothing. What's up with you?"

"Not much to report."

"What was Andy's last name?"

"Spadarino," Mike answered.

As he said the name, his demeanor changed and a somber expression came over him.

"When I saw him in the hospital, he told me I was lucky to have a brother to talk to—to confide in."

"That must have been hard. What did you say?"

"I told him he could confide in me."

"Did he?"

"A bit. He never came out to his folks, and it tore him up inside."

"I remember when you told me about sitting up on Potrero Hill with him, after work one day, watching the fog roll in."

"He was a good kid," Mike said, with a sad realization in his voice.

"I'm sorry, Mike. I know he was more than a neighbor or some stranger we worked with. You got him his job, didn't you?

Mike nodded.

"You should have told me."

"Nah, you and Laura were dealing with Rob and . . ."

"That's not a reason not to tell us."

"You're right."

"To happier times," I said, raising my glass.

We each took a sip of our drinks and went out to the deck, where Stephen was still chuckling over Mike's Italian accent comment.

"Has he always been like this?" I asked Stephen.

"Like what, a dick?"

"Hey!" Mike objected.

"Just kidding. No, Mike's always been opinionated and impatient. He always wanted to stay up late when we were kids even if there wasn't anything going on."

"He must have driven your parents crazy."

"You know, I'm standing right here," Mike said.

"Yeah, our father especially. He was always Mom's favorite, but Dad, man, he'd get pretty frustrated with old Mike—me too sometimes."

"I would have thought you were the perfect child," I said.

"Stephen? Hell no. He was just clever and didn't get caught," Mike replied.

"I guess that's sort of true," Stephen laughed. "If you're looking for the perfect child, that would have been Laura."

"In spades," Mike added.

"Was she a happy child?" I asked.

"She was a persevering child. Whatever it was school, soccer, piano—she strived to excel and always did," Stephen said.

"But, was she happy doing those things?"

"I believe her happiness came from her success in everything she perceived as her father's dream for her," Mike said.

"Those achievements helped fill the gap in her life. She couldn't gain his praise, so she sought recognition elsewhere," Stephen added.

"Was she sad? I mean about not having her father?"

"She didn't dwell on Uncle John not being there. She had us, and the rest of the family— Rob too. She just lost a very special connection and carried that reminder with her every day of her life," Mike offered.

"She still does. The drive, the ambition, is masking what she can never recoup," Stephen said.

"That's where you come in, my friend," Mike said, putting his hand on my shoulder.

"Yeah, well," I replied.

"Yeah well, what?" Mike asked.

"We love each other I have no doubt about that. I just wish I could make her feel more secure, convince her that everything is going to be wonderful and last forever."

"Things can't always be wonderful," Stephen said.

"Or last forever," Mike added. "You want to protect her, that's natural."

"I want her to feel safe and reassure her that no matter what, I'll always be there for her."

"That's all you can do. You can't predict the future, and even if you could, you wouldn't be able to alter it," Stephen replied.

"She lost her father and that fact will never change. It's not your job to fix the way she feels. Your job is to love our cousin and know we'll kick your ass if you ever hurt her," Mike grinned.

"Since when did you become so mature?"

"Since Spadarino."

"Who?" Stephen asked.

"Never mind, brother. I bet those shrimp and clams are done."

We returned to the living room and everyone sat on the floor around the cocktail table eating hors d'oeuvres.

"Stephen, do you mind if I use your phone?" I asked.

"No, not at all," he replied, pointing to the wall phone in the kitchen.

"I wonder if you have a more private . . ."

"Yes, in the bedroom."

I sat on the edge of the bed and dialed Rob's room. It was almost nine o'clock curfew, so I knew he would likely answer.

"Hello."

"Rob, it's Will."

"Hi, Will. How are you doing?"

"I'm fine, Rob. How are things?"

"Oh, I'm good. I've got soda and popcorn. We're going to watch *It's a Wonderful Life* in a few minutes in the community room."

"Oh, I love that movie."

"Me too."

"I just called to wish you a Happy New Year."

"Happy New Year to you too."

"Well, if it's almost movie time, I'll let you go."

"Okay, Will, I hope to see you soon."

"Yes, absolutely. Remember, we have that trip to Point Reyes."

"I didn't forget. Thanks for calling."

"Good night, Rob. I'll see you next year."

"Oh right, I'll see you next year too."

When I returned to the living room, Laura asked whom I called.

"Your brother."

"Is he okay?"

"Yes, he's fine. He's about to watch *It's a Wonderful Life*."

"I called him earlier. He seemed upbeat."

"He seemed that way just now too. We don't need to dwell on this."

"I know," she said, getting up from the floor to kiss me. I kissed her back.

"Hey, get a room you two," Mike yelled.

I gave him the finger and kept kissing Laura.

"You taste like strawberry."

"I found an old lip gloss in my overnight bag."

"That's what you tasted like the first time we kissed."

"Oh my God! What is this, *Days of Our Lives*?" Mike shouted.

"I think it's sweet," Jane said.

"So do I," Caroline seconded.

"Stephen, help me out here?" Mike pleaded.

"No, I think it's three to one on this," Stephen replied.

"I see," Mike responded.

Laura and I sat back down on the floor.

"Mike, we all love you here, even this third-date Dr. Jane, so there's no need to mask your true emotions behind some macho caricature," I said.

"Boy, have you lived in San Francisco too long," he retorted.

"Dinner is served," Caroline announced, from the candle-lit dining room.

After we were seated, Stephen raised his glass and proposed a toast.

"To my wonderful, smart, and talented cousin Laura and her unemployed fiancé, to my employed brother and his charming and brilliant date, and especially to my lovely and beautiful wife; thank you, all, for sharing this evening and tomorrow with us. I wish us all much happiness, love, and success in the New Year."

"Can I get a late check out?" Mike joked.

"I got a job offer as a securities analyst," I announced.

"What firm?" Mike asked.

"Yours."

"You're coming to Witter?"

"Yep," I replied.

Mike came over and shook my hand as Stephen amended his toast. After several courses of salads, seafood, and fish, we were all sated and a little drunk.

"Okay, kids, it's time to change into swim suits," Mike announced.

The order fell on deaf ears. No one wanted to move, no less change and move, from where we were seated.

"I can't believe no one wants to swim in the ocean at midnight!"

"Mike, we appreciate your enthusiasm, but the water is very cold and there's a new moon, so it's pitch dark on the beach, besides no one wants to leave this comfortable condo with all this great food and drink," Laura said, trying to reason with him.

"So you're all saying you don't want to ring in 1984 in the ocean?" he continued.

"We want to celebrate it near the ocean," she countered.

"When was the last time you were in the ocean?" Stephen asked.

"It's been a while, that's why I thought tonight could be special."

"Maybe we could go for a walk on the beach in the morning when it's light out," Laura suggested.

"Yes, that's a great idea. We can all start the New Year off with a contemplative walk," Caroline added.

"Well, then, how about a champagne toast on the deck?" Mike asked.

"Sounds like a good compromise," Stephen replied.

We all stepped out onto the porch and passed flutes of champagne. It was pitch dark, except for the candle glow from inside.

"We should all make a wish—a wish for something we want in the New Year. I'll go first," Jane said. "I want an end to so much heartache and sickness."

"Amen," Mike echoed.

"I want a baby," Caroline said.

"Amen to that," Stephen replied.

"You know, you have to be home long enough to make that happen, Stephen," Mike interjected.

"I want a happy year with Will, to pass the bar, and have a fantastic wedding," Laura announced.

After Stephen and I said our wishes, I added, "Success is getting what you want. Happiness is wanting what you get."

"Who said that?" Caroline asked.

"My mother used to say it to us," I replied.

"Us?" Jane wondered.

"My brother and me. He's no longer with us."

"I hate that euphemism," Laura said.

"So do I. It's sanitary, so neat and tidy with no regard to the actual person whose life had meaning . . . like it wasn't all for naught. I had a brother and he died."

I suddenly realized how drunk I was and apologized. We all went back inside and Laura sat down at the piano and started playing "What Are You Doing New Year's Eve?" A bit later, Mike and I found ourselves outside, emptying bags of smelly garbage.

"Geez, Mike, I don't know why I said that. I guess it's the holidays. They remind me of when I was a kid with my parents and Tommy."

"Hey, it's okay to miss them. I'm sorry you lost them. It must have been awful," he replied.

"Thank you."

"That's what a best man is for."

"I lost Tommy, but I feel like I've gained three brothers."

"I heard you got through to Rob—that's a remarkable accomplishment," Mike said.

"Timing. Maybe it was just the right time. It's something your grandfather mentioned to me once."

"He's a wise, old man—my grandpa," Mike agreed.

"Come here," I said, hugging him just as Stephen came down the stairs with more garbage.

"I assume this is consensual?" Stephen laughed.

Stephen and I looked at one another, and he realized that the conversation inside about my brother had likely continued. We returned upstairs where Laura was playing more carols. I sat down next to her at the piano and watched her play. By one thirty in the morning, Stephen and Caroline had gone to bed. Jane and Laura were stoking the fireplace and sipping more champagne. The four of us sat and talked for another hour. Mike set up his double sleeping bag in front of the fire and offered us the guest room. Laura and I walked to the bedroom and drifted off to sleep almost immediately.

The next morning, Laura and I were having coffee as we looked out on a cool, overcast, gray sky with huge waves rolling in across the way. Caroline, smelling the coffee, joined us in her pajamas and robe. It was one of the few times Laura was not wearing her faded Berkeley sweatshirt, but instead, a heavy, oatmeal-colored Irish knit sweater her mother had given her for Christmas.

"Should we go for a walk on the beach?" Caroline asked. "Stephen's awake, I know he would join us."

"Yes, that sounds nice," Laura replied.

"Okay, let me go tell him."

"Tell me what?" he said, walking into the kitchen in his underwear and T-shirt.

"Stephen, can't you put some clothes on? We have guests."

"Guests? Will and I take saunas together at the gym and Laura's my cousin—almost like a sister."

"Well, what about Jane?"

"Jane's asleep, besides she's a doctor."

"Hey, it's New Year's. Let's not start the year off with a domestic dispute," I said, handing him a mug of hot coffee.

"Thank you, you're a gentleman and a scholar."

"So, tell me what?" he asked again.

"We're going for a walk on the beach. Want to come?" Laura replied.

"Sure, let me put some clothes on," he said, walking back to the bedroom.

Caroline shook her head, "Men."

It was windy as we made our way up the beach to the Cliff House restaurant, so Laura and Caroline could use the ladies' room. Then we headed back south along the water as the sky brightened and the wind died down a bit.

"So, any New Year's resolutions?" I asked, to no one in particular.

"Bechtel is trying to put us on the same projects, so when the team goes to China or India, we'll be together. I'm not sure that's a resolution but it's the best-case scenario we're hoping for," Caroline replied.

"I want to be a better sister to Rob. Will helped him so much this past year, and I've been so preoccupied," Laura said.

"I think that's a noble gesture," Stephen offered.

"No, it's not noble, it's just the right thing to do," she replied.

I took Laura's hand. I wanted to say something encouraging, but she was right. She needed to face the fact that she had been delinquent and would now make amends.

"What about you, Will?" Caroline asked.

"My resolution is to embrace every day and be thankful for family and friends. Mike made me realize last night that even though my family is gone, I'm blessed to be part of Laura's."

"Does this have anything to do with hugging him?" Stephen asked.

"You could say that."

"You sound like a priest," Stephen said.

"Because I'm searching for answers to questions without explanation?"

"Doesn't everyone search for some deeper meaning?" Caroline asked.

"No, not really. I think most people just coast through their lives with little introspection or contemplation," I replied.

"The unexamined life," Stephen offered.

"Will doesn't talk to me about his parents or brother because he thinks it will remind me of my father. He feels if he brings up the subject, it will make me sad. Am I right?" Laura asked.

"Yes," I admitted.

"Listen to me, Will. I love you. You can tell me anything. If you hurt, I hurt too."

"Okay," I replied, hugging her.

The women were getting cold, so they headed back to the condo. Stephen and I lingered on the beach, watching two surfers gliding out on the water.

"I knew you were compatible with her all this time—high achievers, tenacious, both hating to lose."

"That's why we're always partners at Trivial Pursuit—we avoid disappointment."

"That's smart of you."

"I'm sorry, I interrupted your thought," I said.

"No, it's just I'm realizing how you both have been so pro-foundly affected by death. I know that's obvious, but it doesn't make it any less true."

"There's a difference though. I was practically an adult when my parents and brother died, but for Laura, it's something she's lived with almost her entire life. I have to believe that's much harder—wondering what life would have been like, how her father's presence would have affected the course of her life through childhood and adolescence—even now."

"Perhaps you're right," Stephen conceded. "After all, I'm an engineer not a shrink."

"Neither am I," I replied.

"Hey, wanna head back?"

"Yes, I'm getting cold standing here."

When we arrived back at the condo, Jane and Laura had a crackling fire going. Caroline and Mike were preparing breakfast in the kitchen.

"What can we do?" Stephen asked.

"Pour some champagne," Mike shouted.

We looked at each other and followed his instruction.

"Hey, Will, you look a little cold standing there, why don't you stir this waffle batter for me," Mike said.

"That will warm me up?"

"No, but if you stir with one hand and sip champagne with the other, it might."

"I think I can manage that," I replied.

Laura came up behind me and put her arms around my waist.

"Hey, you're not doing anything to help," Mike said to her.

"I'm providing moral support," she replied, in a giddy tone.

"Well, what I need is someone to slice those melons."

"Oh, I'll do that," Jane offered.

"Yes, she knows her way around a scalpel—I mean knife," Laura said.

"So you're just going to stand there and look pretty?" Mike jested.

"Yes, and I think I do it fairly well if I don't say so."

"So do I," I said.

"You don't count," Mike shouted.

"So do I," Caroline interjected.

"Me too," Stephen said.

"Me three," Jane added.

"You should never argue with the chef," Mike replied.

"Hey, co-chef!" Caroline demanded.

"Mike, you're so sensitive. I just love it when you show off your creative talents," Laura teased.

"It's not easy slaving away in the kitchen all morning for a bunch of ingrates."

"You got up fifteen minutes ago," Jane cried.

"Et tu, Brute?"

"God, now he's got a paranoia complex," Stephen laughed.

"Ah, young Michael has a lean and hungry look—such men are dangerous," I warned.

"Mike, we're sorry your creative temperament has been impugned. We just want to be supportive of your outstanding culinary efforts," Laura replied.

"God, you sound like a lawyer. How about a refill on the Moet?" he said.

"That I can do."

"Grazie."

"Prego."

We enjoyed brunch until after 2:00 p.m., and Stephen and Caroline insisted no one rush to put things away. They had two more vacation days before a business trip together to Singapore and offered to clean up. Laura called her mother, and then we all spoke with Andrew and Betsy to wish them a Happy New Year. By four o'clock, we were back at the apartment, doing laundry and drinking mass quantities of water. I stepped out later to pick up some Shrimp Lo Mein and a garlic eggplant dish we liked. When I returned, Laura had changed back into her old sweatshirt. We sat on the living room floor using the cocktail table for our plates and water glasses.

"I feel bloated," she announced, placing her hand over her stomach.

"Yes, well, that happens with copious amounts of alcohol."

"Will you love me when I'm fat?" she asked.

"I doubt it."

"Then I better lay off the stuff for a while," she smiled back.

After dinner, I opened my fortune cookie and read it aloud.

"A good way to lose weight is to make love after Chinese dinner."

I leaned over and kissed her. We made love there on the floor with Laura on top, still wearing her sweatshirt.

We rose early the next morning. I drove to pick up Rob while Laura made us sandwiches, snacks, and hot chocolate. Rob was standing outside when I pulled up at 8:00 a.m.

"Where's Laura?"

"She's making our lunches. We'll swing by and pick her up."

"Did she remember the cocoa?"

"Absolutely," I said, gesturing toward two cases. "Open those up and wipe the binocular lenses with that soft cloth inside. Hey, did you bring a hat?"

"Right here, in my pocket."

"Okay good, you'll need that."

The trip to Point Reyes was fun but cold. We spent over two hours sitting on the rocks, overlooking the Pacific. Through the binoculars, we spotted dozens of humpbacks. Laura brought a wool blanket, which we draped around ourselves to keep warm. The sun was out, but even on a clear, dry day, there was a constant chill from the gusting wind. By one o'clock, with food and hot chocolate consumed, she suggested we head back to the city. In the car, Rob couldn't stop talking about whales, specifically their plumes and breaches.

"Somebody really likes whales," I said.

"Yes, they're majestic."

"He's loved whales ever since he was a little kid," Laura said.

"That's true, Laura."

Halfway home, Rob fell asleep in the back seat.

"This was sweet of you. I think it was the perfect Christmas gift—not to mention the clothes you bought him," she said.

"I'm glad he enjoyed himself. He needs to feel connected."

She took my hand as we crossed the Golden Gate Bridge. We were now back in the city underneath a beautiful blue sky, which heralded the first Monday of the New Year. After we dropped Rob off, we drove back to the apartment and took a short nap before we showered and changed. Laura's mother and grandparents were coming over from the East Bay to meet us for a New Year's celebration dinner. There was discussion about inviting Rob, but they decided to wait until he finished the program before including him in things outside the family home. They also wanted to discuss the wedding—another reason for excluding him and the other grandchildren.

"Where are we meeting them?" I asked.

"We're not, they're picking us up. Gramps hired a limo."

"Really, a limo? I'd have thought he'd consider that an extravagance."

"He is frugal, but he's also sensible enough to know when to leave the driving to someone else."

"I guess BART was out of the question?"

Laura looked at me like I had two heads.

"We could have gone to Berkeley," I said.

"I offered, but they wanted to make this special for us— for me, I guess. I think they realize this might be the last time they will be entertaining their only granddaughter as a single woman."

"So, a suit?" I called to her in the bathroom.

"Yes, your new navy," she said, as she returned to the bedroom in an incredible black cocktail dress.

"Wow, you look stunning."

"Really?"

"Yes, really. And to think, a few hours ago, you were sitting on a cliff, eating a peanut butter and jelly sandwich."

"Do you like my shoes?"

"I like them very much. Are they suede?"

"Yes, and expensive."

"Good thing we're not paying for dinner."

A few minutes later, the phone rang. It was Betsy calling from the limo, telling us they were here. We went downstairs and entered a limo for the second time in almost as many days. I sat back on the leather seat as we headed up Russian Hill. I peered out the window, trying to figure out our destination, which appeared to be Nob Hill. As the limo headed north, I realized I was wrong. *Maybe North Beach*, I thought. Then the driver made an abrupt turn up Telegraph Hill and stopped at Julius' Castle. Apparently, it was Andrew and Betsy's favorite place from long ago. The restaurant overlooked the entire San Francisco Bay with a panoramic view from the East Bay all the way to the Golden Gate Bridge and the Marin Headlands. When the champagne arrived, Andrew raised his glass.

"To the most beautiful and precious women I know."

I didn't want to steal his thunder, so I simply said, "I feel the same, cheers."

"Well, I'd like to propose a toast," Ellen said, somewhat unexpectedly. "To my wonderful daughter and my soon-to-be son-in-law, I wish you much joy and happiness in this New Year when you will become husband and wife."

It was an enjoyable evening. We talked about wedding plans and discussed our upcoming lunch on Wednesday with the Wilkinsons, at their home in Belvedere. When we arrived back at the apartment, I kissed Laura's mother and grandmother goodnight and shook Andrew's hand. He leaned forward and kissed me on the cheek.

"I've rarely seen him do that, Will," Laura said, once we were upstairs.

"He's very kind. You're lucky."

"I know I am. And I'm lucky to have you too," she replied.

"Come here. Did I tell you how sexy you look in that dress?"

"I think you mentioned something subtle in passing. Perhaps I'd better take it off, so it doesn't get wrinkled."

"Good idea, maybe I should hang up my new suit, so it doesn't get wrinkled either."

"Look how much we're saving on dry cleaning," she remarked.

"Right. We better start saving. It's going to be an expensive year."

"I'm thinking of something we can do that doesn't cost anything," she replied, standing there in a black satin half-slip. She slipped off the garment as I turned the light off and we both met in the middle of the bed, embracing each other.

On Tuesday, I had a follow-up lunch with Carl Maddox to discuss the securities analyst position. We talked about the tech sector and companies he was most interested in. He asked for my opinion on a wide range of issues: financing, hardware production capability, technological innovation, R&D, customer needs for both business and personal use. On the latter, we found key common ground—in five or so years, certainly in the '90s, PCs would hit the retail market, which offered a huge profit potential. Microsoft had already capitulated to the hardware industry. Capital would drive the financing needs, for both established companies and start-ups, demanding a keen analytic sense of where to invest. At the end of lunch, feeling very satisfied with my responses to his questions, I asked when he expected I could start.

"I know you've got one semester left, and with your background and experience, we can hold off until May, when you finish your degree. We would like you to sit for the Series 86 and

87 Research Analyst exams sometime between now and then, but I don't see that as much of an issue, do you?"

"No, not at all," I replied.

"Good, so we have a deal?"

"We do."

"Listen, I've got to get back to the office. I'm going to have HR send you a mountain of paperwork, and we'll schedule something with the whole team in four or five weeks."

"That's sounds great," I said.

"Okay, Will, I got to run," he said, as he rose from his chair. "I'll see you soon."

"Thank you again, Carl, and Happy New Year."

After I finished my iced tea, I headed over to the bookstore to buy my textbooks, which I put in my locker and then walked across Market Street over to Sutter to catch the bus home. When I arrived, Laura was in the kitchen, making vegetable soup, which filled the apartment with a wonderful smell.

"Mmm, it smells delicious."

"Thanks. I thought it might warm us up after our run. How was your lunch meeting?"

I pulled Maddox's business card from my shirt pocket and handed it to her.

"Carl P. Maddox, Senior Vice President, Institutional Sales & Investment Management, Dean Witter Reynolds," she read out loud. "I wonder what the P stands for," she teased, knowing I had more to tell her.

"The P stands for Preston. Turn it over," I said.

"Fifty-two. What's fifty-two?" she asked.

"$52,000 a year starting salary."

"Will, that's fantastic, I'm so happy for you," she replied, hugging me.

"For us, happy for us."

"For us," she repeated.

Running five miles against the cold wind sapped our energy, but it felt good to get some exercise and even better to soak in a warm bath afterwards, which Laura scented with eucalyptus oil. She lit candles and put on a Yo-Yo Ma tape of Bach cello concertos.

"On the ride home, all I could think about was telling you. I don't think it would have mattered half as much if I didn't have you to share it with."

Laura leaned forward in the tub and kissed me.

"I love you."

"I love you. You make me feel like I'm the most special person in the world," she whispered.

"You are the most special person in my world. You give me a reason to want to be the best person I can be."

A tear ran down her cheek.

"I didn't mean to make you cry."

"Tears of happiness."

After the warm bath and hearty soup, we reopened our Christmas gifts and read all the cards and notes from friends and family until it was time for some much-needed rest.

Wednesday was Laura's last day before starting her externship. My classes started on Thursday as well. She spent the morning on the phone, making appointments with the florist, the caterer, and the printer. We were due at the Wilkinsons in Belvedere at one o'clock for lunch and a tour of the property. Belvedere is located at the southernmost point of Tiberon peninsula and most homes have expansive views of the Bay and the San Francisco skyline. In the car, Laura told me about her call with Jane.

"I talked to Jane today about helping with the fundraiser for Ward 5 at SF General."

"Oh, I heard her mention it to Mike the other night," I replied.

"Yes, he's co-chairing the event."

"Really, I didn't know that."

"Have you been there?" I asked.

"No, have you?"

"Once," I replied.

"When?"

"When I first moved here, just before we met. My friend Ken from school had a brother who was a patient and asked if I'd visit him."

"Did he . . ."

"Yes, he died two weeks later. That's why I only saw him once."

"That must have been terrible."

"Ken was planning to come out the following month and spend his vacation time with him. Neither of them knew the end was so near."

"That's so sad. Did he come out for the funeral?"

"No, they shipped the body back to New York. I think it's great you're doing this."

"It's an important cause—you know that as much as I do."

We arrived with a bottle of wine and a bouquet of flowers for our hosts.

"I see you found the place all right. How was the drive?" Phil asked.

"Not much traffic this time of day," I replied.

"Good. Well, come in," he said.

"I'm glad we could finally get together," Carol said, greeting us warmly.

"Yes, it's delightful to see you again, Carol," Laura replied.

"It's my fault," Phil insisted.

"I believe it," Carol joked.

"No, it's probably ours. These past few months have been hectic for us," I offered.

"I can imagine, and now a wedding to plan," Carol said.

Carol and Laura toured the house, while Phil and I stood in the main room, looking out the floor-to-ceiling windows toward the city in the distance.

"Does the temperature dip in the summer when the fog comes in, like it does in the city?" I asked.

"No, that's the beauty of Marin; it stays temperate though sometimes the fog can obscure the view most of the day."

"How did you handle the parking for the party that Laura and I attended?"

"The valet company has a deal with a few of the nearby marinas. How many people are you expecting?" he asked.

"Ah, that's a Laura question—about sixty, I think. Her grandparents are hosting a pre-wedding reception at the Sheraton Palace the week before, so we can keep the number of actual wedding guests to a reasonable number."

"You just go on believing that, Will," Phil smiled, handing me a Heineken.

"Thank you," I said, taking a sip.

"So, what else is new?"

"I was offered a job at Witter."

"Congratulations."

"Thank you. It's a securities analyst position for the tech sector."

"Tech sector? That's a senior SA position."

"I know."

"And a nice comp level for a young guy like you, no doubt?"

"Yes, and I'm sure my time at the Exchange working for you went a long way in their decision."

"That's terrific. You might need a copy of the NDA you signed for me."

"Yes, well, this just became official yesterday."

"What happened yesterday?" Carol asked, when they rejoined us.

"Will's accepted a position at Dean Witter," Phil replied.

"That's marvelous, congratulations. Phil, this calls for champagne."

"Yes, good idea."

"And, Laura, tell us what's new in your life?" Phil asked.

"Well, I'm finished with classes and I start my externship tomorrow with the Department of the Interior in the Solicitor's Office."

"That sounds very impressive," Carol said.

"And then what?" Phil asked.

"The bar exam in July."

"And the wedding," Carol interjected.

"Yes, the wedding, and then we'll see. I'd like to go back to the Sierra Club if there's an opening. I interned there last summer."

"You two certainly have a lot on your plate," Phil commented.

"And the San Francisco General Dinner Gala," Carol added.

I looked at Laura.

"Will, Carol is involved in the fundraising with sponsorships," she explained.

"Really, that's great," I said.

"And I'm happy to do it. It was your cousin Michael's doing. He called me up and sold me on the real need to raise money now rather than wait for the government to wake up and increase funding."

"Good for you, Carol. We were just talking about it on the ride here. Mike can be very persuasive about things he's passionate about," I added.

"And Jane, his new girlfriend, has been a good influence on him. She's an OB/GYN doc at SF General," Laura explained.

"I hear 5B might be opening soon, solely dedicated to AIDS patients. It's such a tragic thing to think so many more may die before a cure or vaccine is found. My best friend just lost her only child," Carol said.

"I'm so sorry," Laura replied.

"Yes, my condolences, Carol."

"Thank you, both, I certainly didn't mean to make this about me. Perhaps we should take a walk outside and we'll show you how we've set up things in the past—you know tents, the bar, a place for the band."

"Yes, that would be great," Laura replied, as we stepped out into the cool January air.

Lunch followed with Laura answering a myriad of wedding-related questions for Carol. When we left, it was almost four o'clock and I could tell her head was spinning. The champagne and the wedding talk had taken a toll, so I put KSFO on the radio while she closed her eyes. Back at the apartment, Laura seemed tired but relieved.

"Do you want to go for Chinese later?" she asked.

The statement wasn't really a question—it was an interrogative, but meant she wanted Chinese.

"Sure."

"I think I'll take a nap first," she replied. "You?"

"I've got some reading for classes tomorrow, so I'd better do that."

"Okay, well, wake me in an hour if I'm still asleep."

"Okay."

We walked up to Polk Street for dim sum and tea. She wore the navy pea coat I bought her for Christmas, the matching navy beret, and a gold cashmere scarf wrapped around her neck. After dinner, we walked down to Cannery Row for baklava, where my friend Alex was helping behind the counter.

"Will, Laura, it's great to see you," she said, coming around the counter to give us each a hug. "Happy New Year!"

"Happy New Year, Alex. Any news?" I asked.

"Oh, I passed the CPA exam. I got the results just before Christmas."

"That's a wonderful Christmas gift," I said.

"Congratulations," Laura added.

"So now I will work with my brother, and my uncle, and my cousin Nikos. Do you remember him?"

"Yes, I remember Nikos," I replied. I looked at Laura. "He was a runner at the Exchange and used to show up at 6:00 a.m. directly from the dance clubs."

"But no more. He passed too, so now we are the next generation, along with my brother Pete, to carry on one of the family businesses," Alex said proudly.

"One of many," I replied.

"Yes well, my family, my parents, my aunts and uncles always believed in hard work."

"It certainly paid off. How many businesses are there?" Laura asked.

"Well, we have the accounting firm and the bakery—this you know—and then we have a travel agency, an import business, and the restaurant in Berkeley."

"What restaurant?" Laura asked.

"It's called Rojbas Grill on University Avenue."

"Oh my gosh, I practically lived there as an undergrad. The falafel is amazing."

"Thank you, Laura. I'm glad that you liked it."

"The food is fabulous," Laura replied.

"What is all this talking going on out here?" Her father Nick returned from the kitchen.

"Will, of course, I should have known. Happy New Year, my dear friend."

"Happy New Year to you. Nick, you remember Laura?"

"Of course. How could I forget such a lovely face? But she doesn't eat so much sweets as you."

"Papa," Alex chided.

"What? It is not true? You see how skinny she is?"

"Well, not really," Laura remarked.

"Come, sit down. Alexandra, you join your friends," he insisted, as we made our way to one of the eight tables.

"So, Nick, how is your wife Sophie?" I asked.

"She is well. I will say hello for you. She'll be sorry she missed you."

"Tell her Happy New Year from us."

Nick repeated Happy New Year in Greek. "Yes, I will."

Laura, Alex, and I sat and enjoyed baklava and an assortment of cookies which Nick insisted we try. After an hour, we said our goodbyes with Nick refusing to accept any money.

"It is true you tutored my Alex in statistics?" he asked, pointing his index finger at me.

I looked at Alex and then back at Nick.

"Yes, but she helped . . ."

"No, no. You helped her, yes?"

"Yes, Nick."

"Okay then," he said, putting his hand up. "I think you helped my nephew Nikos too, no?"

"A little bit."

"Say no more. When you are here, you are my guest, understood?" he said, pointing to the floor.

"Okay, Nick."

"Good, I'm glad we understand each other."

Alex caught me slipping a five-dollar bill into the tip jar on the way out. I put my finger to my lips and she smiled waving goodbye.

"I hope I can get to sleep after all that sugar," Laura said, as we entered our apartment.

In bed, I rubbed her neck and back until I heard, or thought I heard, her faint snoring.

"I'm fading, Will."

"Go to sleep," I whispered.

Despite it being her first day at Interior, and my first day of classes, Thursday was rather mundane. Laura had a meeting after work with the fundraising committee that Mike and a woman I didn't know from Crocker Bank were co-chairing. After my last class ended at 7:00 p.m., I stopped by the Tadich to wish Fred a Happy New Year.

"Hey, kid, you're a sight for sore eyes," he said, as I sat down at my usual spot at the bar.

"Happy New Year, Fred. What's wrong?"

"Don't mind me, I'm always cranky during the holidays. Yeah, Happy New Year."

"Why is that?"

"Ah, it's just the same old, same old. Whatta drinking, Will?"

"I'm fancying one of those famous Manhattans of yours," I replied.

"Manhattan, okay, you got it. How's Laura?"

"Laura's good. She started an externship today—it's like a nonpaid job for law school credit."

"Oh, that's great. She'll get some real experience, am I right?"

"Yes, exactly."

"Here you go," he said, putting the drink down. "Will you excuse me for a minute?"

"Sure, Fred."

Fred left the bar and went into the kitchen. The barback, a young guy named Stewart, was at the other end of the bar, stocking the cooler. I waved him over.

"Hey, Stewart, how's it going?"

"Pretty good, Will. How are you doing?"

"I'm good. I'm just wondering what's up with Fred? He seems a little down."

"I don't know, Will. He's kind of been like that for a couple of weeks now."

Fred returned and waited on some casually dressed tourist types before he came back over.

"Texans! They think they own the joint."

"What's wrong?" I asked.

"Nah, it's nothing. It's just I miss . . ."

"What?"

"You know, around the holidays, I just remember what it was like as a kid. I miss those days. My ma and pa have passed. We lost my brother Jimmy in Nam. It just gets me this time of year; that's all, kid."

Fred refilled a couple of lagers for two men sitting nearby and then returned to our conversation.

"Hey, Fred."

"Yes."

"I don't think I ever told you, but I lost my mom and dad and my younger brother."

"God, that's awful, Will, I'm sorry."

"I didn't tell you for sympathy. I told you because we all have our sad stories. I'm not saying we can't be sad about them—feeling sad is natural. I'm just saying that you're not alone in your sorrow."

"Thanks, Will, I appreciate that."

"I mean it, Fred. I know what I'm talking about. Don't let this haunt you."

"What are you saying?" he asked.

"You should talk this out with someone—a professional."

"Will, relax. I am talking . . . about my daughter I haven't seen in quite a while."

"Really?"

"Yes."

I decided not to pursue the inquiry and instead asked for another drink before I headed home.

"Sure, and it's on me. Happy New Year, Will, and I mean that," he said, sounding sentimental.

"Thank you," I replied, satisfied that I had made that connection with him.

I was half asleep when Laura got home.

"Did I wake you? I'm sorry," she said.

"No, I just fell asleep, it's okay. Tell me how it went."

"It was fantastic. It's so professional. The attorneys are very bright and committed and the staff is wonderful and dedicated and you're looking at me like I drank the Kool-Aid."

"Laura Elizabeth, I am not."

"Okay, my mistake. Oh, Will, it's just so great, all these incredible projects."

"In the Reagan administration?"

"I know, that's what everyone thinks. I'm not on board with everything, but they really seem to understand the issues here in California."

"And you've got the Ninth Circuit."

"Don't be cynical."

"I'm sorry. I'm happy for you, I am."

"Somehow, I don't quite believe that."

"Look at it this way, you work at Interior for six months and then, if you go back to the Sierra Club, you'll have all those insights."

"That still sounds cynical."

"Am I wrong?"

"No, not exactly, but there are some good people there."

"I don't doubt it. I'm not a Democrat or a Republican, you know that."

"Don't let my grandpa hear you say that."

Laura sat on the edge of the bed and took off her shoes.

"My feet hurt."

"Ms. McKenzie, I could give you a complimentary foot massage."

"Ah, I know that look."

"I said complimentary."

"Yes, I heard that, but what's it going to cost me?"

"Did you say hello to me?" I asked, pulling her close.

"Not sufficiently," she replied, kissing me on the lips.

We lay there, holding each other until she finally sighed, "It's begun—real life, I mean, hasn't it?"

"I'm afraid it has. It's not easy being green."

"But you're still marrying me, right?"

"Yes, I'm still marrying you."

Laura got up to change her clothes.

"Are you hungry? There's homemade vegetable soup that my female roommate made."

"Yes."

I went to the kitchen, heated a bowl, and brought it back to the bedroom.

"This chick roommate of yours makes delicious soup," she said, sitting on the bed in her sweatshirt with the bowl in her lap while I massaged her feet.

"Yeah well, you better finish it and get out of here before she gets back."

"Or what?"

"Or we'll both be in trouble," I smiled.

"Can you do that a little longer?"

"Why do you need to wear high heels?"

"Because, I'm five foot three. I need to look people in the eye—at least somewhat. It's a power thing."

"So this will be a daily struggle?"

"It's not easy being green, Will."

"I get it," I said, now moving up to lie next to her.

"Thank you."

"For the massage?"

"Yes, and for the tacit understanding."

"You're welcome."

"Now you can do me."

"Really?"

"Yes, do I need to convince you?"

"No. I didn't know a foot massage was all it took."

"No, it's not just that."

"Yeah, I'd be getting hot all day too, if I had a Ronny Reagan portrait hanging in my office."

"Stop!"

"What?" I asked, as I was putting my hand under her sweatshirt.

"No, I don't mean stop that," she laughed.

There was no more talking.

By the following week, another semester's routine set in—a cycle of hard work and fun on the weekends. For Valentine's Day, I got tickets to the ABT—Natalia Makarova was dancing *Paquita*. I had Sunil meet us at Laura's office, where we ate the sushi I brought since we didn't have much time before the performance. He drove to the Civic Center and dropped us in front of City Hall on Van Ness, where we crossed the street and walked up the steps of the Opera House. Laura loved it. Makarova was incredible even to a novice like me. Afterwards we decided to walk home, so Laura changed into the Adidas sneakers she had in her bag. Impulsively, we stopped at the piano lounge at Harris' Steakhouse for dessert. She went to the ladies' room while I ordered us wine. When she returned, Jane was with her.

"Look whom I ran into?"

"Hi, Jane, how are you?" I asked.

"Terrific. Mike and I just finished dinner."

"Perfect, would you like to join us for dessert?" Laura asked.

"Yes, let me go get him."

"No, let me go. You take my wine here and I'll go fetch the lad," I said.

"Okay," she agreed, pointing to their table before sitting down next to Laura.

I intercepted the waiter as he was about to return Mike's bill and credit card.

"Hey, let me do that. He's my best man."

The waiter looked at me oddly, so I handed him a few singles of cash. He handed over the leather folio as I walked over to the table.

"I'm sorry, sir, there appears to be a problem with this card."

"Problem," he said, looking up at me. "Will, you moonlighting?"

"I thought I had you!"

"Nah, I glanced over when you were talking to the waiter."

"I can't get anything by you," I replied. "Laura and I just stopped in for dessert—she ran into Jane in the bathroom."

"Oh, you out in the lounge?"

"Yes."

"Okay, let me just add the tip here."

He put his card back in his wallet and closed the folio, handing it to the waiter as we both walked by him.

"Here you go," Mike said.

"Thank you, sir . . . sirs."

"You're welcome," Mike said.

"You're welcome," I repeated.

"Hi, Laura," Mike said, leaning down to hug her. "Look at you, all dressed up in business clothes."

"I didn't have time to change."

"Will and Laura have just come from the American Ballet Theatre performance," Jane said.

"Yes, it was wonderful," Laura said.

"Will?" Mike asked.

"Yes?"

"What did you think of it?" he smirked.

"I thought it was remarkable, a true inspiration with a bold, new transcendent interpretation," I replied.

"You read that in the playbill!" Laura cried.

"So? They got it right."

"These two are incorrigible when they're together," Jane said.

"Hey, Will, I've been meaning to talk to you about the bachelor party."

"Now's probably not the time," I replied.

"I'm thinking Reno or Vegas," he continued.

"Mike, no Reno or Vegas."

"Really?"

"Really."

"Jeez, it's like you're married already."

"Okay, why don't we order a few things to share?" Laura suggested.

"What did you learn in school today, Michael?" I asked mockingly.

In a child's voice, he replied, "Sharing."

Laura and Jane ordered three desserts while Mike went to the men's room, and I excused myself to say hello to a broker I knew. When we returned, Laura raised her glass and said, "To love and happiness."

We all repeated the words and drank our wine.

"So, how is the new job and how are the wedding plans coming?" Jane asked.

I watched as Laura sat back in her chair, wine glass in her right hand, talking and smiling and laughing. Every once in a while, she would look at me and her smile would broaden. It was true—she loved me. We sat and drank and ate and drank until the pianist played a final song for the evening.

"Hey, do you want to walk out to the end of Aquatic Park Pier?" Mike asked.

The concrete pier extends out into the Bay at the northernmost part of Van Ness.

"Ah, I think it's kind of late," Jane replied.

"I'll go," Laura answered quickly.

"Really?" I asked.

"Sure, we haven't been out in weeks."

"Okay," I replied.

Mike got us a cab and shortly thereafter we were heading down the pier. Unlike New Year's Eve, there was a full moon. The water was calm, and the moonlight reflected on it with a radiant brilliance.

"God, I love this city, especially at night," Mike confessed.

"It's magical," Laura added.

"Look at the Transamerica Pyramid and Coit Tower, and all those buildings downtown," I said.

"Will and I come down here occasionally, but never this late at night. The water looks so deceivingly serene, yet it's treacherous. The sky is so clear, but then in summer, the fog obscures everything. It's like a metaphor for life," Laura continued.

"Hey, see now. What did I tell you? This little walk has made poets of you all," Mike said proudly.

We stood there a few minutes longer, just taking in the evening's splendor. The music from the grand pas lingered in my head, and I could tell Laura shared in the magical moment. *Little moments*, I thought. Each of these comprise our lives strung together in some oft-remembered tapestry of pleasantries. The imagery was interrupted by Mike's pragmatism.

"Let's head back to the cab before someone says they need use the bathroom."

Mike and Jane started back first.

Laura pulled me close to her and whispered, "Thank you for a wonderful evening."

"You're welcome," I replied, leaning down to kiss her.

Mike looked back and yelled, "Merritt, stop molesting my cousin."

"She may be your cousin, but she's my fiancée."

"Okay, then hurry up if you want a ride home," he commanded.

Mike and Jane dropped us at our building and we climbed the stairs to our apartment, feeling both tired and elated.

"Can you unzip me?" she asked.

"Anytime."

"Hey, Merritt, it isn't happening tonight, but I need you to hold me."

"Okay, why?"

"Because I'm cold, and you know how to warm me up."

When she got into bed, after her bathroom routine, she pressed her feet against my body.

"You are cold."

I warmed her feet with my hands and then gently kissed the back of her neck.

"I'm fading, Will," she whispered.

We fell asleep lying close together all warm and comfy and happy.

The rest of the month passed quickly. Laura was occupied with work and wedding plans, and I was busy with classes and studying for the Research Analyst exams. Occasionally, I would stop at the Witter offices now that my paperwork had cleared HR and the NASD. Two nights a week Rob came over. Laura fed him dinner, and I tutored him in math for his surveyor's exam. Uncle David got him into an apprenticeship program with the state, which was scheduled to start in April once his rehab was completed.

It was during the course of those winter months that Laura reached out to her brother. In addition to the twice weekly visits, they began to get together on the weekends—sometimes for breakfast—and other times she accompanied him to Narcotics Anonymous meetings. Somehow it all seemed to be working. Rob was turning his life around, and I was enormously happy that Laura was a part of that remarkable change. Things were hopeful. This renewed constancy of family in his life was making a profound impact on his behavior and outlook for the future.

As for Laura and me, on weekends when Stephen and Caroline were out of town, we would babysit their condo at Ocean Beach. We toyed with the idea of buying the one next door when it went on the market, but decided against it until we felt more secure in our employment situations.

Our plan to host a St. Patrick's Day party was thwarted when I was asked to attend the Spring Comdex trade show by my soon-to-be manager at Witter. With midterms over, I didn't think I could say no, so I spent four days in Atlanta. The flight home on Sunday had a stop in Dallas–Fort Worth before the leg up to San Francisco. Serendipitously, my seat mate on the first leg was a nineteen-year-old, named Michael Dell, who had just started a company called PCs Limited. We struck up a conversation when I noticed his tote bag from the trade show. For the next two hours, he bombarded me with questions about Silicon Valley companies and venture capital firms in the Bay Area. When he departed, to catch his connection to Austin, I gave him my newly minted business card and told him to keep in touch, which he assured me he would. My flight landed at SFO at four o'clock and I took a cab to the apartment, stopping at a florist first to buy flowers. When I arrived home, I knocked on the door, having forgotten my keys. Mike opened the door.

"Hey, stranger, how was Hotlanta?"

"Great, the show was great."

"Strip clubs?"

"Not a one."

"You're home," Laura said, as she came to the door.

"I am."

"I missed you."

"I missed you too."

"Oh jeez, let me get out of the way of this lovefest," Mike cried.

I hugged and kissed her and then handed her the flowers.

"Happy Birthday."

"Calla lilies, my favorite. Thank you."

"I'm sorry I couldn't get back yesterday."

"I know. It's okay. You're here now and that's all that matters."

"So, what's going on?"

"Oh, Mike invited himself and the gang over. They brought wine, pizza, and cake."

"Wow, okay, let me throw my bag in the bedroom and I'll come say hello."

"Hey, there's the traveling man," Stephen said, standing to shake my hand.

"More like Willy Loman," Mike joked.

"Michael!" Jane admonished.

"What? He knows I'm kidding."

"So, how was Geek Week?" Caroline asked.

"Geeky, but it was only half a week for me. It was good. I met Bill Gates last night."

"Really?" Laura asked.

"Who's Bill Gates?" Jane asked.

"He's the CEO of Microsoft," Mike replied.

"Yes, the investment and finance group hosted a dinner and he was the speaker. After the program, someone had a cake sent over. Everyone started singing and he came over to the Witter table to wish me Happy Birthday."

"Really?" Stephen said, in astonishment.

"Yes, someone took a photo of the two of us."

"Cool, Will. You'll have to put that picture on your desk next to the obligatory wedding photo—you know, the one to keep the babes at bay," Mike said.

"I thought you were the one who told me they liked young, married men?"

"Can we change the subject?" Laura demanded.

"Yes, and may I have a slice of pizza, and a glass of the Cab that no doubt Stephen and Caroline brought?" I asked.

"Hey, I brought the cake," Mike replied.

"We brought the cake," Jane quickly corrected.

The conversation turned to the wedding and then back to work. Stephen and Caroline would be spending most of April in China, so Laura and I had a weekend retreat again. Jane mentioned how well Rob seemed to be doing.

"Much thanks to Will," Laura said proudly.

"You too, Laura," I added.

"I think it's more than that, Will," Jane injected. "He's doing mandatory volunteer work at the hospital."

"Isn't that an oxymoron?" Mike interrupted.

Jane ignored him and continued, "Whenever I see him, it's 'Will did this for me' or 'Will said this' or 'Will took me here or there'—you should be proud," she said.

"You've done well, Will," Caroline added.

"Well, coming from the only other Easterner here, I appreciate that."

"So, how is the fundraiser coming?" I asked.

"Saturday, April 28. We finally got confirmation from Tony Bennett," Mike announced. "And Witter's buying four tables—that's forty grand."

"Bechtel's in for three," Caroline said.

"Will, you should see Laura work the phones—she's amazing," Mike said.

"I have no doubt," I replied.

"How many tables have you booked so far?" Mike asked.

"Eighteen," Laura confessed.

"That's amazing," Jane commented.

"Guess I need to rent a tux. Where will I be sitting?" I asked.

"Gramps bought a family table, so you and I will be sitting with them and my mom and Rob and Jane," Laura replied.

"And we'll be back in time for the event, so we'll be there too at one of the Bechtel tables," Caroline explained.

"I invited the executive director of the Sierra Club and his wife and daughter to round out our table," Laura added.

"It sounds like things are in good shape. Mike, I assume you'll be on the dais? Let me know if you need any help with your remarks," I said, expecting him to make a joke.

"Thanks, Will," was his reply.

"Will, can you take Rob for his tux?" Laura asked.

"Sure. Can I get another glass of wine? I've been drinking club soda for the last four days."

The sun was setting over the Golden Gate Bridge as Stephen, Mike, and I shared a cigar on the outdoor patio. Afterwards, everyone sang "Happy Birthday" and Laura and I blew out the candles together. Laura made tea for herself and Caroline, while Jane and the rest of us opted for brandy. After everyone left, Laura cleaned up while I took a shower and unpacked. She joined me in the bedroom afterwards.

"I'm . . ."

"I know—I saw the bathroom basket."

"But I want you to hold me," she replied, as she changed into her Berkeley sweatshirt and slipped into bed.

"I missed you. I haven't slept alone since Labor Day weekend up at the cottage," I said.

"You're right. But you had Sergeant," she joked.

I told her more about the trade show until I could see she was about to drift off. I kissed her forehead and lay there watching her sleep.

Rob finished his program at the end of March and moved back home with Ellen. Stephen gave him his old Saab, so he could get around. As for me, Witter was giving me more 10Ks and 10Qs to read, having passed the securities analyst exams. All that was left for school were final exams. Laura's path was more challenging, but after three interviews, she was offered a full-time legal position at the Sierra Club the day before the San Francisco General Hospital Gala.

The dinner was a huge success with over twelve hundred people attending. The affair raised just over $2.1 million. Laura and I spent much of the evening circulating among the tables, as she introduced me to everyone she knew or had recently met: lawyers, government officials, politicians, health-care executives, socialites, members of the media, and, of course, prominent gay community activists and advocates. I introduced her to people in investment banking, finance, the brokerage business, and even a few sports figures I had managed to meet through business connections. After dinner, several of Jane's colleagues were recognized. Later, they congregated around a couple of tables and Jane introduced us to them. One particularly loquacious fellow, a Dr. Philips, was in the middle of a discussion when we approached him.

"Because the AIDS agent is a retrovirus, it needs to perform an extra step before reproducing in a cell—copying its RNA into DNA."

"With its reverse transcriptase?" Laura asked.

"Yes, exactly. Are you a physician?" he asked.

"No, a law student," she replied modestly.

I was impressed that she knew so much about cell biology, but then, she was constantly impressing me with her knowledge and kindness and compassion. After talking with the doctors, we returned to our table for dessert. Tony Bennett took the stage and sang four songs, beginning with "I Left My Heart in San Francisco" and then two more songs before he went into a moving diatribe about AIDS and how important it was to support causes working to fight this dreadful curse. He was gracious and wonderful, then I saw Mike on the dais, making a pointing gesture toward Tony.

"I'd like to finish the evening with a wonderful song by Johnny Mercer and David Raksin, and I'd like to dedicate it to all those out there who worked tirelessly to make this evening such a success."

And then he sang "Laura."

CHAPTER 7

THINGS WERE HEATING up in Silicon Valley. In late April, I got a message from my manager, Tim Williams. When I phoned him back, he was in a meeting, but took my call anyway.

"Will, sorry for such short notice, but we need you to start May 1."

"Okay, Tim, I'll make that work," I replied.

"Good, glad to hear it. I can't talk right now, but I'll see you then," he said briskly, as he hung up the phone.

I approached all three of my professors and asked if I could take their finals, explaining the situation. Surprisingly, they agreed and I sat for the exams on Monday, April 30, and started at Dean Witter the next morning.

Sunday, May 13 of 1984, was not only Mother's Day, but Laura's law school graduation. Graduating summa, she had a role in the ceremony. While there were no speeches from the graduates, she played a prominent part in welcoming guests and introducing faculty. Besides *Law Review*, she was recognized as the Editor-in-Chief of the *Environmental Law Review* and for the highest grade point average in the Environmental Law track. She also received some cash awards from BNA Publishers, Prentiss-Hall, and Commerce Clearing House. The ceremony ended in traditional Capshaw–McKenzie fashion by celebrating at the Sheraton Palace.

"I was so nervous up there," she confessed.

"Oh my, that's not like you, Laura," her mother remarked.

"Laura, I thought you were great," Rob said.

"Thank you, Rob."

Andrew raised his glass with a slight wavering feebleness, "Laura, your grandmother and I are so proud of you today, for everything you set out to do, for everything you've achieved, and for everything you will accomplish in your life."

The lunch continued with toast after toast for both her and the mothers. At one point, Ellen whispered a consoling thought, knowing I was likely thinking of my own mother. I sensed some added joy now that I had a professional position and Laura would also be employed post bar exam.

After lunch, I suggested we stop at the Tadich, which was normally closed on Sundays. Fred was picking up an extra shift to help his daughter through college—a daughter he never mentioned until recently. Laura and I, along with Mike and Jane, made our way over.

"To what do I owe the pleasure?" Fred asked, when the four of us approached the bar.

"Laura just graduated," I said.

"Hey, Laura, congratulations, honey. I wish you all the best," he replied.

"Thanks, Fred. I'm not sure you've met Jane Nolan, Mike's girlfriend."

"Jane, it's very nice to meet you. Fred Connors."

"Nice to meet you too, Fred," Jane replied.

"Hey, Mike, good to see you again."

"And, Will," he said, extending his hand across the bar, "glad to see you."

"You too, Fred. I know it's been a while, that's why I suggested we stop by and see how you're doing."

"Doing fine, kid. Hey, let me see if I can't get you a bottle of Dom on the house."

"Fred, that's nice, but I don't want you to get into any trouble."

"No, it's okay, I owe you for your kindness and concern," he replied.

"I appreciate the offer, but get us a bottle and let me pay for it," I said.

He nodded his head to the side and walked down the bar as I followed him.

"Are things better?" I asked.

"Yes. I talked to my daughter and she wants me to be a part of her life," he said, with some emotion.

"That's good news."

"Yes, it is."

"That's what matters, Fred, family."

"You're right, kid. When you're right, you're right."

"Okay, get that bottle of Dom and I'll get Mike to pay for it—that way we both win."

"You got it."

I returned to the others. Fred brought the bottle of champagne and poured four glasses.

"Pour yourself a glass," Mike insisted.

"Okay, for Laura, I will."

"When's the bar exam?" Jane asked.

"July 18 and 19. I start review classes on Tuesday."

"Ouch, the day after tomorrow. Best of luck."

"Thanks, Jane."

"And when do you start your new job?"

"Not until after our honeymoon," Laura smiled.

We lingered that Sunday afternoon because we knew reality was closing in. Laura had the bar to sit for, and I was being asked to analyze all kinds of tech companies springing up in Silicon Valley. Witter was expecting a lot—trying to forecast the future, but our tasks didn't seem daunting. The excitement of taking on responsibility was a welcome challenge. Yet, I couldn't help thinking our time together was about to be encroached upon. We were entering a new chapter of our lives. I was happy for Laura, I truly was. I saw the amount of work and determination it took to graduate summa from law school. But now, I guess I felt I was about to lose the exclusivity I had with her—I would have to share her from now on. It was selfish, I thought, sitting there at the bar, vaguely listening to the conversation. She will still be the most important person in my life, I reminded myself. I couldn't put my finger on it, I couldn't figure out why I was so reticent about the future, our future. After all, we had set a wedding date, which is what I wanted more than anything. I recalled the cab ride home after the reception she organized before Christmas and how she wanted it to last a little longer—maybe this was my turn to ask the same. I had been deep in thought until I heard her say my name.

"Will has been incredibly supportive."

"You deserve all the credit. You worked very hard to achieve this," I said.

I was feeling sad inside in this most happy of times. I couldn't explain it. I felt like I had lost something—some unique relationship that I would never get back. The irony was clear to me—after all, I was the one after the holiday party telling her she would go on to do great things.

"You are the most amazing woman I've ever met, and I am the luckiest man in the world."

The words came out in an emotional outpouring. In that moment, I just needed to say them. I wanted to explain, but after a prolonged silence, I no longer felt the need. It would be okay, I thought, it would be okay and wonderful with Laura in my life even if I had to share her with the rest of the world.

PART TWO

"MISERY"

JULY 1984–MAY 1986

CHAPTER 8

LAURA ALTERED HER routine for the ten weeks between graduation and the bar exam with constant studying. I took over all the household chores: laundry, grocery shopping, cooking, cleaning, running errands. By the Fourth of July, she was feeling confident, having done well on the practice exams, and took the day off. We spent the afternoon at Golden Gate Park, strolling around the gardens and groves of trees, feeding the geese and blue herons at Stow Lake. It was like old times, recalling our first date there. She reminded me of her comment about my "soulful eyes and reserved sense of kindness."

"Well, all I can say is, you're an excellent judge of character," I smirked.

"Yes, I am," she smiled, taking my hand.

"I love you."

"I know you do. Hey, I never made you hug a tree, did I?"

"I don't believe you did. You were too distracted by my charming personality."

"Okay, Merritt, go hug that one," she said, pointing to a huge Monterey Cypress.

"Yes, my lady."

She walked toward me, putting her arms around my neck.

"I love you too, Will."

By late afternoon, Laura was feeling tired, so when we returned home, she took a nap. That evening, we sat on the roof and watched the fireworks display at Aquatic Park.

The next day brought a return to her studies with the bar exam two weeks away. I was busy too, sitting in on earnings calls and dissecting second quarter P&Ls. The day before part one of the exam, on Tuesday, July 17, I took the afternoon off and we drove to Stinson Beach in Marin. I knew she needed to get her mind off the exam, and a few hours at the beach seemed like the perfect indulgence. That evening, Laura fell asleep earlier than usual, which I interpreted as a good sign. I made sure I was up early the next morning, so she had plenty of time to get ready before driving downtown. I drove her because I was headed to appointments in Silicon Valley. I reassured her as best I could that the outcome would be positive, knowing how hard she had studied and how well she had done the past three years. Still, there was an air of nervousness as we said goodbye. My day went well, with onsite meetings and then lunch at the Witter office in Palo Alto. Just past 4:00 p.m., I got a page from my office. When I called in, the receptionist told me I had received an urgent call from Ellen McKenzie asking that I call as soon as possible.

"Ellen, I got your message, what is it?"

"Will, I can't reach Laura. Rob's been shot."

"What? How?"

"I don't know. I got a call from the Highway Patrol. He's at Stanford Hospital—that's all I know."

"Ellen, listen, I'm in Sunnyvale. I'm twenty minutes away. I'll go there and call you back as soon as I know anything, okay?"

"Yes, okay. I'll stay by the phone until I hear from you."

I arrived to learn he was in surgery from a gunshot wound to the thigh, which had damaged his femoral artery, and called Ellen to tell her. By six o'clock, Rob was out of surgery with the doctor telling me he was in stable condition. I called Ellen back to give her the news.

"I think it might be best not to tell Laura until tomorrow afternoon when she's finished with her exam."

"Whatever you think, Will, I trust you know best."

"I'll stay with Rob all night—if anything changes, I'll call you."

"All right, but please call me in the morning. I should be there no later than noon."

"Of course," I said.

Then I dialed the apartment. Laura answered and the tone of her voice sounded reassuring when I asked how the first day went.

"It went well. I'm feeling really good about my answers and had enough time to review them all."

"Two of my appointments got rescheduled for tomorrow, plus I've got a dinner meeting I can't get out of. I'm going to stay down here tonight and head to my meetings in the morning."

It was the first and only time I ever lied to her, except for that fib about not being out of breath when she called to invite me to join her family over Labor Day weekend.

"Well, okay. I'm pretty beat. I think I'm just going to take a warm bath and then try to get some sleep," she replied.

We talked a few more minutes before hanging up. Rob was in recovery for several hours after surgery and then, before the midnight shift change, was transferred to the ICU. They wouldn't allow me to see him until ten o'clock the next morning.

I had checked in with Ellen, but had no real news. Rob was awake when I entered his room.

"Will, I didn't expect you'd be here."

"What do you mean—of course, I'm going to be here. How are you feeling?"

"I'm not sure. I feel dizzy, like they gave me something."

"Rob, do you know what happened to you?"

"I was shot."

"You're okay. The surgery went well. You're going to be all right. Do you understand?"

I think I was feeling more upset at that point than he was.

"Yes, the doctor was in a little while ago and said the same thing."

"How did it happen? Do you remember?"

"I was down here for a surveying assignment. I stopped at the Burger King in Menlo Park and ran into someone I used to know. He asked for a ride to his cousin's in East Palo Alto and when we got there, the next thing I knew—pop, pop, pop—they were shooting at us."

I sat with him for a few minutes and then called Ellen again. She told me she was about to leave with Anne and David. I returned to the ICU and sat with Rob, who dozed off and on until Ellen arrived with her sister and brother-in-law. I drove back home to pick up Laura after her exam and was able to get home in time to shower and change before I drove to pick her up. When Laura and I arrived at the hospital, Rob had spiked a fever and the doctor ordered an increase in antibiotic medication. A few hours later, an EKG revealed an irregular heartbeat. Another test determined internal bleeding. The doctors suspected a suture wasn't holding and he would need a second surgery. Finally, at eight o'clock, they decided the surgery couldn't wait when his blood pressure dropped. We all sat in the waiting room until the surgeon returned two-and-a-half hours later to say the vessel had been repaired. There was still a risk of infection, especially because Rob had undergone invasive surgery twice, but he was stable and resting in recovery, where they expected he would stay the night. In the morning, he was transferred back to the Intensive Care Unit.

Three days later, Jane pulled some strings and got Rob transferred to San Francisco General. David arranged for an ambulance with a private company. Everything seemed fine for the first few hours. The fever was down as was the swelling. Then suddenly, he went into cardiac arrest; a blood clot had traveled to his heart. He needed an emergency thrombectomy because the drug protocol they administered wasn't working. The condition was life-threatening. I called Mike and Stephen, and by the time Rob was wheeled into surgery, the entire family, including Andrew and Betsy, were there. David, Stephen, Caroline, Mike, Laura, and I gave blood while Anne and Ellen sat in the chapel with their parents. Jane joined us after her shift and tried to keep us informed as best she could.

Tuesday morning, four days before our wedding, with Rob still in critical condition, we decided to postpone. We enlisted friends and family to make calls to the caterer, florist, a variety of others, and, of course, the invited guests. By Thursday, everyone had been contacted and Rob was upgraded to serious condition, though now he was fighting a blood infection. The sepsis was concerning—no doubt his past drug abuse had contributed to a compromised immune system.

Everyone was exhausted from lack of sleep. Laura seemed particularly worn out. We drove home, so she could rest, but that was short-lived when we listened to a message on the answering machine. It was the hospital blood bank asking her to return the call as soon as possible. When she did, the doctor who had called was unavailable. He called back an hour later, informing her there were cell abnormalities in the blood she donated and advised her to contact her primary care physician. He was unable to give her any further information, indicating that additional testing would be necessary to rule out certain things and make a proper diagnosis. Laura hung up and dialed Jane's pager. When Jane called, she basically told her the same thing, but offered to set up an appointment at the OB/GYN clinic at SF General for the next morning and do the CBC herself. Laura agreed and then tried to rest.

The complete blood count was indeed abnormal. Her red cell count was low and her white count high. Jane called a friend at UCSF Medical Center and got her an appointment with the associate chief of hematology for the following Monday, July 30, for tests and a bone marrow biopsy. We scheduled a follow-up appointment for August 2. The biopsy confirmed the presence of immature myeloid cells, called blasts, at a level of 30%. A number greater than 20% was a positive diagnosis for leukemia, specifically acute myeloid leukemia, or AML. A cytogenetics test also showed an adverse chromosomal change—a t(8;21) translocation—which meant part of chromosome 8 was located on chromosome 21 and vice versa. Genetic abnormalities, we learned, were a complicating factor in a prognosis. On August 6, Laura was admitted for remission induction therapy—a seven-day regimen of chemotherapy. Two weeks later, a second bone marrow biopsy was performed. The decrease in the level of leukemic cells was not as significant as they had hoped with the doctor characterizing it as a partial remission. A second round of induction took place followed by a third biopsy and, by the end of September, complete remission was achieved. I moved Laura to her mother's home, where Rob was now also recovering, so she could care for her. She was still weak and tired, but glad to be out of the hospital. Post-remission therapy began almost immediately—these were less intensive doses of drugs which didn't require overnight hospital stays.

The week before Christmas, we got two pieces of good news. After three months of post-remission therapy, her hematologist reconfirmed the AML remained in complete remission. The next day, we learned she passed the California bar exam. On Friday of that week, I moved into her mother's house for the holidays, having taken the last week of the year off from work. I asked Ellen to invite her parents for dinner and brought Greek takeout from the Rojbas Grill in Berkeley. Laura had a surprisingly good appetite and was happy we'd be spending the next week under the same roof together. On Christmas Eve, she wasn't up to Midnight Mass, so we watched *Miracle on 34th Street* with Rob. She had delegated her Christmas shopping to her mother and Caroline, but pitched in with the baking. Christmas morning, Rob and I finished decorating the house while Ellen was in the kitchen cooking with Laura supervising everyone. That day was filled with happiness and laughter as the entire family celebrated together. I bought Laura a pair of bedroom slippers to wear around the house for which she feigned thankfulness. After dinner, I handed her another, much smaller box.

"This is from Santa," I said.

She opened it to find a diamond-and-aquamarine tennis bracelet.

"Oh, Will, this is beautiful—aquamarine, my birthstone," she smiled, coming over to sit on my lap and kiss me.

"It's my birthstone too, so maybe I'll borrow it when I have an important meeting where I need to impress someone." The joke was lame, but at least we were laughing again after so many months without any laughter.

That night, we made love for the first time since her diagnosis in August. Laura was timid, and somewhat self-conscious, because her gums were still bleeding a bit, but we slowly reconnected, rediscovering that familiarity only lovers know. It was sweet and passionate, and I told her I loved her more than ever, because it was true.

"Do you think our lives will ever be normal again?"

It was an odd question given the context in which it was asked.

"Well, this is a start," I said, holding her close to me.

"Yes, this is nice. I just want to know it will be the way it was . . . before. I need that certainty in my life."

"Nothing in life is certain, except my love for you."

"I guess I'd rather have that, than knowing for sure if I'm going to be okay."

"Oh, Laura, you can't obsess about the illness. You were sick, and now you're better. God wouldn't punish you twice."

"You don't believe in God."

"No, but I believe in some transcendental justice."

"Like karma?"

"Yes, and you certainly deserve it."

"Did I tell you I love you?" she asked.

"It never gets old."

"I love you, Will."

"And I love you too," I repeated.

"I know you do, and it makes me very happy."

On New Year's Eve, I brought up the subject of a wedding date. She was adamant in her unwillingness to consider it until the doctors were "totally convinced" in her words that she was cured. I didn't want to spoil the evening, so I let it go. Her appointments in January were all positive. I got Rob to work on her. Every day he asked her, he argued with her, he pleaded with her. Every night after work, I took the train over to spend time with her. My days were long by the time I got back to the apartment in the city. Work was a helpful distraction and I was upbeat about the remission. Mike, Stephen, and I lunched a few times since Stephen was home for a while. Things were okay. They could be worse, I kept telling myself. Weeks passed, and Rob kept me informed of his progress—both his physical recovery and his raison d'etre—getting Laura to agree to a date. I called him Cyrano.

The Saturday before Valentine's Day, I took Laura to a spa for a massage and then to lunch at Chez Panisse.

"Did you enjoy the massage?"

"Yes, it was wonderful. Thank you again."

"We made love for the first time after we had dinner here, do you remember?" I asked, trying to soften the mood.

"Of course, I remember. How could you think I forgot that?" she replied, looking a little fatigued.

The conversation seemed strained. I assumed she was tired from her medication when she ate so little. I was getting exasperated and blurted out, "McKenzie, if you love me, you'll marry me."

Surprisingly, it broke the ice and she laughed out loud. I hadn't heard her laugh like that in a long time, and sensed she finally realized this was paramount to everything else.

"Yes! Between you, and Rob, and Caroline, and Jane—yes, I will marry you!"

On Valentine's Day, I had a late-afternoon meeting in Oakland and afterwards stopped by Ellen's with two dozen red roses for Laura. We spent the evening sitting on the living room sofa, kissing like we were teenagers. Ellen was out at church for the evening and I pressed her on a date for the wedding.

"You sure are pushy," Laura mused.

"I am," I agreed.

"All right then, March 17, on our birthdays."

The next day, I called Mike, Stephen, and Caroline and invited them to lunch at the Tadich Grill—now that I could afford to eat there on a regular basis. They were all available on such short notice—or more likely made themselves available, sensing I had news. Fred was off, so I sat at a table. Stephen and Caroline arrived first and Mike a few minutes later. Having been completely focused on Laura's health, I hadn't considered the mental toll it took on me. The three of them listened to my relief after so many months of anguish, which I had kept to myself. It was a cathartic recognition, which I didn't realize I needed to express until that moment. Then I shared the news that Laura had agreed to a date, and they congratulated me. Mike, sensing my emotional state, ordered us each a Martini. It was my first alcoholic drink since her diagnosis, and sitting there with those three wonderful friends, I realized how fortunate I was. Still, I worried how a relapse might affect Laura. I knew she worried about that possibility—it was the only reason she had been so hesitant to set a date. Stephen and Caroline headed back to work, but Mike, aware of my anxiety, ordered us espressos. I shared my thoughts and he confided that Jane was concerned too. Apparently, Laura called her about a recent blood test that was inconclusive. Jane relayed to him that such results, so soon after complete remission, could be a potential sign of reversion.

"I'm going to make her my wife, and we are going to live a long and happy life together. Maybe that's wishful thinking, but I need to hold on to that hope."

Mike looked down at the table, and then back up at me, and in a cheerful and sincere voice responded, "Yes, I know you will."

At that moment, we both needed to believe in that wish. We parted, hesitating outside the restaurant, neither of us sure if we had finished our conversation probably because there was no suitable resolution. It's not that we tiptoed around the subject, but without specific information, we were only left with uncertainty. I tried to focus on the wedding, knowing that event would be a wonderful celebration of our love and devotion.

March 17, 1985, our wedding day, was a Sunday. It was a clear sunny day with an azure blue sky overhead. I was twenty-nine—my twenties almost behind me. That realization didn't concern me because a new life with Laura was beginning. We were married at the Claremont Club in the Berkeley Hills, overlooking lush green gardens with palm and eucalyptus trees. The San Francisco skyline glimmered in the distance, and the air had a spring-like dewy freshness to it. I arranged for twenty-five vases each with a single calla lily representing one year of Laura's life. Other than a handful of friends, it was an intimate family affair. A solo cellist played during the ceremony, and Rob walked his sister down the aisle. She looked radiant, though noticeably thin; makeup hid her pale complexion but her loving smile lit up the room. When it was my turn to repeat the words "Till death do us part," my voice cracked conspicuously. Laura took my hand and squeezed it reassuringly. We spent three nights in the honeymoon suite. I arranged massage and beauty treatments at the spa, and in the afternoons, we enjoyed sitting on the large outdoor veranda, soaking in the warmth of the sun. Color was returning to her face and she seemed reinvigorated and happy.

We moved back to the apartment—together for the first time since September. The next month was idyllic, "wedded bliss," Laura called it. Her strength was returning with each passing day. Evenings we would drive to the Marina Green, where she would sit on a bench with a book while I ran on the track. She made dinner every night and we would sit together and talk for hours.

Then in late April, the fatigue returned—along with nausea and vomiting. She was hospitalized for dehydration. Tests revealed an infection in her blood and febrile neutropenia—a fever due to an abnormally low number of neutrophil granulocytes, a type of white blood cell. The leukemia had relapsed aggressively. Days went by, and another round of chemo was considered, but the doctors concluded she was too weak for the drug cocktail that would be necessary.

I took her to her mother's on the first of May and spent the next twelve days at her bedside.

"Will, I need you to promise me something."

"Anything."

"After I'm gone . . ."

"No," I objected, putting my hand up, signaling for her to stop.

"You have to get up every day and do the things that are important to you. Can you do that for me?"

"I can't think about it."

"I need you to promise me."

"I don't want to think about . . . I mean—no."

"Will, I'm going to die, and you are going to go on living. I need to know you'll be okay—I'm your wife after all."

"Yes, and you always will be."

"No, that's my point. You have to go on living and following your dreams, your passions, and succeed in what you've worked so hard to achieve."

"None of it matters, if I don't have you to share it with."

"Listen to me, my time is near, and I love you so much— please keep our memory alive by continuing what you're destined to do."

Laura's concern was selfless—it was her nature ever since she was a child. I couldn't continue to protest her wishes.

"Okay," I replied, in a resigned voice.

"Good. And after a while, you'll find someone you care about—someone who understands you, makes you laugh, makes you feel good inside, someone you look forward to seeing. I don't want you to go on mourning me. You need to allow yourself to be open to finding that someone who will love you as I have—you deserve that, Will. I know you will always love me, I have no doubt, but I also know you have a boundless capacity to love, and to go on living without it would be such a waste, such a loss. You need love in your life because without it, you will become bitter and lonely, and I can't bear the thought my death was responsible for that."

She paused for a moment to catch her breath and then continued.

"I need you to promise me you'll open your heart to that person when you find her."

"I don't think that could ever happen," I said, wanting the conversation to end.

"Promise me," she pleaded, with what little strength she could muster.

"Laura, you're asking me to . . ."

"You want to make me happy, don't you?" she implored, with a sense of determination.

"I do," I uttered, barely loud enough for her to hear just to stop the torture of her words. They were the exact same words I had spoken on that clear, sunny day in March.

On the evening of May 11, at Jane's insistence, we summoned the family and kept an all-night vigil. At first light, Laura opened her eyes. Ellen was awake, sitting at the foot of the bed.

"Happy Mother's Day, Momma," she said.

"Thank you, dear. How do you feel?" she asked, with a mother's hopefulness.

Laura hesitated, and then announced in a serene, telling voice, "I think it's time, Momma."

Rob and I rose from our chairs and went to her bedside. Ellen went downstairs and, two at a time, sent the family up to her room. David and Anne, then Mike and Jane, Stephen and Caroline, and Andrew and Betsy. When they had seen Laura, Ellen came back to the room and stood in the doorway. I joined her, so Rob could talk with his sister alone. He leaned down, squeezed her hand, and kissed her cheek. Ellen walked over and hugged him tightly. I could see a slight smile form on Laura's face—things had come full circle. Before he started to cry, Rob left the room to join the others downstairs. Ellen sat down in the chair beside the bed and took Laura's hand. I went to the other side and stood, taking her hand in mine. She put her finger over my wedding band and whispered, "Companion of my heart," referring to the inscription she had engraved on the inside of the ring.

"Forever," I replied, fighting the tears streaming down my face.

"Will?"

"Yes."

"I love you. I'm fading, I can't . . . I'm fading, Will," she murmured, as she closed her eyes.

I leaned down and buried my face into the blanket, sobbing.

I have little recollection of how long I cried before I stood when Jane came into the room with her stethoscope. I walked over to Ellen and embraced her. Jane checked for a pulse, then listened for a heartbeat.

She turned to us and said, "I'm so sorry. I'm so terribly sorry."

Jane hugged us both and left the room with Ellen. I leaned down and kissed Laura's cheek.

"I'll love you forever, Laura. I'll love you forever."

We held her funeral at Ellen's church—St. Ambrose on Gilman Street in Berkeley. Mike read what I had written—a montage of stories about how Laura and I met, our first kiss, spending time at the summer cottage, quiet dinners, our evening walks, and the long hours we spent together in the library, doing what we dreamed would lead to a successful and wonderful life together. He did an admirable job and threw in a couple of ad-libs, which received a few smiles in an otherwise tearful eulogy.

Rob read a portion of a Wordsworth poem that Laura loved:

> Though nothing can bring back the hour
> Of splendor in the grass, of glory in the flower;
> We will grieve not, rather find
> Strength in what remains behind;
> In the primal sympathy
> Which having been must ever be;
> In the soothing thoughts that spring
> Out of human suffering;
> In the faith that looks through death,
> In years that bring the philosophic mind.

After a short service at the crematorium, there was a reception at Ellen's for family and friends, which included high school, college, and law school classmates and professors, people from the Sierra Club, Bechtel, Witter, the PSE, and many older friends of Andrew and Betsy.

The following afternoon, David arranged a charter from the St. Francis Yacht Club. There were nine of us, as Andrew and Betsy chose not to go. We traveled out under the Golden Gate

Bridge and then for some reason south. From a distance, we could make out Stephen and Caroline's condominium. Before I scattered Laura's ashes, I recited the Yeats poem *When You Are Old*. I don't recall much about the trip back, nor the ride to Stephen and Caroline's. My mind was in a daze. I remember drinking a cup of black coffee and wondering why it tasted strange, not realizing at that moment I usually drank mine with milk. At some point, I went for a walk.

"Where's Will?" Caroline asked.

Mike, staring out the window, answered, "He's standing out there on the beach."

"Shouldn't someone go see if he's okay?" she asked.

"But he's not okay," he replied, in a somber voice.

"I'll go," Caroline said.

"No, let me," Jane insisted.

"Hey," Jane said, as she approached me.

"Is everyone worried I might wade into the Pacific?"

"Is that what you're contemplating?"

"If I thought it would help Ellen and Rob and everyone else, I would, but I know it wouldn't. It would only end my pain."

"Will, there's nothing I can say, or anyone can say, to ease the heartache you're going through. But you need to understand there are people who love and care about you."

I looked at her plaintively.

"Love is most nearly itself when here and now cease to matter."

"Who wrote that?"

"T.S. Eliot," I replied, in an inconsolable voice.

"Should I go back? Do you want to be alone?" she asked.

"I am alone. I'm all alone."

I started to cry, quietly but then louder and louder until it was uncontrollable sobbing. Jane hugged me, and I put my head on her shoulder. She patted my back and kept repeating, "It's okay, let it out, it's okay, Will, let it all out."

We stood there embracing tightly until I finally stopped crying.

"Do you want to go back now?" she asked.

"No, but yes," I said.

Before we entered the condo, I thanked her.

"Anytime," she replied consolingly.

She had seen enough people in grief to know it's best not to say too much. She placed her hand on my cheek. I grasped it and kissed her palm.

"I know everyone is hurting. I'm sorry I can't be a comfort to them, Jane. I hurt too much."

"They know you love them—that's all that matters."

"I'd crawl to the ends of the earth to have her back . . . even for a day, even for a moment, so I could tell her again how much I love her."

Jane was crying now.

"Laura loved you too, Will, and she would hate to see you like this."

"What am I supposed to do, Jane? The love of my life, the person who brought true happiness is gone."

"I know, and I'm so very, very sorry."

"I know you are. Thank you for not telling me everything will be all right because it won't. It will never be that way again."

I took my remaining two weeks of vacation before I returned to Witter. For the next six months, I threw myself into work—getting to the office an hour before everyone else, skipping lunch, and then running almost every night. I lost almost twenty pounds, and my suits looked baggy on me. My face was gaunt. I stayed in touch with Rob and Ellen and couldn't avoid seeing Mike at least once a week in the office. Remarkably, my sector and company analyses improved to where I was getting calls from our New York office. I made a trip there in the fall and met several of the firm's senior leadership. On the flight back, it crossed my mind to request a transfer, but realistically it made little sense, since most of the tech companies were in California. I guess it was more a desire to do something else somewhere else, I realized.

Despite continuous invites, I never set foot in the HC that year, and I could have counted on one hand the number of times I stopped to see Fred, where I'd sip half a glass of soda water. Mostly I walked alone at night around our old haunts—Fisherman's Wharf and Aquatic Park pier, the Marina Green—sometimes as far as Crissy Field. Once, when I was feeling really down, I stopped into the Buena Vista on Hyde. I sat there at the end of the bar, watching happy tourists drink Irish coffee because someone had claimed it was invented there. It made no sense to me—people patronizing an establishment because of coffee and Irish whiskey.

The apartment became my sanctuary. Laura's Berkeley sweatshirt was neatly folded on the pillow next to mine, and all her things were as she left them. I would walk through the rooms picking up a book, a note, sometimes a scarf or sweater and hold it to my nose, hoping for a scent of her. And, when I could detect a faint familiarity, I would melt into tears and set the item back down where I found it. This went on for months until Rob convinced me it might be best if those constant reminders were removed. We argued about it on the phone the night before Thanksgiving after I told him I would not be joining the family for dinner.

"Will, don't you see the cruel irony here? For years, it was me who stayed away, too afraid to face my fears."

"What's your point?" I yelled back at him over the phone.

"Will, we all care about you, your welfare."

"I can't do it, Rob. It hurts too much to be around the people who are a reminder of her."

"Will, I owe you my life, so I'm not about to question your decision."

"Please give everyone my best, Rob," I said, before I hung up the phone.

December was a fog. I slept just to pass the time, trying to escape the reality of the holiday season. Finally, somehow, I woke up and realized I couldn't continue. I needed a change. I needed to make some changes. It's what I had promised Laura.

CHAPTER 9

I RESOLVED TO spend Christmas Eve boxing up Laura's belongings. Her books and clothes and jewelry fit in the trunk and back seat of my car. The visual image of their compactness wounded me like a knife through my heart. Except for the private, cherished memories, these physical belongings, these tangible items, were all that was left of her. At that moment, I promised myself I would find a way to create a true legacy of this wonderful human being whom I missed terribly. More immediately, I felt obligated to return these possessions to Ellen, and decided to do it on the day I thought I'd be most miserable; I figured doing this chore couldn't possibly depress me anymore. I was wrong. By six o'clock, I was on the Oakland Bay Bridge before I realized I had forgotten to call to tell her I was coming. When I arrived, the lights were on and her parents' car was in the driveway. I made my way up the red brick steps, remembering the first time when Laura answered the door in her special occasion lilac dress. I fought off the memory as Ellen greeted me.

"Will, what a nice surprise!"

"Ellen, I'm so sorry. I got halfway here and realized I forgot to call first."

"You're always welcome, you know that."

"Thank you. Are your parents here?"

"Yes, come in, they'll be so glad to see you."

I entered the living room, which was adorned with Christmas ornaments and a white pine tree. It didn't seem overly decorated as in past years and I wondered if it was intentional or just my imagination. Betsy and Andrew greeted me warmly, and after a few minutes, I felt the need to explain my visit.

"Ellen, my lease is up in a few months and I'm not sure I'm going to stay—you know, after Laura moved in, it was our place and now, I don't know, I'm feeling . . ."

"I understand, Will," she interjected, trying to spare me from having to continue.

"The thing is, I brought Laura's belongings—her books and clothes and things."

"You brought them here?"

"Yes, I have them in my car. I thought you might want to go through them and decide what to do."

"Well, that was thoughtful of you, Will. Rob should be home any minute and can help carry them in."

"I hope this won't make you feel worse than you must already feel on Christmas? Maybe it was a mistake for me to do this during the holidays?"

"Will, stop—it's okay. We all miss her. This will give me something to do. Are you sure you don't want any of it?"

"I kept a few books and some cards and photographs, mostly from summers at the cottage and . . ."

Ellen looked at me consolingly.

"Her wedding ring."

"Yes, you should keep that; after all, it was your mother's."

"I'm sorry to have barged in, thinking only of myself."

"Nonsense," Andrew said.

"Don't be silly, Will, we understand completely," Betsy added.

"And we hope to see you tomorrow when the whole family is over," Ellen said.

"I'm sorry, I'm afraid I won't be able—I'm flying to Japan in the morning on business. Nobody in the office wanted to leave during the holidays, so I offered."

"We'll miss you," Andrew said.

"I'll miss you too. I'll miss all of you."

We heard Rob coming in through the kitchen door with bags of groceries.

"Is that Rob?"

"It sure sounds like it," Ellen replied.

"I'm going to say hello, if you don't mind?"

"No, go ahead."

"Hey, Rob," I said, walking into the kitchen.

"Will, wow, I didn't know you were coming over."

"No one did. I kind of just found my way here."

"Well, good. I'm going to make hot turkey sandwiches with gravy for everyone."

"I can't stay."

"Why not? Got somewhere else to be?"

"No."

"I didn't think so. It's settled, you're staying. How about a beer?"

"No, thanks. I stopped drinking when Laura got sick."

"On the straight and narrow huh—join the club."

"So, how you doing? I mean physically—is the pain gone?"

"Yeah, pretty much. I'm back to work, almost eight months now. I'm a journeyman."

"Good for you, Rob, I'm really happy things turned out so well."

"Hey, want to help me make dinner?"

"Sure, just tell me what to do."

Rob and I prepared dinner and the five of us gathered around the dining room table, talking about past Christmas holidays, the cottage, anything we could think of that didn't have to do with Laura's illness. After Betsy and Andrew left, Rob and I carried the boxes from my car into the house and up the stairs to Laura's room. A melancholy feeling came over me, remembering how she had lain there in bed after chemo, so weak and nauseous. Back downstairs, it was after ten o'clock when I said goodnight to Ellen and Rob, wishing them a merry Christmas.

I drove back to the city where all the lights were shining brightly on the tall buildings. Somehow, I ended up in North Beach. I parked near Saints Peter and Paul Church and went in. The organist was already playing Christmas hymns. I sat in the back of the still nearly empty church and closed my eyes. I heard Laura's voice in my head, urging, "Sing, Will, sing," and became overwhelmed with sadness. I started weeping to the point that I had to go outside. I walked until I felt in control enough to drive home. The next thing I remember was waking to the alarm clock radio at 5:00 a.m. I had arranged with Sunil, knowing as a Hindu he wouldn't be celebrating Christmas, to pick me up at six o'clock for a ride to SFO.

"Merry Christmas, Will," was the first thing he said when I got into the cab.

"Thank you, Sunil," I replied bleary-eyed. He knew me well enough not to engage in conversation at that hour and remained silent for the entire ride. When we got to the airport, I leaned forward and said, "Sunil, I'm flying Japan Airlines."

"Okay, then we go to the International Terminal."

As we pulled up to the JAL sign, he got out of the cab and retrieved my bag from the trunk, placing it on the curb beside me.

"You look like you want to say something."

"It is just that I am sorry for you, Will, having to leave here on Christmas."

"I appreciate your sentiment, but it's best. I don't think I could handle being here for Christmas."

I handed him one hundred dollars and added, "This is for your kindness."

"Oh, Will, it is too much."

"Please take it, I insist—for your family."

"Okay, very well. Please have a safe journey, my friend."

"Thank you," I replied, picking up my bag and turning toward the terminal.

The eleven-hour flight was uneventful and I was able to sleep most of the way. I had a driver from the airport to the Marriott in downtown Tokyo. By the time I checked in and got to my room, it was 11:00 a.m. the next day, but seemed like seven at night to me. The next six days were a whirlwind of lunch and dinner meetings and factory tours at NEC, Hitachi, and Toshiba. I also spent some time at the Dean Witter office, trying out my limited Japanese. For my reward, or my Hosho, I was allowed on the floor of the Tosho, the Tokyo Stock Exchange for a private tour.

On my last night, New Year's Eve, after I worked out in the hotel gym and made a few calls, I headed to the Business Center, where I spent several hours typing my report on a new

IBM Personal Computer/AT. It was the first one I'd ever seen. When I finished, I copied it to a floppy disk, which I placed in a hard plastic case for safe-keeping. I looked at the clock on the wall—it was one thirty in the morning. The soundproof glass walls prevented me from hearing fireworks or celebration outside. I was partly relieved I missed it. After all, the whole point of this trip was to avoid dealing with my personal reality. I decided to take in one last view of Tokyo from the rooftop lounge. I stopped on my floor to leave my briefcase and grab a sports coat. When the elevator opened on the top floor the room was nearly empty—most likely guests had already gone to bed or were still out on the town. As I walked over to the large floor to ceiling windows and gazed out onto 1986, the notion that I would soon be back in San Francisco hit me in the pit of my stomach. As I turned, a table of people caught my eye and a young, attractive Black woman waved me over. I knew I wouldn't be able to sleep and welcomed the distraction. As I approached, she said, "Come join us, we seem to be the only Americans here."

"The only people," I corrected her. "Thank you," I said, as I approached and reached out to shake her hand. "Hi, Will Merritt."

"Happy New Year, Will. I'm Whitney."

"Happy New Year. Nice to meet you."

Everyone introduced themselves in turn with a friendly, welcoming demeanor and I sat down at the one empty seat.

"Were you out celebrating tonight?" she asked.

"No, I missed it. I was working."

"Really, well, so was I," she replied.

Everyone at the table snickered at the inside joke. I looked at her more closely.

"You're Whitney Houston."

"You got it, baby, though maybe not a fan?"

"No, I loved your first album."

"My only album so far."

"I like 'You Give Good Love' . . . Never stopping, I was always searching for that perfect love."

"The man's got good 'tase," someone at the table laughed, sipping on his Hennessey.

A waiter came by and asked if I'd like something from the bar.

"Club soda, and another bottle of champagne for the table," I said.

"You don't need to do that, Will, I invited you over."

"I'd like to, Whitney. I've been here six days on business and have yet to spend a dime on my expense account."

"Thank you. Traveling during the holidays—how does your wife feel about that?" she asked, noticing my wedding ring.

"She doesn't. I mean, it's okay. It was a last-minute thing, I drew the short straw," I lied.

"Well, I wish we'd met before tonight, I would have comped you a ticket for one of my shows."

"Thanks. How did it go tonight?"

"Very well, the audience was really into the music. Plus, it being New Year's Eve, everyone was ready to have fun."

Within an hour, everyone except Whitney had headed to their rooms. She was sitting next to me now, and as I was talking, she put her hand over mine, which was resting on the table.

"Will, you seem so sad, no, so lonely. Is it that you're missing your wife on New Year's Eve?"

"I miss her every day," I confessed. "She died seven months ago."

"Oh, Will, I'm so sorry," she said, linking her hand in mine. "Thank you."

I hesitated and then mentioned a song title, "How Will I Know."

"You mean my song?"

"Yes, I heard it on the plane here. The lyrics are beautiful."

"They are. I didn't write them though."

"I keep hearing that one line over and over in my head."

"Which one?"

"I fall in love whenever we meet."

"Ah, yes."

I walked Whitney to her room and thanked her for inviting me to join her party. She kissed me on the cheek as we said goodnight. I returned to my room and packed, then headed to the airport rather than try to sleep.

When everyone arrived at work on Monday, January 6, each manager's desk, and all the tech sector analysts' desks, had file folders on it with my report inside. I had come in on the weekend to edit the text, add some graphics, and make copies. I didn't do it to impress anyone. I did it just to get it done, like checking off one more box in a long list of unfilled boxes. Much of the next few months were the same. I was sleepwalking through the job like a mindless robot, producing reports and projections and presentations over and over again.

My thirtieth birthday came and went without acknowledgement, except for Mike Foster, who took me to lunch. He was astute enough to keep quiet, knowing I wouldn't want anyone to know. He bought sandwiches from a cart vendor and we sat outside on a park bench, oblivious to a few perplexed tourists who were eyeing the stark Vaillancourt Fountain behind us. I think he appreciated the street distractions and bleak March weather since it fit the mood and didn't require much conversation on either of our parts. Mike was being Mike in his own way—perfunctory—which was considerate because we both knew there wasn't anything to celebrate.

Spring finally arrived after a cool and unusually wet April. May 12 was a Monday. In the morning, I called Ellen to tell her I was thinking of her and that I planned to go to Ocean Beach where we scattered Laura's ashes in the sea. She asked how I was doing—a question I had been asked a thousand times in the last year and still had no answer for. As we hung up, I promised to visit, knowing she was missing Laura as much as I was. I walked the entire beach twice and then sat for a long time looking out on the vast, endless ocean. Occasionally, a seagull would land nearby and then take flight again. Hours passed until I decided to leave, not wanting to see the sun set on that sacred place. My memory is hazy about how I got home. I recall it involved a walk up to the Cliff House and a cab ride back to my empty apartment. Once there, I collapsed from emotional exhaustion. It was a somber day and, except for talking with Ellen, I hadn't spoken other than stating my address in the cab.

On Tuesday, I had a four o'clock appointment with Carl Maddox—the man who offered me my position at Witter. I walked into his office and began to speak immediately, knowing if I hesitated, the right words might never come.

"Yesterday was the anniversary of Laura's death. I've stayed this whole second year out of loyalty to you and this company but I've come to realize I can't anymore. I've got to get out of here, out of this city—at least for a while."

"Will, I can't say I'm surprised. I wish I could change your mind, but I understand your decision," he said, in a resigned voice.

"Thank you, Carl, I appreciate that."

"Can I ask one final favor?"

"Of course."

"Will, you'd be a great asset representing us at the Spring Comdex Show. Can you see your way to doing that?"

"Yes," I said, realizing Dean Witter Reynolds shouldn't suffer because of my personal situation.

"Thank you. We'll miss you around here, but I understand what you feel you must do."

"Thank you, Carl," I said, shaking his hand as he got up from his chair.

He put his hand on my shoulder as he walked me to the door and wished me well. I was sad I was leaving, but knew it was necessary for my well-being. Moreover, it was something Laura would have wanted me to do. My future was now more uncertain than ever.

PART THREE

"REDEMPTION"

MAY 1986–JUNE 1989

CHAPTER 10

THERE ARE SEMINAL moments in one's life, and for me, one of those was reintroducing myself to Michael Dell at the Peachtree Center in Atlanta during the 1986 Spring Comdex Show, where he unveiled the industry's fastest performing PC—a 12-megahertz, 286-based system. We ended up talking late one night, at a small corner table in the hotel lounge, where he elicited my entire resume, asking insightful questions that required long complex responses. He explained where the company was heading having just secured their first letter of credit for $10 million, their manufacturing expansion, international business plans, and his overall vision for the company.

"Sounds like you're undercapitalized for what you want to do," I said candidly.

"Will, Lee Walker, and I are putting a new finance team together to explore further funding sources. Would you consider coming down to Texas to meet with him?"

In between his barrage of questions about my background and experience, and him telling me his plans for Dell, I confided about resigning from Witter and why. He was saddened about Laura's illness and death and offered very kind and thoughtful sentiments. I hadn't wanted to dwell on it, so I turned the conversation to his company.

"You mean to discuss an employment position?" I asked.

"Yes, to see if you're a good fit for Dell and whether we're a good fit for you."

And that is how I ended up in Round Rock, Texas.

By the end of the following year, 1987, we completed a $21.5 million private placement of convertible preferred stock with the offering handled by Goldman Sachs. I returned to San Francisco only once that year—the week of May 12. Then another year passed, and I found myself back that same week in May. This time, after my Ocean Beach ritual, I stopped to see Stephen and Caroline, who still lived in the condo where Laura and I had spent weekends together when they were away on business.

"I'm so glad you called," Caroline said, as she opened the door to greet me.

It was strange to be there, but its familiarity was also comforting.

"Where's the baby?" I asked.

"He's with Grandma and Grandpa for a couple of days."

"Oh, I hope I didn't interrupt a romantic weekend."

"No, we just needed a little break to relax and get some sleep," she replied.

After talking for an hour, I felt it was time to head back to my hotel and said as much.

"So, are you going to stay at Dell?" Stephen asked.

"You mean after the IPO next month?"

"Yes."

"No, once we go public in June, I'll be leaving."

"And then what?" Caroline asked.

"And then, I don't know. I'm going to take some time off—maybe travel. I think I'd like to see India. I've been reading about Hinduism and Buddhism. It's helped me," I confessed.

"That's wonderful, Will. Stephen will be there for six weeks this summer while I stay here and pack up the condo."

"You're moving?"

"Yes, with the baby, we need more space. We're buying my parents' place on Russian Hill. There're moving back to the East Bay now that my father's law firm relocated to Oakland," Stephen explained.

"What about this place? Do you have a buyer?"

"We haven't listed it yet," Caroline replied.

"I'd like to buy it."

"Really?" Stephen said.

"Yes, really. I'd like to buy it if you feel comfortable selling it to me."

"Well, we don't even know what's it worth—we haven't had it appraised," Stephen replied.

We talked about the condo for a few more minutes and realized it would require a longer conversation with me leaving the country in a month or so.

"Hey, can I take you out to dinner? I mean, if you don't have plans," I said.

Caroline looked at Stephen and he replied, "That sounds like a nice idea, but let's split the check—you haven't exercised your stock options yet."

I agreed, saying, "Pacific Café?"

"I love that place," Caroline smiled.

The Pacific Café was a local fish and seafood restaurant on Geary and Thirty-Fourth. In lieu of accepting reservations, they offered complimentary glasses of wine to patrons waiting for a table.

"Can you get good seafood in Austin?" Caroline asked, after we were seated.

"I imagine so, it's not far from the Gulf of Mexico."

I could see my answer perplexed her.

"Caroline, I don't go out much—actually, I don't go out at all. I eat lunch in meetings and dinner at my desk."

"Perhaps we should talk about the condo?" Stephen suggested, moving the conversation away from my personal life. After dinner, they were adamant about driving me back to my hotel downtown, after I insisted on paying.

"So, let Caroline know if you end up traveling to India this summer, and she'll give you my local contact information," Stephen offered, as we said our goodbyes at the Hyatt Regency.

I took the escalator up to the lobby level, and slowly walked toward the bank of elevators. Memories of Laura's law school Happy Hour parties filled my head. I was remembering the big band music. One particular holiday gathering in her third year stuck out in my mind, when she wore the black velvet pantsuit with the silver sequins on the jacket that sparkled, making her the center of attention, or least the center of my attention. As painful as the memories were here, and all over town, I realized it was better than not having any reminders like in Texas. Thankfully, the IPO was only a month away, I thought as I stepped into the elevator.

"What are you going to do now, Will, head back to Silicon Valley and work for the competition?"

It was a question one of the junior hardware engineers, inebriated from cheap champagne and lack of sleep, asked at the going away party I didn't want. I wouldn't dignify the question with the obvious answer that I had signed a noncompete agreement, nor the fact that I had an equity position in Dell. Instead, I answered, "I'm going to see the Taj Mahal."

Admittedly, I didn't make many friends in Texas. In my two years in Round Rock, I was at the office, or traveling on business, six or seven days a week, except for the two personal trips to San Francisco. I'm not suggesting people at Dell weren't hardworking or committed to their jobs—just the opposite. As an upstart going against IBM, HP, and Apple, Dell was an underdog. But what was instilled in the workforce was to embrace it and that made everyone work harder. No one conveyed that better than Michael Dell. I slept in my office some nights during those two years. I was an outsider, an iconoclast, a lonely widower—as some of the older women in the office referred to me. But I know it never interfered with how I treated anyone. In fact, the more aloof I was, the more endearing I became to some of those people—not all, but some. I was an enigma, but someone who always took anyone's call and always responded to anyone's inquiry or concern about something going on at Dell. But yes, I put up a wall, and even though I knew the names of each child of all the parents I interacted with daily, no one, not even Lee or Michael, knew what was going on inside my head—no one had insight into my deepest thoughts and feelings. So, it really surprised no one when I told them I was planning a trip to India. They just wished me well, knowing I had enough of a head on my shoulders to traverse the landscape and culture of a foreign country.

My last conversation with Michael, before I left, had to do with his children. He went on a couple of minutes and then, sensing he was being overbearing, stopped. I prodded him to continue as he was enjoying talking about them. I remember him telling me fondly about his son scoring the winning goal at his soccer game, and at that moment, it put everything into perspective. His life was a remindful insight into happiness, which for me was only a faded dream.

I landed in the capital city of New Delhi on the Fourth of July. Stephen had arranged an invitation to the Independence Day celebration at the American Embassy—compliments of Bechtel. I was feeling weary, but made an appearance. I didn't come to India to socialize—if anything, it was to get away from people. The past few months before the IPO, my job had taken on a role more resembling public relations than finance, and I was tired of all the questions. It wasn't about me, it was about the company—its products, its technology, the innovation, expanding distribution channels. It wasn't about my private life. I had gotten into it with Don Collis, the CFO, one afternoon in early June.

"It's about us, Will," he argued. "Dell is its people, and its people have lives and families and real-life stories that customers and investors, who also have lives and families, can relate to. It's called relationship-building."

I was reliving the whole conversation now on the train from New Delhi to Calcutta, where I was traveling to see the Bechtel project Stephen was working on. The heat was stifling, and the sounds and smells were overpowering. When I met up with him,

I was in a depressed mood. Not working sixteen-hour days gave me too much time to dwell on the past. He gave me a tour of the plant they were building along the Hooghly River, and invited me to join him for lunch before my train left for Agra.

"Will, my father sent word through Caroline that we closed on the condominium. I've been wondering though—do you think it's a good idea for you to live there? I mean, so close to Laura's final resting place."

"It's what I want. I don't care if it's a good idea or not."

"We're worried about you—the whole family is concerned."

"Family? I had a family once, but they all died—first my father, then my brother, then my mother. And then I met Laura, and for a while, she was my family. I don't think there's such a thing as third chances, Stephen."

"So, you're going to live like a hermit out there on Ocean Beach, and shut everyone out of your life?"

"The deal's done, right?"

"I heard you gave $1 million to the Leukemia Society and pledged another million to the Sierra Club. Is that true?"

"Why?"

"Will, I'm not trying to pry into your affairs. I'm just trying to understand what's in your heart."

"My heart, that's rich. What heart? It was ripped out of me and thrown to the ground and trampled on. I have no heart."

"Is it true?" he persisted.

As he spoke, the oppressive heat became overwhelming.

"Yes, it's true. It was selfish."

"Selfish?"

"I was trying to buy my way out of this anguish. I thought it would make me feel better, but the only thing I feel is pain. It's just brought everything back into focus. I go off to Texas for two years and spend all my time working just to occupy my mind, so I didn't have to think about it, about her, and now it's all come back, sitting here in this godforsaken yet somehow beautiful place. Laura was my whole life and now there's nothing inside me except pain and anger. What's the point of all this? Why didn't He just finish off my family completely rather than take her? What did she ever do to deserve that death sentence? She was sweet and kind and loving. She never hurt anyone. That feckless SOB—strike me down, I dare you, God in Heaven, strike me down!"

"Will, get a hold of yourself."

"Why? Why should I get a hold of myself? What the hell difference does it make? Do you know how long I knew her, Stephen? How long I knew Laura?"

"What?"

"One thousand three hundred and ninety days. That's three years, nine months, and twenty days. I could tell you the hours and the minutes, if I wasn't so infuriated."

"So that's the reason you're moving back to San Francisco?"

"Yes, that's the reason."

"Will, I know you loved her."

"Loved her? I haven't stopped loving her!"

"You can't live in the past."

"Why not? It's all I have. It's all that matters to me—nothing else makes any sense in this world. Look at this place. They don't even have clean water to drink."

"We're trying to help with that, but we can only do so much."

"Well, it's not enough! It doesn't matter, nothing matters anymore."

"Will, Laura wouldn't want you to go through life like this, this obsessed, self-tortured person you've become."

"I've got a train to catch," I said. "Good luck with the project."

"Will, don't go like this."

"This is what I am, Stephen. I can't change. I'm not even sure I could, if I wanted to. I'm stuck in time."

My life changed in Agra. While India is primarily Hindu, my newfound interest in Buddhism drew me to the teachers I could find there. I began attending both Hindu and Buddhist dharma sermons and reading about the spiritual nature of things. Soon, I was taking lessons from a guru and spending the entire day either listening, talking, or reflecting on the *sutra* teachings. I began to practice meditation. By the sixth week, I felt a calmness take hold of me and my inner self. I learned self-control, breathing techniques, and how to channel energy into positive action. A few weeks later, I got a small smelting factory in a nearby village to stop dumping their metal waste into a stream by buying them a dump truck. Without the metal deposits in the river, the water could be treated faster and purified to a higher quality.

When the guru heard the news, he asked me, "Do you know the difference between altruism and selfishness?"

"I suppose any difference is meaningless as long as it involves an active striving," I responded.

"This is true, Will Merritt. You must go home now and put what you have learned into daily practice."

"I don't know how to thank you. I think you may have saved my life, and my soul."

"Your gratitude, and your newfound wisdom, is enough. It is my hope you will use it well to heal your suffering, so you can do great things and live a long and happy life."

I spent my last day in Agra the same as my first—visiting the Taj Mahal. Only on that second visit, I felt a connection. I somewhat understood the spiritual enlightenment that is ultimately possible through devotion to the teachings.

I arranged with Carol Wilkinson, who had graciously agreed along with her husband Phil to host our wedding, to have the condo painted, carpeted, and decorated. When she asked about furniture, I told her to go ahead. She had been an interior designer before she married and I knew she took pleasure in projects like this.

"Where are you now?" she asked, when I called from the airport.

"New Delhi. I'm flying to New York for a few days. I'll be back early next week."

"Well, it's all finished, and your things from Texas arrived. I bought you some kitchen appliances and stocked the cupboards with basic nonperishables."

"Carol, I can't thank you enough."

"Safe travels, Will. Let me know how you like it when you get home."

"I will and thank you again."

As I hung up, her words resounded in my head: "Let me know how you like it, when you get home."

Home. I was returning to a place that was indeed my home—another gift, I realized.

CHAPTER 11

UPON MY RETURN to San Francisco in mid-September, I spent the first couple of weeks adjusting to a new routine. In the mornings, I ran on the beach, and at sunset, I walked it. It felt strange to be back and odd to be unemployed. Occasionally, I walked over to Golden Gate Park to smell the eucalyptus trees to remind myself of something Laura and I enjoyed. I had a phone line installed and bought a BMW. My first call was to Carol to thank her for the impressive job she did. I checked in with a few people at Dell to see how things were going. I visited Ellen, and I wrote Stephen a note apologizing for my behavior. He wrote back, saying he understood and would have felt the same had it been Caroline. I wasn't as close with Stephen, but nonetheless invited him and Caroline to Sunday brunch at the Mark Hopkins a couple of weeks later to catch up. As for Mike, with whom I was much closer, I didn't contact him. Mike, Laura, and I had hung out together in grad school and, despite feeling somewhat stable, I wasn't sure seeing him wouldn't cause me to regress into a state of despair. I was working on my practice and my meditation, but it was a slow process. Every day, I felt a little bit better, a little bit stronger.

At the end of October, I met with the president of the board of trustees and the dean of the Law School at Golden Gate University. The purpose of the meeting was to discuss an endowment in Laura's memory—to fulfill the promise I made to myself. I asked Barbara Kenny if she would attend to lend moral support, which she agreed to do.

"Will, that's a very touching tribute," she said, when I called her.

William Burgess, the trustee, was running late. I hated tardy people, so when he finally arrived and joined us in the dean's office, I didn't feel compelled to recap the conversation.

"I'd like it to be a permanent chair in Environmental Law."

"That's very generous, Will," the dean remarked.

"Dean Wright, this isn't about me, I want Laura's name to be remembered for something she felt very passionate about."

"Will, you don't need to be defensive," Wright replied.

"I'm sorry, it's difficult to be here in this building again."

"We understand, Will," Burgess said.

"So, I don't mean to be crass, but what are we talking about in dollars?" I asked.

Burgess started again, "Well, this is a board matter, so I'll need to get it on the agenda for the next meeting and discuss—"

"Historically, what is the standard amount?"

"Well, I guess somewhere between half a million to maybe triple that."

"So, one-and-a-half would work for the board?"

"$1.5 million?"

"Yes, that's what I just said."

"I'm certain it would," Burgess replied.

"In that case, here's my attorney's card. Please send her the paperwork. I'd like this completed in sixty days by Christmas. And any details that remain, I will work out through Dr. Kenny if acceptable to you gentlemen?"

"That sounds acceptable, Will."

"Good. Then I won't take up any more of your time. Thank you, Mr. Burgess, Dean Wright, Dr. Kenny."

I left the meeting and went straight to the men's room to throw up. I had no idea being there, where we spent so much time together, would affect me like it did. I was still fragile in so many ways I didn't even realize. When I exited the bathroom, Barbara was standing in the hallway.

"Are you okay?"

"No, I didn't think this would be so damn hard."

"Oh, Will, I'm so sorry."

"Thank you for being in there."

"You were a little rough on Burgess."

"He's a pompous ass," I replied.

We both laughed and I started to feel better.

"Who is your attorney, if you don't mind me asking?"

"Samantha Symons. She's at Morrison and Foerster. Sam was a good friend of Laura's."

"I remember her—very bright and conscientious."

"You're a good friend too."

"Likewise, Will. I'll make sure this gets done by Christmas."

"Thank you, Barbara."

I said goodbye and headed downstairs to the lobby—the lobby where Laura and I first met. Before I could even think about that, I heard someone calling my name. I turned to see Rob McKenzie.

"Hey, Rob," I said, giving him a hug.

"I heard you were back. Sorry I missed you when you stopped by to see my mom."

"Yes, I've been back about six weeks. Say, what are you doing here?"

"I'm taking a couple courses in construction management."

"Construction management, that's great."

"Yeah, I got my associate degree, and thought I'd try for my bachelor's."

"Try? No, you have to, you have to, Rob."

"Well, we'll see. I'm working full-time for the state, so I'm busy, but they're paying my tuition, so that's a big incentive."

"And everything else?"

"It's going pretty good. I still go to NA meetings, but I'm clean and sober and doing all right."

"That's wonderful. I'm glad to hear it."

"Say, Will, are you going to Mike and Jane's wedding?"

"To tell you the truth, I'm not sure. Some days I feel all right, and others I'm, it's . . ."

"Difficult?"

"Yes, that's putting it mildly."

"You can't let your grief consume you. I know how much you must still love Laura, but you have to live your life."

"Look at you, all Joe College, with the psychological insights."

"Hey, you know what? I realized after you left, I never thanked you for everything you did for me."

"Sure, you did."

"I was just saying the words. I was still so scared. I didn't know what would happen to me—but you believed in me."

"It was you who put in the work."

"That you made possible, Will. I'm telling you, if it wasn't for you, I'd most likely be dead. You saved my life, and I just want you to know how much I appreciate what you did, and how much I cherish every day now."

"You're welcome," I managed, in a sober voice.

"So, come to the wedding, and help Mike celebrate his future with Jane."

"I'll think about it."

"Don't think too much, just listen to your heart, it will tell you what to do."

Rob and I said goodbye. I walked up Market Street over to Montgomery, looking up at all the buildings I had been in and out of so many times. I didn't have a desire to go back to that past. I enjoyed it at the time, but couldn't see myself in a nine-to-five job anymore. *Listen to your heart, it will tell you what to do*, I thought.

I drove down to Fisherman's Wharf and walked the pier at Aquatic Park. I saw mothers pushing strollers, a few joggers, some tourists sightseeing, and the ubiquitous seagulls. Nearby, young children played on the sand-covered beach. I was remembering the walk on that cold Valentine's Day evening, and how clear the sky had been. I missed her so much.

I went home and tried to focus on the positives of the day. Somehow, I found the energy to read. Reading had become another foil to distract me from the present, or the past, depending on how you looked at it. Here, it transported me to nineteenth-century England, reading *A Tale of Two Cities*. Surely any book that began with "It was the best of times, it was the worst of times" was the one I could relate to. When I read the line, "It is a far, far better thing that I do, than I have ever done; it is a far, far better rest that I go to than I have ever known," the sun was rising, and its first light provided a view of the ocean. I took the

RSVP card from the wedding invitation, wrote my name on it, and sealed the envelope. I walked up the hill until I reached the front door of the Cliff House. A mailbox was located there for tourists to deposit post cards, and I mailed the invitation.

Most mornings, I made calls to principals of venture capital firms in the Bay Area. By mid-November, my network had grown and job offers started coming. I wasn't necessarily looking to join a VC company, but felt it was important to let people in Silicon Valley know I was engaged in the conversation. I sent Don Collis a mea culpa letter, telling him he was right. He wrote back a gushing note about how much I contributed to his team, and how badly he felt for never acknowledging that publicly. I put the note on the refrigerator, held there ironically with an Apple Computer magnet. Shortly thereafter, I learned that he had cut back on the long hours at work to devote more time to his family. Family—I couldn't seem to avoid its vital nature in everyone's life, including, for better or worse, my own.

Another invitation arrived—it was for Mike's bachelor party the Thursday before Thanksgiving at The Holding Company from 4:00 to 7:00 p.m. When I arrived a little after five o'clock, there was a sign on the door "Private Party for Mike Foster and Guests." Beer was flowing, and the odor of cigar smoke hung heavily in the air. I made my way through the crowd, saying hello to familiar faces. I knew many of the people in the room, so it took me an hour to make my way to the far end where Mike and Stephen were standing smoking cigars.

"Will, glad you could make it," Mike said, hugging me hello.

"Mike, I know I've been a shit for not calling."

"Yes, you have, but I forgive you."

"Hey, Will," Stephen said.

"Thank you again for the note," I replied.

"Will, I'm not going to ask you to do a shot, but you are coming to the wedding, right?" Mike asked.

"I wouldn't miss it. I'm going to let you enjoy your night, but yes, I promise I will be there."

We talked about his recent promotion, and Jane's new position at a fertility clinic on Nob Hill. After catching up and promising him again I would see him at the wedding, I said my goodbyes. It took almost another hour to make my way back to the door. By the time I reached it, I had at least five dozen business cards in my pocket. I went to the bar for a glass of ice water, and when I looked up, Lynn McCracken was standing there sipping a Martini.

"Will, is that you?"

"Hi, Lynn, it's been a while, you look great."

"Thank you. I feel great too," she said, taking another sip of her drink. "I haven't seen you in ages. I heard you took Dell public."

"Well, Goldman did that, but I was involved."

"How long have you been gone now?"

"Two-and-a-half years. Two years in Texas, and then I traveled for a while. What are you doing now other than crashing a stag party?"

"I'm still at Merrill—still on the retail side, but my client list is growing," she said.

"That's great."

"Can you believe Mike Foster is getting hitched?"

"Oh, Jane is wonderful. I think he's found his soulmate in her," I replied.

"You sound like an authority."

"I know love when I see it."

"Are you on your way out by any chance?"

"As a matter of fact, yes."

"Would you mind walking me home? I just bought a condo overlooking Walton Square, and I'm not used to being alone on these streets after dark."

"Sure, I hear those condos are nice," I added.

"They are."

We left the Embarcadero Center and headed over to Davis Street. When we arrived at her complex, she asked if I wanted to look inside. We walked up a flight of stairs to the second floor and entered her condominium.

"Boy, this is large and very nice."

"You know what else are large and very nice?" she said, in that seductive voice of hers. She unbuttoned her blouse and tossed it to the floor. "These," she announced, standing there in a black, D-cup brassiere pushing her chest out to accentuate her huge breasts.

I grabbed and kissed her, unzipping her skirt from behind, which fell to the floor. She unbuttoned my shirt and kissed my chest, moving down, lower and lower, until she was on her knees in front of me unzipping my pants.

"Wait," I said.

"What's the matter?"

"I can't."

"What?"

"I can't. I thought I could, but I can't. It's too . . . soon."

"Will, it's been over three years!"

"I know how long it's been. Believe me, I know exactly how long it's been, but I can't do this. I'm sorry."

"So am I."

"I think maybe I should go."

"Yes, that might be best," she said, reaching for her clothes.

I turned and left without saying another word.

On Thanksgiving, I borrowed my neighbor's old, beat-up Chevy to avoid any pretense and drove to the Castro to help serve dinner. I stayed late to help clean up, and then drove a couple of people home who lived in The Haight. It had been a good few weeks, and even though I had already said I was going to attend Mike's wedding, after this pivotal day, I decided for certain. Seeing the bleakness of those poor souls made me realize how much Mike and Jane's friendship meant to me. I needed to stop being selfish and start thinking about others who had lost Laura too.

Mike and Jane's wedding ceremony and reception was being held at the Sheraton Palace Hotel. Strike one, I thought, especially after my episode at the University. Laura and I had danced the night away at Stephen and Caroline's wedding in that room. Still, I resolved to at least make an appearance. It crossed my mind to ask Lynn to go with me, but after the fiasco at her place, I didn't want to send mixed signals and besides, I didn't need a date, I would know most of the guests. Strike two. Could I really endure the cavalcade of concerned questions: "How are you doing Will?", "How are you managing Will?", or my favorite, "How are you coping, Will?" "Fine and dandy, couldn't be better, I feel like a million bucks, I'm on top of the world."

Right. It was black tie optional. Good news—I owned a tuxedo, so the question of what to wear was settled. I read the invitation again, noticing the line, "Complimentary valet parking." Okay, I thought, not ideal for a quick getaway, but I could manage. A gift? I had forgotten about a gift. In desperation, I called Caroline for a suggestion. She told me they were planning to remodel Jane's place on Potrero Hill and needed new furnishings, wall coverings, sconces, and recessed lighting. Perfect, I thought. I made a quick call to Carol Wilkinson and explained the situation.

"I'm in, Will. What's my budget?"

"Well, besides your decorator's fee."

"Which you know I won't accept."

"Which I know you won't accept," I repeated, and then mentioned a figure.

"That works for me."

"Great, so now I owe you two lunches."

"You bet you do," she said, hanging up.

Saturday, the wedding day, arrived and I did my usual morning run on the beach. I volunteered to help serve another Thanksgiving meal at lunchtime in the Castro. I borrowed my neighbor's Chevy again, which he didn't mind since it was a reciprocal arrangement, allowing him to tool around in my BMW 740. I couldn't delay any longer. I showered, put on my cleaned and pressed tux, and drove downtown. I think I was almost the last one through the receiving line. It felt overwhelming, but I got through the ordeal. My first instinct was to turn around and leave until Jane explained that after their first dance, I was to be Ellen's partner.

"What about Rob?" I protested.

"Rob has a girlfriend, and it's important for him to pay attention to her. Besides, it was his idea. It's just one dance," Jane said pleadingly.

I thought back to our conversation on the beach after Laura's death, and how she helped me get through my grief that day.

"Okay, if that will make you happy," I smiled.

"Thank you," she replied, kissing me on the cheek, which seemingly acknowledged my reticence.

Strike three. Widowed son-in-law dancing with his widowed mother-in-law. I decided to have a drink.

"By the way, I have someone I want you to meet later," she added.

There is no strike four.

I mingled through the crowd, talking with many of the Witter people I knew, and then spent time with Rob and his girlfriend Allison, whom I took a genuine liking to. I could tell she was a good influence and told him so. I sat down to chat with Betsy and Andrew. They were glad to see me and happy I decided to attend.

"So, what's next for you?" Andrew inquired.

"I'm not sure, sir."

"Since when did you start calling me sir?"

"I'm sorry, Andrew, I've just had so many people ask me so many questions."

"It's okay, son," he said.

"Since when did you start calling me son?"

"I don't know. I think of you as a son, well, a grandson. You've been very kind to Betsy and me."

"Laura used to tell me I had a reserved sense of kindness," I said, being reminded of how happy we had been at Stephen and Caroline's wedding in that same room five years ago.

"She would be very proud of what you've accomplished these past two years. I know, I read *The Wall Street Journal*, and Mike tells me what's going on with you and this Dell Computer—a $30 million IPO that you helped mastermind."

"Well, that's a bit of a stretch, there were dozens of people involved."

"Including you! My point is that you've done something good that will benefit many people, not just investors, but all those people Dell can employ—and their families, who'll have better lives because of those jobs. You should be proud of that."

Andrew's words reminded me of my argument with Don Collis.

"Thank you, Andrew. It's nice of you to say so."

The time for the dance with Ellen arrived. She looked happy and still youthful at fifty-four. I had asked Laura once why she thought her mother never remarried. She told me that after her father's death, her mother had thrown her life into her children, and by the time they were out of high school, she had become set in her ways. Ellen preferred music, a good book, and her family to anything more social that required putting herself in new or unfamiliar situations. Who was I to question, I thought as the song ended.

"Thank you, Will. Laura told me you were a good dancer, and you are."

"Maybe a little rusty. Not many opportunities in Texas."

"So, how is it living out there at Ocean Beach?"

"It's peaceful, Ellen. It's just what I need right now."

"I'm glad, but don't be a stranger."

"I promise I won't," I said.

As we returned to the table to sit down, I noticed Jane talking with a strikingly beautiful woman with long dark brown hair, wearing an elegant red dress. She looked to be about thirty. Jane waved to me and I excused myself to walk over to them.

"Will, I'd like you to meet Sherry Adams. Sherry, this is William Merritt."

"William? No one calls me that; Will, nice to meet you, Sherry," I said, shaking her delicate hand.

"Well, I'm going to leave you two to get to know one another," Jane said, as she walked away.

"So, I guess this is the classic wedding set-up?" Sherry said.

"It's an iconic maneuver undertaken by a well-meaning friend who feels compelled, compelled mind you, to introduce the single male and female guests who are dateless and within proximity in age."

"That sounds about right."

"Very subtle, Jane!" I shouted, in her direction.

"Well, she's never been the shy, demure type."

"How could she be? She married him," I replied.

"I heard you and Mike were best friends in grad school."

"He paid me a lot of money to hang out with him."

"I'm afraid I have you at a disadvantage."

"Ah, so Jane's basically told you everything?"

"Pretty much."

"I see," I said, with a noticeable sigh.

"If it's any consolation, I lost my husband three years ago to cancer."

"Oh, Sherry, I wasn't expecting that. I'm so sorry, that's terrible."

"Thank you, but we don't need to dwell on it at this beautiful wedding."

"So, how do you know Jane?"

"We met in med school at Stanford."

"You're a doctor?"

"Yes, a neonatologist at Children's Hospital."

"That must be tough a lot of the time, but I'm sure very rewarding too."

"Yes, that's a good way to describe it. And you just moved back?"

"Yes, in September."

"You were in Austin, working at Dell?"

"Round Rock, it's a suburb of Austin. What did she give you, a dossier to read?"

"I'm sorry, I ask questions all day—it's my nature."

"You ask preemies and newborns questions?" I said smiling.

"Jane didn't tell me you had such a sense of humor."

"That was probably redacted from the dossier, you know, to maintain my image as a lonely widower. Would you like to dance?"

"I would."

"You know what they say?"

"What?"

"You can't have a bad time dancing."

"Who said that?"

"I think I just did."

We danced a while and then the band started playing a slow song, "Someone to Watch Over You." I couldn't remember the last time I held a woman's body so close to mine—at least I didn't want to remember because I knew the only possible answer. Halfway through, Sherry asked, "Is this awkward for you?"

"A little," I replied.

"Do you want to stop?"

"No, do you?"

"No, but thank you for asking."

The band went on break after the song ended, and we went to the bar for a drink. I switched to ice water and she ordered a Martini. What was it with beautiful women and Martinis I wondered—being reminded of Lynn.

"It's my first drink," she confessed.

"Ever?"

"No, tonight," she smiled.

"You don't need to explain yourself to me," I said.

"One's my limit when I'm driving. Oh wait, I came with the Olivers."

"Are you sure that's your first drink?"

"Yes, I'm sure," she replied, slightly embarrassed.

"Tim and Liz Oliver?"

"You know them?"

"Liz and I were at Witter together. She's an analyst for the aerospace industry. I didn't see them here."

"Actually, Tim was on call, and had to go to the hospital."

"That's right, he's a pediatric surgeon."

"Yes, I work with him at Children's. So, Liz and I were planning to take a cab back to Marin."

"I'll drive you."

"Really?"

"Yes, look, I'm drinking ice water."

"Well, if you're sure?"

"I'm sure."

"Would you mind if we leave soon? I only have a sitter until ten thirty."

"No, not at all. You have a child?"

"A daughter, Claire. She's nine years old."

"That's a beautiful name. Does she look like you?"

"No, she's blonde with blue eyes like Eric."

"Your husband."

"My late husband. We can't seem to escape the constant reminder that our spouses are deceased."

"I think that's an impossibility—at least it is for me," I replied.

"Yes, though I don't pretend to know how you feel. I try not to dwell on it because it only makes it worse."

"You're right, Sherry. It's difficult to understand and even harder to explain. I love Mike and Jane, but they don't understand I'm not on some timetable. I'm not on any timetable."

"You're absolutely right. They have good intentions, but you can't just make something happen that way. I miss Eric every day."

"I'm sure you do."

"Is it the same for you? I'm sorry, that's a foolish question."

"Say, why don't we find Liz and say our goodbyes?"

"Good idea, William."

"What?"

"I'm sorry. I was just trying to lighten the mood."

We found Liz and said goodnight to the bride and groom. Sherry took a piece of wedding cake for Claire and we drove off to Mill Valley.

"Say, Will, ever think about coming back to Witter?" Liz asked, from the back seat.

"Not you too? No, not after having worked for a start-up like Dell. It was incredible— like walking a tight rope without a net and blindfolded. I couldn't go back to a nine-to-five job after that experience."

"Well, you could come back and take the gang out for drinks—you know, Thursdays at the HC."

"What's the HC?" Sherry asked.

"The Holding Company, it's a bar in the Embarcadero Center where traders and brokers hang out after work—actually not so much anymore. It's not like the old days when we were all young and single," Liz said.

"Nothing is," I answered.

"Are you avoiding my question?"

"I don't drink anymore. Well, hardly anymore."

I glanced over at Sherry in the passenger seat.

"So, tell me more about Claire, other than she's nine years old and has her father's eye and hair color."

"She's smart and beautiful. She likes animals, especially horses, plays soccer, and takes ballet and piano lessons."

"Whose idea were the ballet and piano lessons?"

"Hers. I took her to see *The Nutcracker* when she was seven. She liked the lead because her name was Clara and loved Tchaikovsky's music. She couldn't decide between dance and piano, so she chose both."

"Sounds like she's ambitious—maybe like her mother?"

"Perhaps."

I observed through the rearview mirror that Liz had leaned her head back and closed her eyes.

"Our friend is asleep back there," I said to Sherry.

"I heard that," Liz said. "I'm just pretending, so you don't think I'm listening to your conversation."

"Well, pretend then. But don't fall asleep because we're ten minutes away," Sherry told her.

We dropped Liz off and I drove down the block to Sherry's house, which was preceded by a long driveway.

"You live on a farm?" I asked.

"Well, yes, sort of."

I pulled up to the front door, got out, and walked around the car to open the passenger door for her.

"Thanks," she said, getting out. "And thank you for making this evening so enjoyable. If I hadn't met you, I don't know what I would have done."

"Probably drank more Martinis and regretted it in the morning?"

"Possibly."

"Well, I'd better let you go."

"Thanks for the taxi service too. What do I owe you?"

We realized we were likely thinking the same thing.

"Sherry, I had a nice time getting to know you. You're a very attractive woman, but I can't be impulsive, it only makes things more confusing, and I don't want to be confused about how I feel about you, or rather, how I might feel about you. That is, if you want to see me again? I'm babbling, aren't I?"

"You'd like to see me again?" she asked, in a slow, quiet staccato.

"I would. I still feel vulnerable and I understand if you feel that way too."

"I would like to see you again too."

"So you felt something?" I asked.

"We were both a little flirtatious and it felt comfortable—it felt good dancing and laughing together. I haven't done either in a long time."

"I'm just going to say goodnight, so you can go inside and send your babysitter home."

We stood there for a moment, staring at each other. And then, we embraced. I was so conflicted in that moment. It felt both wonderful and wrong. I let it go. I needed some time to figure out what was happening.

"Drive safely."

"I will."

"Okay, good night."

"Good night, Sherry."

I drove away, uncertain about how I felt. *Would she change her mind? Would I?* I put a cassette of cello music on to avoid thinking about it too much. I needed to better understand why I felt the way I did, but that would require sleep first. I crashed on my bed as soon as I got out of my tux.

I called Liz on Sunday. It turned out Sherry had attended Columbia in New York as an undergrad and was thirty-three, a year older than me. Her late husband Eric Adams, an advertising executive, had died of pancreatic cancer. I unconsciously jotted down "cancer" on the pad in front of me as I listened to Liz expound on his unsuccessful treatment. The irony was uncanny and all too familiar. As soon as we hung up, I headed out for a jog on the beach. I needed a distraction and knew running could ease my torment. It was cold and windy, and I only managed three miles before my face and hands were freezing, but I didn't mind. I craved the numbness—it dulled my sense of loss, and I realized then, in that moment, the enormity of everyone else's loss. Sherry was right—we both shared a constant reminder that no matter how happy we might ever become, there would always be that sense of loss. We would carry it with us forever.

She's nine years old, I kept thinking to myself over and over. I knew it had some significance, but couldn't figure out what. Then in the shower it came to me—Claire's father died three years ago . . . when she was . . . six. Laura was six when her father died. The coincidence was too surreal to comprehend. Did it have some deeper meaning? Was this a sign? Was Laura trying to tell me I had a role to play in their lives? I honestly didn't know what to think. I called Ellen.

"Hello."

"Ellen, it's Will."

"Will, it was so nice to see you last night."

"Yes, it was a beautiful wedding, wasn't it?"

"Yes, it was."

"Listen, Ellen, I have a rather strange question to ask."

"Oh my, what is it?"

"Growing up, Laura had a doll. She took it everywhere with her."

"Yes, she did."

"What was the doll's name?"

"Why would you possibly want to know the name of Laura's doll, Will? I'm worried about you living out there where we scattered her ashes."

"Ellen, please tell me."

There was long silence and then she said, "Claire."

"Thank you, Ellen, thank you. I have to go, but I'll talk with you soon."

Claire. The doll's name was Claire. I started to hyperventilate and took slow deep breaths to calm myself. I lay down on the bed and fell asleep. While I slept, I had a dream about Laura as a little girl living in squalor in Calcutta. She held her doll tightly and was walking down a dirt road alone on a hot summer day. Then she disappeared from view. I woke up in a sweat—my T-shirt was drenched. I got up and looked out the living room window. I had slept all afternoon and missed the sunset. It was only six o'clock, but everything was dark outside. I went back to bed, fell asleep, and this time slept uninterrupted until the phone rang at six thirty the next morning. It was Lee Walker, who immediately apologized, forgetting it was an hour earlier in the Pacific Time Zone. Lee was Dell's president and COO. He was calling to ask if I'd help with a new advertising campaign now that their market cap had reached $80 million.

"Will, I know you're not a marketing guy, but we need someone in the room who can offer opinions about our customers and insights into our competitors. We've hired a firm from San Francisco, so you wouldn't even need to travel."

"Sure, Lee, whatever you need, just send me the details."

"Thank you, Will, we appreciate this. I'll let Michael know you're on board."

"Lee, this is a one-time gesture. I just want you to understand that."

"Absolutely, Will. It's just been crazy down here since the IPO, and we need someone we can trust to give educated and informed feedback."

The next week, I was back on Montgomery Street, sitting in concept meetings with a group of twenty-somethings. I didn't mind really. It was new for me and after a couple days, I began to interpret it more as a "collaborative challenge." This is how I remembered my reason for being there when one of the newer guys showed up and asked, "Who's the suit?"

"He was Michael Dell's point man with the investment bankers. If it wasn't for him, none of us would be sitting here," the team leader stated.

"That's right. So, you can blame me for having to sit in these meetings all day—maybe we can just concentrate on the task at hand and consider this a collaborative challenge."

The phrase stuck and I heard even Michael himself used it in a meeting with Dell's new laptop manufacturing team over in Ireland. When it was finished, I was impressed with the campaign—its tone, message, and touch points were all clever and effective. Lee called to thank me; senior management had seen the final presentation and given it a thumbs-up.

Over a week went by and I still hadn't called Sherry. Jane left a message on my machine, basically saying, "You can't wait for love." And then a much less subtle, "Call her." But I wasn't looking for love, was I? Another day passed before I admitted I didn't know the answer to that question. I called Sherry that evening and explained what I had been doing. She surprisingly took quite an interest—perhaps because Eric had been in advertising. After I answered her questions, I apologized for not calling, that despite the last-minute assignment, it was no excuse.

"But you did call. Better late than never," she responded. "Say, what you are doing Sunday afternoon?" she asked.

"Nothing."

"Then you're free to come for lunch?"

"Yes, that would be nice."

"I have to warn you, Claire will be here."

"I look forward to meeting her."

"Okay then, we'll see you Sunday, say, one o'clock?"

"Sounds great," I said, as we hung up.

On Sunday, Sherry greeted me at the door. Claire was standing just behind her, inside the house.

"You must be Claire, I'm Will Merritt."

"Pleased to meet you, Mr. Merritt."

"You can call me Will."

"Pleased to meet you, Will."

"I'm pleased to meet you too. These are for you and for you," I said, as I handed each of them a bouquet.

"Thank you, Will, they're beautiful," Sherry said.

"Do you like them, Claire?" she asked.

"Yes, they smell pretty."

"Come in, let's all go to the kitchen and put these lovely flowers in some water."

After Sherry arranged the flowers in two vases and filled them with water, Claire took hers to her room, which gave us a chance to properly say hello. I impulsively kissed her on the cheek and again apologized for not calling. She gave me a tour of the first floor, and when Claire returned, we sat down at the dining room table.

"Mommy's a wonderful cook."

"I'm sure she is," I replied.

"How do you know?"

"Well, you just told me she is."

"But I'm just a little kid."

"Well, I value the opinions of children as much as I do grown-ups'."

"Really?"

"Yes, really."

Sherry returned from the kitchen with a salad and a large bowl of Cioppino.

"Do you know what that is?" Claire asked, pointing to the bowl.

"I think I do."

"What is it?"

"It looks and smells like Cioppino."

"Mommy, he guessed it," Claire said gleefully.

"Yes, he did, didn't he?"

"Claire, did you know Cioppino originated in North Beach?" I asked.

"Yes, that's where Mommy grew up."

"You grew up in North Beach?"

"I did."

"What's your maiden name?"

"What's a maiden name?" Claire asked.

"It's a woman's last name before she marries and takes her husband's name," Sherry explained.

"Oh," Claire replied.

"Alessi."

"Why did I think you grew up in New York?"

"We moved to New York City when I was eleven, so my father could help his brother run the family business after their father died."

"Oh. What type of business?"

"It was a restoration company, which meant everything from art and artifacts to old, antique furniture. It was quite lucrative. After Columbia, I got accepted to Stanford for medical school and moved back."

"This is kind of boring," Claire said.

"I think it's fascinating."

"Where did you grow up, Will?" Claire asked.

"I grew up in Buffalo, which is also in New York, but at the other end of the state, and then I went to college in Syracuse, which is in the middle."

"Maybe if you moved to New York City, you would have met my mommy."

"Maybe, Claire, but then we wouldn't be sitting here eating this great Cioppino."

"I'd rather be here," she said, after considering the thought.

"So, Claire, what do you want to be when you grow up?"

"I want to be a doctor and make daddies better, so little girls and boys don't have to grow up without one like me."

"Like your mom does."

"Kind of, except she helps little babies get better."

"You know what, Claire? I knew someone who lost her father when she was six just like you."

"Really, what happened to her?"

"She grew up to be a very beautiful and smart young woman."

"Did you like her?"

"Yes, I liked her very much."

"Is she a doctor?"

"She was a lawyer."

"You mean, she's not a lawyer anymore?"

"No," I answered instinctively, not knowing quite what to say next.

"Claire, could you go bring in the apple pie from the kitchen?" her mother asked.

"Okay, Mommy."

"I'm sorry . . ."

"It's fine. She's very bright."

"And very inquisitive," Sherry added.

"That's a good thing," I said.

"What's a good thing?" Claire asked, returning with the pie.

"Dessert," I replied.

"Oh, yes!"

After lunch, Sherry and I took a walk around the farm. We talked about Claire and how she was adjusting, and then the conversation slowly came around to Laura and Eric. Sensing neither of us wanted to dwell on the subject, I asked if she had dated at all.

"Nothing that approaches a real date. You?"

"No, unless you count today."

She smiled.

"You have a beautiful smile."

"Thank you."

"Can I ask you something?"

"Of course."

"Do you ever wonder if it's easier not to remember?"

"You mean in order to move forward?"

"Yes."

"It's hard when you have a constant reminder for whom you need to be both mother and father. Don't get me wrong, I'm not saying it's any easier for you or anyone else."

"I didn't think you were."

"Can I ask you a question?"

"Sure."

"Did you move back here to be closer to her? I mean, closer to the places where all your memories with her were made."

"After Laura's death, everything reminded me of those final months in and out of the hospital, and I just got to where work seemed meaningless. I went to Texas and threw myself into different work. It was a challenge, a big challenge, and I felt like I was contributing to something important and meaningful. And then, when that work was done, I wanted to come home, or at least to the only place I thought of as home. Yes, maybe because of her, but I also knew there were people here who cared about me even though I kept them at a distance."

"So you were sure moving back would be good for you?"

"Not at first, but that changed in India."

"What changed?"

"I tried hard to let go of my anger and focus on the positive. I learned you can gain deliverance from your suffering through your actions and that those actions affect your life path. I learned to meditate. Meditation leads to self-control, an 'active striving' for heart and mind. The powers of love, determination, awareness, all help bring you closer to true enlightenment."

"That's fascinating."

"And it's true. I believe it more and more each day. Maybe it could help you too. I mean, what's the mortality rate in the NICU? You see suffering and death every day . . . I'm sorry I'm talking too much."

"No, I get it, you care . . . about me."

"I do," I said, as I leaned down and kissed her cheek.

She took my hand as we headed back to the house. There was a long silence as we walked, but neither of us felt it was awkward. Finally, she spoke.

"It's hard trying to get to know someone, especially in our circumstances. I guess that's why I haven't really tried."

"What are you saying?" I asked.

"That I'd like to try. Oh, Will, please say something."

"I would too," I said, embracing her.

She put her head on my chest, and I ran my fingers through her long, thick brown hair. She looked up and we kissed. We stood there holding each other, neither wanting to let go of the moment or the emotions we were experiencing.

I drove back to the city, feeling like something was happening to me, that feelings deep inside were trying to surface, to see the light of day. They were mixed emotions, but they were emotions I hadn't felt in a long time. When I got home, I dialed Mike and Jane's number and got their answering machine.

"Jane, it's Will—you were right."

I called Sherry the next day to thank her for lunch. I asked about Claire and she told me how much she liked her flowers—watering them twice a day. I heard her pager go off.

"Is that you?"

"Yes, I'm afraid it is. Hey, Will?"

"Yes."

"Claire wanted me to ask if you'd join us for Midnight Mass on Christmas Eve in North Beach."

"I don't know if I can."

"I understand if you have plans."

"No, I don't have plans. I'm not sure . . . I don't know if I can be in that place filled with all those memories."

"I understand. Listen, I have to answer this page, I'm sorry."

"Yes, okay, I just wanted to thank you again for a wonderful afternoon yesterday."

"You're welcome, Will," she said, as she hung up.

CHAPTER 12

On CHRISTMAS EVE at sunset, I went across the street to walk the beach. It was deserted and uncommonly serene for that time of year. The sun was hidden behind a bank of clouds and I felt a calmness descend over me. Was it like the guru preached, that external objects of reverence could be a source of compassion and serenity? Minutes passed, the sun now set, and the sky darkened. I looked up and could see the first star. It reminded me of something from *Romeo and Juliet*:

> "When he shall die, take him and cut him
> out in little stars, and he will make the face
> of heaven so fine that all the world will be
> in love with night."

Where was she, I wondered, *my pilgrim, my Laura?* Surely still here somewhere, if only in my thoughts and memories. I would have to reckon with the fact that those recollections would be all I'd have left of her for the rest of my lifetime. *What of my life. What of my life!* I shouted it aloud, "What of my life?" I sat down on the cold sand and cried, rocking myself back and forth, my eyes half closed, my mind frozen in time. A large wave of cold salt water came crashing down, soaking me completely in its wake. I slowly stood up, took off my wedding band, and threw it as far as I could into the ocean. I turned and walked back across the street.

A few hours later, I walked into the Tadich Grill for the first time in almost three years. To my delight, Fred was behind the nearly empty bar.

"Will, you're the last person I expected to see tonight," Fred said.

"I didn't expect to be here either, but somehow fate interceded."

"Can I get you something?"

"Redemption."

He looked at me quizzically.

"I'm sorry, Fred—whiskey neat."

"I thought you gave up booze after . . ." he stopped midsentence.

"I'm sure she wouldn't mind. I need to summon all the courage I can."

"For what?"

"Courage to move on, to find peace, maybe even happiness."

"I'll make it a double," he said, in a solemn voice.

"It's been a long journey I've had to take alone," I offered, as way of explanation.

"Will, you don't owe me any explanation. You went through hell, kid. I get it—no hard feelings."

"Thanks, Fred, I knew you'd understand."

I finished my drink, put a twenty on the bar, and got up to say goodnight when the cab I had called arrived.

"Heading out?" he asked, sensing my pensiveness.

"Yes, I'm . . . meeting someone," I hesitantly revealed.

"If anything is worth a risk in life, it's a second chance at love," he offered.

His comment was unexpected and I suspected he was thinking about his daughter. Perhaps a harbinger of things to come was my other thought. I didn't show any emotion, but replied, "Merry Christmas, Fred," as I walked out onto the cold, damp sidewalk and got into the cab.

"Where to?" the cabbie asked.

"North Beach. Saints Peter and Paul."

When I arrived, they were walking up the front steps of the church. Sherry was dressed in a black skirt with a red sweater and cream-colored cashmere coat. Claire was wearing a red dress and a short green jacket with white stockings and black patent leather shoes.

"Claire," I called.

They both turned around and she called back, "Will, you came!"

"I did," I said, joining them as we entered that nostalgically bittersweet place.

The sound of the organ music and the smell of candlewax were familiar and telling. It was the first time since I lost her that I felt hopeful about the future and grateful I might have someone to share it with. We sat in a pew about halfway to the front with Claire between us. The altar was decorated with several planters of red and white poinsettias.

"Isn't it beautiful?" Claire remarked joyfully.

I looked at Sherry and replied, "Yes, very beautiful."

"Mommy, I think Will is talking about you!"

"You're very perceptive for a nine-year-old," I said.

"What's perceptive?"

"It means you're observant and aware of things around you."

"So, you like Mommy?"

"Yes, Claire, I do," I repeated, in a sincere voice.

"I think Mommy likes you too, Will," she offered, in a giddy tone.

When mass began, Claire unexpectedly handed me a song book and said, "Sing, Will."

I closed my eyes, thinking of Laura repeating those same words to me. I opened them, and then surprisingly opened my mouth, and slowly joined her in singing. Something happened in those moments of song. I wasn't sure what exactly, but I felt some connection between the past and present. After mass, we sat there listening to the organist play. I finally leaned over and asked, not quite knowing if she still believed, "What do you want Santa to bring you for Christmas?"

"I want my mommy not to feel sad anymore."

Whether she believed no longer mattered, what struck me was her awareness of her mother's loneliness. I looked at Sherry and then Claire.

"Well, I'm not sure Santa can help, but maybe I can."

"Really?"

"Yes, really. Merry Christmas, Claire."

"Merry Christmas, Will; Merry Christmas, Mommy."

Sherry's eyes were tearful as she replied, "Merry Christmas, dear."

Outside, a mounted policeman was stationed at the curb. Claire asked if she could go over to pet his horse. As we stood there together, I took Sherry's hands in mine.

"That was very sweet of you," she said.

"I meant it."

Sherry stared down at the ground.

"What's wrong?" I asked.

She looked back up, "I can't believe how genuinely happy I feel."

"I can't believe I feel this way too."

Claire came back over and said, "Did you ask him?"

"Claire and I would like to invite you for Christmas dinner."

Without hesitating, I said, "I'd love to join you for Christmas dinner."

I walked them to their car where Claire said goodnight and got in, tuning the radio to Christmas music.

"Thank you for coming, it meant a lot to me."

"I spent most of today thinking about us and knew I wanted to be here tonight with you."

"I'm glad. It made me very happy to see you. And I'll see you tomorrow—well, actually later today."

"Yes, what time?"

"We should be back from Eric's parents' by four."

She leaned down to look in the car; Claire was still awake.

"I'd better get her home."

"Yes, drive safely."

"Merry Christmas, Will."

"Merry Christmas," I replied.

Sherry kissed me goodnight and got into the car. As they drove away, I gazed up into the darkness and could see the sky now filled with stars. *All the world will be in love with night*, I thought. Laura was my night sky, looking down on me and somehow guiding me along a path to peace and happiness.

I slept fitfully and rose late. After a run on the beach, I wrapped the gifts for Sherry and Claire, read the paper, and then showered and dressed. I stopped at a florist to buy flowers for Ellen. Just past two o'clock, I rang the doorbell at the McKenzie home. Mike answered the door, which seemed a fitting welcome after my lengthy absence.

"Will, Merry Christmas—come in."

"How was Maui?" I asked.

"Wonderful, we had a great time."

After I said hello, and gave Ellen the flowers, I mingled, talking with everyone. Rob had done well in his classes, which Ellen was pleased about. Andrew and Betsy were in good health. Stephen and Caroline were pregnant again, which was happy news, especially for Anne and David, the expectant grandparents. And Mike and Jane, just back from their honeymoon, looked relaxed and in love.

"I heard you went to Sherry's for dinner," Jane smiled.

"Actually, it was lunch."

"Did you meet Claire?"

"I did."

"Isn't she precious?"

"Yes, and quite precocious."

"And?" Jane said, waiting for more.

"And . . . I like her."

"Claire?"

"I meant Sherry, but Claire too. I met them last night for Midnight Mass in North Beach."

"Really?" she said surprised. "Was it . . . okay for you?"

"It was all right, Jane. I wasn't sure it would be, but something made me want to be there with her."

Mike, who had been listening, finally asked, "That's good, right, Will?"

"I feel like it is, Mike, I really do."

"You aren't feeling guilty or anything, are you?" Jane asked.

I thought about the question a moment and then replied, "No, not with Sherry. Say, Mike, I'm thinking about selling the condo."

"Where would you move?" he asked.

"You remember Henry Wilson?"

"Of course."

"Well, I called him last month and he's looking to downsize. He's got a five-bedroom house in Presidio Heights. Anyway, he invited me over last week, and I like the place."

"It sounds lovely," Jane said. "And five bedrooms," she added, smiling.

I glanced at my watch, "Listen, I'm going to need to leave shortly."

"Are you going to Sherry's?" Jane asked.

"Yes, but I have something I need to tell everyone."

We chatted a few minutes longer about their honeymoon and then Mike summoned everyone's attention. I walked over to Ellen and took her hand.

"I don't need to tell anyone what Laura meant to me, and in so many ways, still does. When I was in India this past summer, searching for answers—immortal answers to questions immemorial—I thought of something I could do to honor and remember her, something I think she would have appreciated. I've endowed a permanent professorship at the law school in her memory. It will be named the Laura Elizabeth McKenzie Merritt Chair in Environmental Law."

"Oh, Will, that's a wonderful gesture," Ellen said, hugging me.

"Thank you, it means a great deal that I can do this, more than you can possibly know. The school would like to have a small ceremony and reception for her classmates and friends, and family, of course."

"When will it be?" Mike asked.

"I wanted to check with you all first, but I was thinking on her birthday."

"That sounds very appropriate," Ellen said.

The conversation continued another twenty minutes until I apologized for having to leave.

I felt emotionally exhausted when I arrived at Sherry's. Claire was in her room changing as I relayed the whole story to Sherry. When I finished, she hugged me.

"The more I learn about you, the more I discover how wonderful you are."

"Sherry, please. I didn't tell you for that reason, I told you because I'm feeling drained and I don't want you to think it's because I'm not happy to be here."

"Come sit with me in the living room," she instructed.

We sat on the sofa and she took my hand in hers.

"How was it seeing Eric's parents?"

"It was okay, a few sad moments, but with Claire being the center of attention, it was fine. They asked if they could take her over New Year's."

"What did you say?"

"I told them I wasn't scheduled to be on call, though that can change, but they insisted, so I said yes. Will you excuse me a minute?"

"Of course."

When Sherry came back downstairs, she told me Claire was asleep in her bed.

"Poor kid, tired from Midnight Mass, and I bet she was up early?"

"5:00 a.m."

"I'm sorry, you must be tired too."

"I am a little, but I did make dinner."

We decided to let Claire sleep and ate without her. Afterwards, I took a small package from my sport coat pocket and set it on the table in front of her.

"Merry Christmas," I said.

"Oh, Will, you didn't have to get me a present."

"Of course, I did."

She unwrapped and opened the Tiffany's box, "Oh my, these are beautiful."

"You like them?"

"I love them and I don't have diamond earrings—at least not real ones."

She leaned over to kiss me and I grasped her forearm, pulling her gently toward me. She got up from her chair and slid herself onto my lap. We embraced each other and started kissing—slowly and then more and more passionately until she gasped for air and laid her head on my shoulder.

"Oh, Will, this feels so right. I never expected this to happen again. I haven't been with anyone since Eric. I'm not sure I'm ready."

"It's all right. I'm not sure either. I tried once, but shut it down; I couldn't go through with it. But now, for the first time I want to, I mean, when you feel ready."

"Rather pathetic, isn't it?"

"No, not at all. Why don't you try them on?" I suggested.

She jumped up off my lap, grabbed the box, and left for the bathroom mirror. When she returned, she was smiling broadly.

"Oh, Will, they are exquisite, absolutely stunning. Thank you."

"I'm glad you like them."

"I love them but my gift doesn't even come close to—"

"You've already given me more than you know," I said, as she handed me a package.

It was Daisaku Ikeda's book, *Unlocking the Mysteries of Birth and Death: And Everything in Between.*

"Thank you, Sherry. I've wanted to read this for a few years now. I've only read one of his other books."

"I'm glad it wasn't this one."

I got up from the table and hugged her, then stepped back to admire her earrings.

"You know what?"

"What?"

"I think you need some place to show those off."

"Really? Where would you suggest?"

"I was invited to Art Agnos' for New Year's Eve; I haven't RSVP'd yet."

"You know the Mayor?"

"I've met him a few times, and he's a relative of my friend Alex from grad school."

"It sounds wonderful. I'd love to go."

"Great, I'll call tomorrow."

"Speaking of tomorrow, I've got an early shift."

"Yes, I should go. You'll make sure Claire gets her presents?"

"Absolutely. What did you get her?"

"There's a jewelry making kit and a real doctor kit."

"A real doctor kit?"

"That's what it says on the box and Roald Dahl's newest book *Matilda*."

"Oh, Will, she'll love all three. Thank you for making this a wonderful Christmas for us."

"Likewise," I said, kissing her tenderly.

Heading back to the city, at one point, I turned on the radio to listen to Christmas songs and found myself singing along.

I arranged for a limo on New Year's and called Alex to see if she was going to the party. She told me she was and was bringing her fiancé Chris, whom she just got engaged to on Christmas. I congratulated her and then paused a moment, taking a deep breath.

"What's up?" she asked.

"Alex, I . . . met someone. Her name is Sherry, Sherry Adams. We met at Mike Foster's wedding."

"Oh, Will, that's great. I can't wait to meet her."

"Alex?" I hesitated.

"What is it, Will? You can tell me, you know that."

"She's my date for New Year's. I didn't want you to be surprised."

"Well, I'm sure she's lovely, this new woman in your life."

"But, is it okay? I mean, I really like her, Alex," I said, in an apologetically pleading voice.

"Of course, it's okay. I look forward to seeing you both. I'm thrilled for you, and I'm also happy you value our friendship enough to ask my opinion."

"Thank you. So, we'll see you and Chris then," I replied, as we hung up.

Traffic on the Golden Gate Bridge was heavy. I called Sherry from the limo to tell her, and when I arrived, she came right out when she saw lights coming up the driveway.

"I brought a change of clothes," she announced. "There's a slight chance I might get called into the hospital. OB is expecting fourteen deliveries tonight and NEO is short-staffed. I'm sorry."

"Don't be sorry, I understand."

She was wearing a full-length mink coat with her hair pulled back in an updo and her new earrings, but it wasn't until we entered the Mayor's home when she removed her coat that I saw what she was wearing—a low cut strapless black cocktail dress and black high heels.

"You look amazing," I said.

"Thank you. I bought this yesterday. Jane helped me pick it out."

"Well, you both did a superb job."

We mingled in the large foyer for a few minutes. I said hello to a few investment bankers, while Sherry chatted with a lawyer she knew from the hospital. We moved on to the ballroom where the Mayor and his wife were receiving guests. Alex and her fiancé waved us over.

"Hey, Alex, Happy New Year," I said, hugging and kissing her hello.

"Happy New Year! Will, I'd like you to meet Chris Malagisi—he's half-Greek on his momma's side."

"Alexandra Scouras, Chris, I'd like you to meet Sherry Adams."

"It is so nice to meet you, Sherry," they replied.

"Thank you, it's nice to meet you both. So, you and Will went to grad school together?" Sherry asked Alex.

"Yes, and we used to study together sometimes at my parents' bakery in the Cannery."

"I was addicted to her father's baklava. How are your parents?" I asked.

"They are well. You know, working every day—the same old thing."

"Please give them my best."

"I shall, but you should stop and see them; you should bring Sherry too. Oh, come let me introduce you to Art before it gets too crowded, he's my second cousin."

We met the Mayor and his wife, chatted a few minutes, and then moved on to a second ballroom where a band was playing. The four of us talked for another half hour as the room filled. I noticed more people I knew in venture capital, a couple of institutional brokers, and a few attorneys. Sherry spotted the health commissioner and went over to say hello. I excused myself and made a point of chatting with the venture capital guys. By then, it was well after eleven, and Sherry rejoined me as I was saying goodnight to a gentleman from Hewlett-Packard.

"Would you like to dance?" I asked.

"I'd love to," she smiled.

We danced until midnight when balloons dropped from the ceiling and guests blew noisemakers and the band played "Auld Lang Syne." Several people went outside to watch the fireworks display over the Bay. I grabbed two flutes of champagne and we moved to a corner where it was quieter. I knew the song title meant "To times gone by" but instead said, "To us," as we raised our glasses. We took a sip, set the glasses down, and kissed each other with a newfound and excited familiarity.

"I wish this evening didn't have to end," she said.

"It doesn't. Do you want to get out of here?"

"Yes," she replied.

We hurried to the foyer to collect her coat and made our way to the limo while the fireworks finale was still going. From Pacific Heights, we traveled down the hill through Presidio Heights onto California Street.

"Hey, that's where I work," Sherry remarked, as we drove past Children's Hospital.

"Hopefully not tonight," I said.

Ten minutes later, we were at my condo.

"You can't see it now, but the Pacific Ocean is about four hundred yards out that window."

"Wow, the sunsets must be incredible. Do you mind if I use your phone? I want to check on Claire."

"Go right ahead," I said, pointing to the phone on the kitchen wall.

"Or there's one in the bedroom," I smiled.

"Don't worry, you'll get me in there later."

While she made her call, I lit candles in the living room, bathroom, and bedroom. I took off my shoes and tux jacket and set it on a chair in the bedroom.

Sherry peeked in and said, "Hey, everything is good with Claire."

"Would you like something to drink?" I offered.

"No, I'm good. Are you nervous, Will?"

"No, are you?"

"I don't think so, but I need to use the bathroom."

"Down the hall."

"Okay. You know, I'm kind of sweaty from all that dancing. Do you mind if I take a quick shower?"

"No, go ahead. I'm kind of sweaty myself," I smiled.

"Give me a moment."

A few minutes later, I heard the water running. I undressed and walked down the hall. I could see her naked body in the candle light behind the steamy glass shower door. I opened it and stepped in behind her rubbing my hands against her arms. She turned and put her arms around my waist, pulling me close. We kissed as the warm water ran down our bodies. It felt like the water was melding us together and we continued our passionate embrace for several minutes until the temperature started to drop. I leaned over and shut the water off, still tenderly kissing her. Finally, we got out and gently dried each other. I took her hand and led her to the bedroom where we slipped into bed and embraced. I was on top of her, moving my head lower to kiss her breasts. I continued running my tongue down her chest to her belly and abdomen and thighs. She gasped as she parted her legs and I ran my tongue against her.

"I want you inside me."

I entered her and she moaned in pleasure as I moved up and down. A few minutes later, we switched positions with Sherry on top, straddling me. She put her tongue in my mouth as I started thrusting until I climaxed with such intensity that I couldn't move. Moments went by before she gently laid her beautiful naked body down against mine. We held each other in silence until I said, "That was incredible. You are an incredibly sensual woman."

"You're a wonderful lover. Maybe we should try that again in a little while."

"I'm going to need a few minutes, or maybe more than a few minutes."

"We have time."

We drifted off, then woke up to make love again until we finally fell into a deep, tranquil sleep.

About eight in the morning, I got up and walked through the rooms, blowing out the candles that were still burning. I glanced at the stack of mail on the dining room table. One large envelope had a Sierra Club return address. I opened it and pulled out a 1989 calendar. It was the annual gift I received for being a life member—something I conceded to do shortly after I met Laura because I knew it would elicit a smile of approval on that beautiful, loving face of hers.

Occasionally she'd joke about it, saying, "You're a real soft touch, Merritt, aren't you?"

"Only for you, McKenzie," I'd reply.

I took a walk on the beach to clear my head and figure out if what had happened in the last few hours meant what I thought it did. I continued until the chilly January wind numbed my face. When I got three quarters of the way back, I saw Sherry standing near the shoreline and ran the rest of the way to her.

"I thought I'd lost you," she said.

"Lost me?" I replied, hugging her. "No, we've just found each other, and I'm never letting you go."

"I'm never letting you go either."

EPILOGUE

I DIDN'T BUY Henry Wilson's house in Presidio Heights. Sherry and I were married in June of the summer of 1989 in a beautiful open meadow on her farm in Mill Valley, where we lived with Claire and eventually another child, Michael. I started a venture capital firm, ironically with an office on Montgomery Street and Sherry continued to practice medicine, but the most joy and fulfillment we found came from being together and loving each other, knowing how precious and fleeting life could be.